IT WAS A BEAUTIFUL DAY FOR A WEDDING.

The women were forming their line outside before they filed in to sit on the pew benches. Marlene walked past some of the older ladies waiting on the lodge's wide front porch, exchanging greetings with them as she stepped down into the yard. Someone took hold of her sleeve from behind.

Marlene turned and went still. Elverta's expression suggested she'd been sucking lemons for breakfast.

"You're new here, so I should inform you that Lester has *daughters* your age," she muttered disapprovingly. "I'm telling you this for your own *gut*, because men tend to forget about such details."

The *maidel* walked away before Marlene could make a rational reply—or a comeback.

Why had Elverta chosen this moment to inform her of such a fact? As Marlene mulled it over, she recalled that Lester had mentioned the son he'd lost in a traffic accident, so it came as no big surprise that he might have additional children, except . . .

Elverta's trying to shame me—just as she ruthlessly accused Agnes of being chatty and overweight. Lester and I are merely friends, so why would it matter to me if his girls are my age?

Yet, deep down, it did matter.

Family
Gatherings at
PROMISE
LODGE

Charlotte Hubbard

ZEBRA BOOKS
KENSINGTON PUBLISHING CORP.
www.kensingtonbooks.com

Scripture

But the fruit of the Spirit is love, joy, peace, longsuffering, gentleness, goodness, faith. Meekness, temperance: against such there is no law.

—*Galatians 5:22-23*

Acknowledgments

To God alone be all the glory—and my thanks for the energy and imagination to complete this story!

Special thanks to my agent, Evan Marshall, for shepherding my career for more than twenty years!

Thanks, as well, to my editor, Alicia Condon, for her constant support and enthusiasm for the Promise Lodge books. Also, a word of appreciation to Vicki Harding in Jamesport, Missouri, and to the network of Amish friends who answer my questions about the Amish faith as I write my stories.

This book's for my husband, Neal,
who has remained the epitome of patience and
kindness as we came through the pandemic—
and our first year in a new city—together.

Chapter 1

As he tilted his chaise lounge back to stretch out in the afternoon sunshine, Lester Lehman felt like a new man. It was unusually warm for a March day in Missouri, and after spending the winter in his tiny home on the shore of Rainbow Lake, he reveled in the chance to soak up some rays out on his dock. He'd worked hard all morning installing the aluminum siding on Dale Kraybill's new bulk store—a wonderful addition to the other businesses of Promise Lodge—and he'd enjoyed a nice lunch in the lodge's dining room with his friends. And now, nothing was going to stop him from doing absolutely *nothing*.

It felt downright sinful, being this lazy on a Monday afternoon. The gentle lapping of the lake lulled Lester as he reclined full-length on the mesh chaise. He folded his arms beneath his head and let his mind go blissfully blank.

Out-of-town families would start arriving today to attend his niece Gloria's wedding on Wednesday as well as Laura Hershberger's wedding on Thursday, when they married the Helmuth brothers, Cyrus and Jonathan—but for now, Lester could revel in the hush of a solitary sunny afternoon. Living alone in his tidy house all winter had taught him a sense of self-reliance that had cleared his soul—had given him an unencumbered sense of freedom he'd never expected. His bobbing dock rocked him like a cradle. He felt far, far removed from the grief and despair that had followed the loss of his wife and son in a Sugarcreek, Ohio, buggy accident—as well as the passing of his brother, Bishop Floyd, here at Promise Lodge—last spring. As Lester eased into a state of semisleep, he knew the true meaning of inner peace.

At long last, all was well with his life. With the help of his family and friends here at Promise Lodge, he was moving forward . . . floating on the fluffy clouds of a nap. . . .

"Yoo-hoo! Lester, honey! Thanks to Delores, I've found you!"

Lester jerked awake. Whose voice was that? And why had she implied that his dear, deceased wife had led her here?

When he opened one eye, he saw a pudgy little woman starting across the expanse of grass that surrounded Rainbow Lake. Her brown cape dress fluttered around her thick legs as she hurried toward him. Clutching her *kapp* with one hand to keep it from flying off her head, Lester's uninvited guest appeared so excited—and in such a state of overexertion— that he feared she might be bringing on a heart attack. He remained absolutely still, hoping she'd believe he was asleep.

"My stars, here you are at long last!" she blurted out, huffing between phrases. "I've ridden all the way from Sugarcreek—for Gloria's wedding—because with my Harvey gone—Delores has been telling me—for quite some time now—that she wants me to take care of you, Lester! So here I am! Because I know better than to—to ignore heavenly guidance."

Lester sighed. Agnes Plank, his wife's best friend, had never known the meaning of *silence*. She barely drew a breath at the end of one sentence before she shot headlong into her next burst of words. There would be no ignoring her now that she'd almost reached his dock, so Lester reluctantly raised the back of his chaise. All hope for a nap was gone. He felt a headache prickling around his temples.

"I've been *so* excited since our bus arrived about half an hour ago! I looked around, but I didn't see you anywhere," Agnes continued as she struggled to catch her breath. "It was such an adventure to come all the way from Ohio— I've never been to Missouri before—and our friends are so pleased that Gloria's found herself a young man to settle down with—and it's such a joy to attend not one but *two* weddings while I'm here. All that food and visiting time and—and doesn't the sense of springtime *romance* in the air make you feel like you could start all over again, Lester? Don't you just *love* weddings?"

I was indeed looking forward to these weddings—until a few moments ago.

"Of course, ever since you Lehmans moved here, I've been following Promise Lodge's weekly reports in *The Budget*," Agnes went on as she peered at the land and buildings around them. "I was so tickled when Gloria took over as your district's scribe and—well, she's so descriptive, but I had no idea what a *lovely* settlement you'd come to. And of course, you and your brother, Floyd—God rest his soul—installed the windows and siding on these new homes, and with everything except the lodge building being only a couple years old, it seems like the perfect place to start fresh!

"Before that terrible traffic accident took Delores away from us," Agnes continued with a brief frown, "all she talked about was coming here to live in the fine new home you'd built for her. Lately she's been telling me how lonely you've been, Lester, and—well, you know me, I just have to *help* people. The way I see it, Gloria's wedding is a heaven-sent opportunity."

Fully awake now, Lester swung his feet to the dock. When he could get a word in edgewise, he needed to deflate Agnes's high-flying hopes in a hurry, because in her vivid imagination, she was already standing before the bishop with him, repeating her wedding vows. As he opened his mouth to speak, however, another urgent female voice hailed him.

"Lester! Lester Lehman, it's me—your Elverta! I read about Gloria's wedding in the paper, and it seemed like the perfect reason to come and see *you*!"

Lester moaned. His sense of freedom, peace, and unencumbered living had just hit another serious snag.

As the national newspaper for Plain communities, *The Budget* was a wonderful way to keep track of far-flung friends and kin, but he suddenly wished that Gloria—and Rosetta Wickey, their community's original scribe—hadn't been quite so descriptive in detailing the Lehman family's relocation. The tiny town of Promise, Missouri, was out in the middle of nowhere, yet Agnes and Elverta had apparently followed every line of the newspaper's weekly reports right to his doorstep.

As Elverta Horst, dressed in deep green, strode toward his dock, her tall, skinny, ramrod-straight body reminded Lester of a string bean. He knew better than to express that opinion, of course, because the woman he'd broken up with to begin courting his Delores had never been known for her sense of humor.

"Wh-who's this?" Agnes asked him under her breath.

Never one to beat around the bush, Elverta stopped a few yards from the dock. She glanced at Lester before focusing on the flustered woman beside him. "And who might *you* be?" she demanded with a raised eyebrow.

Lester answered as indirectly as possible, because he knew these women would soon find out every little thing about one another. "Elverta, this is Delores's best friend, Agnes Plank. She lives down the road from our former home in Sugarcreek," he explained hastily. "And Agnes, this is Elverta Horst—"

"And I was engaged to Lester before he took up with Delores," Elverta put in purposefully. "First loves are often the strongest, ain't so? The flame may flicker through the years, but it never really goes out."

Immediately Elverta turned to take in the house behind him, pointing her finger. "And what's this? A storage shed for equipment you folks use on the lake?"

"It's a tiny house," Lester informed her. He was accustomed to folks joking about the size of his place, but he suddenly wished he could lock himself inside it until these women went away. "I live here. And I happen to like it just fine."

"My word, Lester, you might as well live in a blue boxcar," Elverta shot back.

"But what about the house you built for Delores?" Agnes asked with a puzzled frown. "She described it as having two stories—like a normal place—and said you and Floyd had installed the windows and siding—"

"You're being funny, right?" Elverta demanded. "Teasing us while you figure out how to send Agnes away so you and I can take up where we left off."

Lester's headache was throbbing full throttle now. "*Jah*, I built a house just up the hill from here," he explained with a sigh, "and in November I sold it to a couple who needed a place before cold weather set in. The young man who lives just up the hill behind us earns his living building these tiny homes, so he's letting me stay in this one—"

"I'll be staying in the lodge," Agnes put in with an eager smile. "My rent's paid up for long enough that you could build us another home—"

"I've got an apartment, too," Elverta interrupted triumphantly. "But the lodge is just for unattached women, so

I won't be living there very long. Lester and I go way back, Agnes. You might as well—"

"Puh!" Agnes spat. "I'll have you know that Delores has been guiding me here for quite some time now, assuring me that I'm destined to take her place. Why do I suspect you're a *maidel*, Elverta, without any experience at being a wife?"

Lester nearly choked as his cheeks went hot, but Elverta wasn't deterred for a second.

"Why would Lester want another man's leavings? Let alone a confused, befuddled woman who claims she's getting advice from his deceased wife?" she asked with a scowl. "If folks get wind that you're hearing voices from beyond the grave, they'll likely have you committed to the loony bin."

Agatha sucked in her breath, which puffed her up like a toad. "You have no right to say that about Delores—my very best friend! I bet she'll find ways to stall you and block your intentions—"

"Oh, if anybody's blocking me it'll be *you*," Elverta spouted. "But not for long!"

As they moved toward each other, Lester stepped between them with his arms extended. "Whoa! Hold it right there," he said, looking from one woman to the other. "I'm telling you both right now that I'm not hitching up with either one of you! So instead of having a catfight, you can just head on back to the lodge—and after the weddings, you might as well get back on your buses to Ohio. Save us all a lot of embarrassment and bad feelings, will you?"

"*I* have nothing to be embarrassed about!" Elverta declared. "And I'm not leaving until *she* does!"

"Well, *I'm* not going anywhere until Lester makes his choice!" Agnes blurted out as she stomped her foot. "I was here first, after all."

"But *I've* known Lester since we were scholars back in the early grades of—"

"Start walking," Lester said, pointing toward the lodge. "And don't think you're going to pester me about this tomorrow, because I'll be at my job site working. Let's go."

As he strode toward the timbered structure across the road, Lester couldn't recall when he'd ever felt so flustered. Not five minutes after these two women had arrived, they'd gone for each other's throats—over *him*. All he wanted was to get Agnes and Elverta out of his sight so he could enlist help from his friends and send the two women packing as fast as possible.

Approaching the lodge's steps, Lester saw that a couple of big buses were parked over in the Helmuth Nursery's lot—and folks were still getting out of them, claiming their suitcases. Agnes and Elverta must've been in such a toot that they'd each rushed to the lodge and inquired about where he lived and then hurried over before they'd even unpacked. When he glanced back at them, the rivals were a distance behind him, focused on him rather than looking at each other. Even so, they appeared ready to spit nails.

Lester entered the lodge and headed straight for the kitchen, hoping to explain his situation before Agnes or Elverta got the facts twisted. Aromas of sugar, cinnamon, and roasting chickens filled the air, and as he passed through the large dining room he saw that the tables were set to serve dinner to several wedding guests. The visitors would be staying in the extra rooms upstairs as well as in the cabins behind the lodge and with residents who owned homes. He was relieved to see Ruby and Beulah Kuhn, *maidel* sisters who lived at the lodge, as well as Rosetta Wickey, who owned the building.

"Ladies, I've got a real problem," Lester blurted when they looked up from the pies they were putting together. "The two gals who're following me have both come to Promise Lodge thinking I'm going to marry them—"

"At the same time?" Beulah teased. "Ooh la la!"

"Why, Lester, you amaze me," Ruby put in with a catlike smile. "Maybe *I* should put my hat in the ring."

He shook his head. These good-natured Mennonite ladies had become his close friends over the past year—and his situation *did* sound too funny to be true. Almost.

"No matter what they tell you—or what information they try to pry out of you to gain the upper hand—I *do not* want to hitch up with either one of them," Lester insisted. "They've already worn out their welcome, and we still have two days of weddings to get through—and they're planning to stay until one of them wins. Just so you know."

Out in the lobby, the sound of the front door opening warned him that Agnes and Elverta had arrived.

"I'm out of here," he said, winding his way between the worktables and counters. The lodge kitchen had once been the hub of a church camp, so the industrial-sized ovens, sinks, and refrigerators required a lot of space. "If I think about possible solutions—and if you gals put your heads together—surely we'll figure out a way to settle this. *Please*? See you later."

Lester ducked through the adjoining mudroom and past another big freezer before exiting through the back door. He'd escaped this initial encounter, but neither Elverta nor Agnes would give up easily.

So much for those peaceful, easy feelings and catching the sunshine. Might as well put in another couple hours at the bulk store and work off my frustrations where those biddies can't find me.

And Delores, I'm not saying you got me into this fix, but if you could help me out of it, I'd be forever grateful, honey. Nobody could ever love me the way you did. I miss you so much.

Chapter 2

Rosetta rinsed her floury hands at the sink, shaking her head. "Sounds like Lester's in quite a pickle," she murmured as the Kuhn sisters nodded. "Now we know why those two ladies hurried in to rent apartments and then rushed out after they'd asked where he lived. I wish I could've warned him first."

"*Jah*, their rent money hadn't even settled on the countertop before they shot out of here," Ruby recalled.

"Just based on my first impressions," Beulah murmured, "I can't picture Lester with either one of those gals. They're as different as night and day, but—oh, hello there, ladies!"

Rosetta turned, immediately noticing the tension on their guests' faces. "Let me see, it's Agnes and—"

"Elverta!" the tall thin one interrupted brusquely. "I'd like to choose my apartment now, before the other wedding guests get over here, please."

"So would I," Agnes chimed in. "And if you'll recall, I paid my rent first."

Rosetta's eyebrows shot up. It wasn't the Plain way to be so aggressive—or so rude. "A couple of other wedding guests from Ohio are already upstairs with Gloria, the apartment manager, so you can come with me. We'll go up those double stairs in the lobby."

When the two women turned, carefully avoiding contact, Rosetta followed them through the dining room. Elverta strode quickly along the side aisle as though she might win a prize for reaching the lobby first, while Agnes hurried down the center aisle between the set tables. Rosetta tried to compose her thoughts, to plan how she'd handle these gals if they started in about spending time with Lester, but they were both moving quickly enough that she didn't have much opportunity to do that.

The lobby was two stories tall with a rustic chandelier of antlers and a gleaming staircase on either side—grandeur that harkened back to the days when Promise Lodge was built. She and her sisters, Mattie and Christine, had acquired this property nearly two years ago when they'd left the Coldstream district and a very oppressive bishop. So much had happened since they'd started out—so many wonderful families had built homes, and their businesses had thrived since then. Several folks had also come alone and had found unexpected love and happiness, including Rosetta and her sisters.

She hoped this tricky situation with Lester's two lady friends wasn't about to mark a low point in life at the lodge. As she gestured for Agnes and Elverta to precede her up the stairs, each woman chose a different staircase as though they couldn't stand to be near one another.

When Rosetta joined them on the second floor, she gestured down the hallway on either side of where they stood. "As you'll see, several of our apartments have been painted and furnished but now stand empty—and we'll have wedding guests in most of them for the next few days."

"What happened to the ladies who lived there?" Agnes asked, as though she feared an ominous reply.

Rosetta smiled. "We've gotten married and moved into

houses," she replied before nodding toward the young woman approaching them. "This is Gloria—"

"Well, of course I know Gloria!" Agnes exclaimed as she rushed forward to hug her. "And now *you're* to be a bride— all grown up, faster than anyone could believe!"

"*Jah*, that's the way it happens, Agnes," Gloria said with a big grin. "I'll catch up with you later, all right? I'm helping other guests from Ohio who need blankets for their beds. Welcome to you, too," she added with a nod at Elverta.

"Well, *I'll* be getting married real soon, too, honey!" Agnes called after the young woman. "Your uncle Lester's going to be a happy man!"

"*Jah*, because he'll be hitching up with *me*," Elverta put in.

Rosetta swallowed a laugh when Gloria shot her a confused glance—even though the situation might not turn out to be so funny. "We all like to think positive thoughts and plan for *happiness* here," she said in a purposeful tone. "Ruby and Beulah—the Mennonite ladies you met in the kitchen—live in the corner to our left, so we'll start by walking to our right. This apartment in front of us is Gloria's, and it'll be vacant after Wednesday when she moves into her new home with Cyrus Helmuth."

When Rosetta had opened Gloria's door, Agnes entered behind her and sucked in her breath. "Oh, my! I've never seen walls that are dark on the bottom and get lighter up by the ceiling—"

"And the ceiling in here is painted like a blue sky with clouds," Elverta remarked from the bedroom she'd ducked into. "That's a little too odd for my taste—"

"It's only paint," Rosetta reminded them. "My sister Mattie originally lived in this apartment, until she married Preacher Amos. The next tenant requested the unusual paint scheme—so you can see that our men are *gut* at fixing up these apartments to suit you. With two weddings coming up, however, it'll be at least next week before they could start remodeling your places."

"No sense in doing that for me," Agnes put in as she headed down the hallway. "I don't intend to live in my apartment very long, after all."

"*Jah*, Lester already knows how I feel about his tiny home," Elverta said with a shake of her head. "He might as well get started on a real house for me instead of spending his time fixing up my apartment."

Rosetta suppressed a sigh as they continued down the hall. "My sister Christine lived in this next empty apartment until she married Bishop Monroe. The corner place was originally mine, but I've also married, and I now live in the white house on the hill that you can see from the big windows."

Before Rosetta could say more, Elverta opened the door and hurried into the corner apartment. "Dibs!" she called out when she reached the windows. "I'll have a great view of the lake, so I can keep track of Lester's comings and goings."

As Rosetta entered the room, she cleared her throat purposefully. "If you'll notice the clothing folded on the bed and the other personal effects," she pointed out, "you'll see that this one's occupied. Irene Wickey, who operates a pie shop in that little white building across the way, lives here. She's in town shopping for last-minute wedding groceries, or you'd have met her in the kitchen with the Kuhn sisters."

Elverta's thick gray eyebrows rose. "What about the apartment next to this one?"

"It's never been occupied, so it's a single room that's been painted, and we've added a few basic furnishings,"

Rosetta explained. "But the men could open it into the next room, which is also empty—"

Elverta hurried into the hallway and immediately entered the room in question. "I'll take it as is!" she crowed. "I can see Lester's boxcar of a house even better from here! I don't need anything fancy because I'm a short-timer, you know."

Agnes looked like a puffed-up hen whose feathers had been ruffled—until she resolutely passed the other unoccupied room in the center of the hallway and opened the door to the apartment in the far corner. "Aha! This place is so fresh it still smells like paint—and it has a *gut* view of the lake, too! I'll take this one."

Rosetta wanted to laugh, but the ladies' attitudes seemed to be getting pettier and more pathetic with each passing moment. "Sorry, but that apartment has just been remodeled for a new tenant who's moving in tomorrow afternoon. She's coming from Coldstream, the town my sisters and Amos and I left, and she put her money down way back in December."

Agnes's shoulders fell. She came back into the hallway, which overlooked the lobby, and watched Elverta bound down the curved staircase to fetch her suitcases. "Well, I'll not be living right next door to *that* one," she muttered. "What's on this other side?"

"These rooms are painted and have basic furnishings for when we have out-of-town guests," Rosetta explained as they looked into each room. "They're smaller because no one's ever rented them, and they look out the front side of the lodge, toward the road. Again, you could ask the men to combine two of the rooms, as the rest of us have done."

Noting no spark of interest on Agnes's face, Rosetta kept walking. "On the fourth side, which overlooks the cabins and faces toward the nursery where your bus is parked, we also have a couple more unoccupied rooms before you get to the Kuhn sisters' corner. I think the two guests Gloria was helping have chosen one of those rooms—but they'll be leaving Friday morning."

Hearing the steady, determined tattoo of Elverta's footfalls ascending the stairs, Agnes straightened to her full height—probably all of five feet—before returning to the hallway on the front of the lodge. "I like this yellow room," she announced loudly. "I'd rather focus on helping Lester design our new house than spend my time remodeling an apartment here. Delores has led me to him, you know—and I bet he already wishes he hadn't sold the home he built for her."

Rosetta refrained from rolling her eyes. *And I'm betting Lester will hole up in his tiny house with no inclination at all to build another home.*

Keeping those thoughts to herself, she smiled at Agnes. "I've always liked this yellow room," she remarked. "Before long, those huge old lilac bushes along the road will be in full bloom. And truth be told," she added in a lower voice, "we leave the doors to the unoccupied rooms open so they won't smell stale. If you ever want to look out the windows on the other side, you'll have that option."

As Agnes's face lit up with gratitude, Rosetta hoped she wouldn't come to regret what she'd just said.

Why am I encouraging Agnes to spy on poor Lester, anyway? These ladies have only been here an hour and they're already annoying me. No wonder he wants them to leave.

Rosetta didn't know why, but she felt a little sorry for short, plump Agnes Plank. Compared to Elverta, she seemed to be such an underdog—a dachshund competing against a greyhound in the race to win Lester's affection.

"Would you like some help with your luggage?" she asked Agnes.

Seeing that Elverta had just topped the stairs carrying three suitcases—and realizing that her rival would have a clear view of her comings and goings, as well—Agnes shook her head. "*Denki*, but I'm stronger than I look—comes from running a household and looking after a husband for more than twenty years, you know," she added more loudly than she needed to.

As Rosetta left the ladies to settle in, she began formulating a strategy. She had a feeling that she—and Lester— would need some support sooner rather than later if the feud between Agnes and Elverta escalated over the next few days.

Lester laid his hammer aside to run his hand over the section of white slatwall paneling he'd just installed. It felt good to pound on something, and if his current state of irritation was any indication, he might complete all the display walls of the new bulk store before the day was done.

"Thought you were taking the afternoon off," Dale Kraybill remarked from the makeshift worktable where he was painting shelves. "I recall something about stretching out in a chaise in the sunshine and letting the world pass you by."

"It was a great plan until a couple of women from Ohio changed it."

Kraybill nodded knowingly. "Women have a way of doing that. Which is one reason I'll remain a bachelor, *denki* very much."

Lester glanced at the middle-aged storekeeper with a twinge of envy. Dale had moved to Promise Lodge to start up a bulk store after selling the very successful one he'd owned in Cloverdale, a few miles up the road. From what Lester had learned while working on the new building next to the Helmuths' nursery, Kraybill was a fine addition to the community—and he came highly recommended by Truman

and Irene Wickey, who knew him from years of attending
Cloverdale's Mennonite church.

"I miss being married to Delores, but I can move on now.
After spending the winter in the tiny home Allen Troyer
loaned me, I know I can make it on my own," Lester confessed softly. "Two women—a former girlfriend and my
wife's best friend—have suddenly shown up to save me
from myself, however. It would be funny if it was happening to somebody else."

"*Two* ladies setting their *kapps* for you. What's your
secret, Lester? No wait—don't tell me!" Dale teased.

Lester chuckled. He might as well get used to this sort of
razzing, because his other friends would take their turns at
it—including the bishop and the preacher who were installing cabinets upstairs in Dale's living quarters.

Whack, whack, whack. The sure, steady beat of a mallet
above them punctuated their conversation

"I'll be sure to introduce these ladies to you," Lester
offered as he picked up the next section of paneling. "If
you like a challenge, Elverta's remained single just as you
have—so she does things her way, just like you. And
Agnes . . . well, Agnes is your typical Amish widow,
making her way as best she can after losing her husband.
You'll never die from *silence* if you take up with Agnes.
The only thing they have in common is that they think
I'm nuts to live in a tiny house."

"So a tiny house sounds like the perfect place from
which to fend them off, ain't so?" Kraybill smoothed his
salt-and-pepper hair back out of his eyes to look at Lester.
He was a slender fellow, neat as a pin even while he was
wielding a paintbrush.

"A man like you doesn't have to settle for just anybody,"
Dale remarked in a thoughtful tone. "You're easy to talk to,
and I suspect plenty of women enjoy your sense of humor

and your unconventional way of looking at things. It doesn't hurt that you're running a very successful business, either—and you still have all your teeth, and a thick head of coal-black hair. Hold out for a woman who's *worth* it, Lester."

Lester blinked. He hadn't expected such a candid assessment of his attributes—much less advice—from a fellow he hadn't known very long.

"*Jah*, well, try telling that to these gals," he said with a sigh. "They're both dead set on hitching up—and instead of returning to Ohio after the weddings, they've rented apartments at the lodge with the idea that I'll soon be building a regular house for our happily-ever-after."

"Don't let down your guard. And don't let either one of them think she's got the upper hand," the storekeeper suggested as he focused on his painting again. "If you try to reason with them or tell them why you won't marry them, you'll only give them ammunition for rebuttal. Best to ignore them altogether, and they'll eventually go away."

Lester let out a humorless laugh. Maybe Kraybill wasn't so wise about the ways of women after all, if he thought either Agnes or Elverta would consent to being *ignored*. It seemed like a good time to change the subject.

Whack, whack, whack.

"When do you figure to open the store?" Lester asked as he positioned his paneling. "When the Kuhn sisters—and the other women—heard you were opening a bulk market here in Promise, they were mighty excited. Saves them a lot of trips to Forest Grove for baking supplies and fabric and such."

Quickly, from years of experience, he tacked the lightweight panel into place with a couple of nails before selecting the section that would finish the wall. The slatwall paneling had horizontal grooves that would allow an infinite

variety of ways for Dale to display merchandise on hooks—
and it looked a lot fresher and more modern than the peg-
board in most Plain stores.

"Originally, I thought it would be mid-April before the
place was ready," Kraybill replied after another round of
pounding above them stopped. "But the men here—a lot of
them skilled carpenters like yourself—have jumped right in
to put the store together. I've notified my suppliers to move
my shipments up to this weekend, so I could feasibly open
by March twenty-fourth. But that's a best-case scenario."

"You'll find most of us here believe in best-case scenar-
ios," Lester put in with a nod. "I've been totally impressed
by the remarkable way these folks—who've come from all
over the country—have formed a large, close-knit community in less than two years. Just say the word, and a whole
group of friends steps up to help you. Moving to Promise
Lodge was my brother Floyd's idea, and coming along with
him was one of the best decisions I've ever made."

"Apparently your two girlfriends have missed you
enough to come after you," Dale teased. But then he waved
off his remark. "Seriously though, I figured I'd be camping
out upstairs with a hot plate and a cot until my quarters got
finished. Staying in a cabin behind the lodge—and eating
those fabulous meals the Kuhn sisters and Irene fix—has
been a much finer welcome than I ever expected."

"Can't beat Ruby and Beulah when it comes to cooking," Lester agreed. "And we're glad Irene moved in with
them after Truman married Rosetta. The pie shop she runs
with Phoebe Troyer is a big hit."

"Their pies—and other products made right here at
Promise Lodge—will be quite a draw for customers. I have
no doubt that this location on the state highway will be an
improvement over my store on a side road in Cloverdale."
Kraybill stood his finished shelf on its end before brushing

a little more paint on a few spots. "I took a gamble when I built this place with nearly twice the space I had before, so I sure *hope* the shoppers will come!"

"You won't be sorry." Lester quickly tacked the final section of paneling into place. Then, with a battery-powered screwdriver, he drove sturdy screws to secure the panels so they could support a lot of merchandise.

Dale stood in the center of the large main floor, gazing around with a satisfied nod. "It's nice to start fresh with lighter, brighter walls and fluorescent lights rather than gas fixtures. Didn't realize how dingy my other store was looking."

"I suppose it's like a lot of things," Lester remarked as he began to put away his tools. "After you've looked at your surroundings for so long, you don't really see them anymore."

"Sounds like a fine topic for a sermon about springtime renewal and Christ's resurrection!" Bishop Monroe Burkholder's booming voice echoed in the stairwell before he emerged onto the main floor.

Preacher Amos Troyer, close behind the bishop, laughed out loud. "*Jah*, file that idea away so you won't be *resurrecting* the same old stuff you've preached about forever," he joked, playfully punching Monroe's arm. "Hard to believe Easter's only a month away."

Lester looked up from the toolbox he was stashing along the wall. These two leaders of Promise Lodge's Old Order congregation had lifted him from the depths of despair more times than he could count after he'd lost his son, his wife, and his brother the previous spring. Along with Preachers Marlin Kurtz and Eli Peterscheim, they'd led their flock to a higher vision of service to God and to the folks in this community—and the Mennonites among them agreed that God had indeed blessed this settlement with steadfast yet open-minded leadership. "Easter will soon have this store looking as colorful as a basketful of eggs," Dale remarked happily. "I've ordered spring fabrics and flower seeds and craft kits—and of course Easter candy—and hams and turkeys and pastel cookie sprinkles. Everything to get folks into the mood for springtime."

Preacher Amos raised his eyebrows at the bishop. "We'll *never* get our wives out of here! But we're awfully glad to have you and your store joining us, Dale," he added quickly.

"Your kitchen and bathroom cabinets are all in, and your appliances are installed," Bishop Monroe put in. "There's maybe another day's worth of finishing to do, but you could feasibly live up there now if you wanted to."

"You guys are fabulous," the storekeeper said. "I was hoping to shift out of my cabin in time for some of your wedding guests to stay in it, so I'll go fetch my clothes right now. I'm sure your wives will want to clean before new folks sleep there."

As the other men started through the warehouse at the back of the store, Lester joined them. Their footsteps echoed in the cavernous space as they passed sturdy steel shelves and large bins that stood ready to store merchandise. Tall double doors in the exterior walls would accommodate delivery vehicles when shipments came in. Two rows of shiny new shopping carts lined one wall, awaiting the day Kraybill's store opened.

When they stepped outside to cross the large, paved back parking lot, Lester felt pleased that he'd played a part in building the Promise Lodge Bulk Market. The new windows glistened in the afternoon sunlight, and the rustic red siding gave the store a down-home countryside look that set it apart from the community's off-white houses and the Helmuth Nursery buildings nearby. Not far away, two new homes would soon welcome his niece Gloria and her new husband, Cyrus Helmuth, as well as Jonathan Helmuth

and his bride, Laura Hershberger. About halfway across
the lawn that separated the bulk store and nursery from the
lodge property, Dale turned to gaze at the back side of his
new market.

"Now that's what you call a dream come true—and in
short order, too," he murmured appreciatively. "*Denki* so
much, fellows. I haven't felt this excited in a long time."

Bishop Monroe clapped Dale on the back. "We all need
something *new* in our lives now and again," he said.
"You've brought us a store that's bound to increase sales for
every one of our residents who own businesses—and for
that, we're grateful."

"I stand amazed at the way Promise Lodge has grown
and prospered," Preacher Amos put in softly. "When I think
back to the abandoned, overgrown campground that Mattie,
Rosetta, and Christine bought two years ago come May, I
thank God for convincing me to go along with what seemed
like an outlandish, impossible idea at the time."

"God is *gut*," the bishop agreed. "All the time—and to all
of His people."

Lester nodded as the four of them resumed their stroll
toward the tall, timbered lodge building and the ten brown
cabins lined up beneath the old trees alongside it. He, too,
had many reasons to be grateful to God—

"Lester! Hell-ooooh, Lester!"

Lester looked up at the second story of the lodge. Agnes
was leaning out of the center front window, waving gaily
at him, as though he was the white knight of her favorite
fairy tale.

Bishop Monroe cleared his throat, probably to cover a
laugh. "Is there something you've not told us about, Lester?"
he asked lightly.

"A not-so-secret admirer," Preacher Amos remarked.
"Do tell!"

"That's Agnes Plank, from my old church district in Ohio," Lester murmured. "Trust me, you'll know more than you want to about her—and about my other unexpected guest—before the week's out."

With that, Lester said goodbye to his friends and broke into a jog. With any luck, he could reach his tiny house on the lake—and firmly close the door—before Agnes could make her way downstairs and out to the lodge's porch to detain him.

You can run, but you can't hide.

As he crossed the lawn alongside the tilled garden plots where Amos's wife, Mattie, grew vegetables for her road-side stand, Lester knew it was only a matter of time before he'd have to deflect both women's attention again. And again.

He had no idea how he was going to do that.

Chapter 3

"Marlene, it's so *gut* to have you and Mose joining us here!" Rosetta said as she led her longtime friend up the main staircase of the lodge on Tuesday afternoon. "Your apartment is all finished—"

"And your brother's new quarters in the barn loft are ready, too," Christine chimed in as she followed Marlene with an armload of boxes. "What a great idea, for him to live above the horses he's going to manage for Monroe."

"*Jah*, it makes for a lot cozier bachelor pad than one of the cabins," Mattie remarked as she brought up the end of their procession. "And truth be told, I think you'll quickly adjust to doing your housework in about fifteen minutes instead of having to clean a whole house. We sisters certainly loved that part of living here in the lodge."

"We did," Rosetta agreed as she opened the door to Marlene's apartment. "But we also recall how hard it was to leave our longtime homes behind, and to clear them out before the new owners took them over. If you need our help with any little thing, feel free to ask!"

Marlene nodded, but she was focused on her new front room. She set her suitcases on the floor and turned slowly in place, a tentative smile easing the tightness of her face.

She and her brother had followed a life path Rosetta was quite familiar with, remaining single and staying at the home place to take care of their aging parents and the farm in Coldstream. At thirty-five, the Fisher twins were tall, broad-shouldered, and attractive, with thick black hair and a faithful patience that had borne them through their *mamm*'s dementia and their *dat*'s debilitating strokes not long after she'd passed. If anyone deserved a fresh start, they did.

"Oh, but this is lovely—even without any furniture in it," Marlene murmured. She went to the windows, gazing out over the expanse of grass at the entry to Promise Lodge, and the tall old trees and lilac bushes that created a green, leafy barricade along the edge of the county road. "I'm so glad we decided to do this. It's not a nice thing to say, but we were so ready to get away from some of the men in our church district."

"We know exactly who you're talking about," Mattie remarked with a nod.

"*Jah*, you don't have to tell us how many times Bishop Obadiah has hounded you to find a husband and live the proper Amish life God intended for you," Christine chimed in. "He was the main reason we Bender sisters sold our farms and pooled our money to buy this property after we lost our husbands and our parents."

As Marlene let out long sigh, she seemed smaller and more vulnerable. "Mose and I sold the farm without advertising it. I'm sure the bishop will give us a piece of his mind when he hears we've left the district without telling him."

"But meanwhile," Rosetta put in as she slipped her arm around Marlene's shoulders, "you and Mose have a new home amongst folks who've known you all your lives—and with other new friends who'll soon make you feel you've known them forever. Obadiah Chupp can't do a thing to stop you, ain't so?"

Marlene nodded but then gazed at Rosetta and her sisters. "Will he be at Laura's wedding on Thursday? I hate to think about him raising a ruckus about Mose and me, or otherwise spoiling your family's big day."

"If he is, we'll handle him," Christine replied confidently. "In the time since we left Coldstream, Monroe and Amos—and Eli Peterscheim—have learned of some financial mismanagement and other irregular activities Obadiah's son Isaac has been involved in. We've sent them both away from here with their proverbial tails between their legs before, and we can do that again."

"I'll be surprised if Obadiah comes on Thursday," Mattie put in. "But if he does, don't you worry about it, dear. Your mission is to make yourself at home—"

"And our job is to welcome you and your brother with open arms," Rosetta said as Christine and Mattie stepped over to encircle Marlene in their embrace. "Ruby and Beulah Kuhn—the sisters you met when you first came to pick out your apartment—and Irene Wickey are delighted that you're joining them here. After the hubbub of our two weddings dies down, you and those gals will have a great time getting better acquainted."

"There's nobody nicer than Irene and the Kuhns," Christine agreed.

Marlene's body relaxed as she hugged Rosetta and her sisters. "I feel better already. I know you ladies are working on the last-minute details for the weddings, so don't feel you have to—"

"Phooey on that! You only have a few more bags and boxes downstairs," Mattie said as she headed for the door.

"By the time we carry those up here, the men will probably be finished unloading Mose's clothes and furniture at the barn, and they'll carry your furniture up for you," Christine put in as she, too, started downstairs to fetch another armload.

Marlene's eyes shone with unshed tears as she let out a grateful sigh. "I can't thank you enough, Rosetta," she said softly. "You're my inspiration, you know—the way you cared for your parents and then came here to start a whole new life. And then you found a man to fall in love with. I keep telling myself that if you can do those things, I can, too."

"So believe what your heart and soul arc saying." Rosetta flashed her a bright smile. "Ever since I came to Promise Lodge, my favorite phrase has been 'Plan for happiness.' We can't sit around waiting for joy to find us, but if we believe we deserve to be happy—and we surround ourselves with *gut* friends and a positive attitude—everything will work out. Trust me on this."

"I do trust you," Marlene whispered with a tentative smile. "After what Mose and I've been through these past months, I'm ready to plan for some happiness *right now*."

"Make yourself at home, Marlene, and let us know how we can help."

Rosetta stepped toward one side of the double staircase, waving at a couple more ladies who'd come from Ohio for Gloria's wedding. As she descended the stairs, she was once again glad that she'd decided the lodge building should be a place for unattached women to stay for such events, as well as to settle into apartments and take charge of their lives—rather than depending upon whichever man in their families would take them in.

When she saw that Mattie and Christine were talking with Agnes Plank in the lobby, she moved a little faster. Agnes's high-pitched voice and furrowed forehead signaled her distress, and Rosetta sensed that she'd better nip a problem in the bud.

"I've been looking all over, and I haven't seen hide nor hair of Lester," Agnes was saying as she clasped her hands at her waist. "I can't imagine where—"

"Lester works full-time, you know," Rosetta reminded Agnes as she gave her sisters a purposeful look. "Now that his brother Floyd has passed on, he handles the siding and window installations by himself—sometimes here on Promise Lodge property, and other days elsewhere."

"Ah. I was hoping he'd take some time off to visit." Agnes's sigh dripped with drama. "I was mighty surprised when Lester didn't stay in Sugarcreek after his son and Delores were killed in that traffic accident. I know all about losing a spouse, and I knew how Delores liked to do things, and—well, I could've been such a comfort to him."

"Around that same time, his brother's health was failing here in Missouri," Mattie pointed out. "Lester felt responsible for Floyd's family when he passed—"

"*Jah*, Floyd's wife—you remember Frances, no doubt—and his daughters, Gloria and Mary Kate, were grateful for Lester's company," Christine added. "He told us he was making a fresh start at Promise Lodge. Most of our residents have come here for that very reason, you see."

"You'll see him at Gloria's wedding tomorrow," Rosetta chimed in again. "Lester has his own schedule, so we don't make a habit of keeping track of him. Is everything all right in your room, Agnes?"

"*Jah*, it's fine."

"*Gut*! If you'll excuse us, we'd better be helping the Kuhns prepare for tomorrow's big meal," Rosetta said as she started toward the dining room. As she passed down the center aisle between the rows of tables covered with fresh white tablecloths, she gave her sisters a chance to catch up with her while there was no one else around to overhear them.

"What was going on back there?" Mattie asked. "You were acting as though you didn't want Agnes to know that Lester's been working at—"

Catching sight of Elverta Horst coming in the front door, Rosetta raised her eyebrows in another warning to her sisters. As she'd anticipated, the tall, slender *maidel* strode right over to speak with them.

"Hello, ladies! I've been putting my time to *gut* use by walking all around Promise Lodge, deciding where I'd like Lester to build our home!" Elverta said matter-of-factly. "This is quite a nice community you've got here—well worth pulling up roots to move from Ohio. Ever since Lester married Delores, I've been waiting patiently for my turn, and I don't intend to let him get away this time!"

Rosetta nodded hesitantly, sensing her sisters were as surprised by Elverta's declaration as she was.

"Lester hasn't aged a day. We'll have a fine time after Gloria's wedding tomorrow, taking up where we left off more than twenty-five years ago. See you then." With a decisive nod, she headed back to the lobby and went upstairs, a woman on a mission.

When Elverta was safely out of earshot, Rosetta's sisters shook their heads.

"Lester's got *two* old flames on his trail?" Christine asked softly.

Mattie let out a short laugh. "*Jah*, and somebody's bound to get burned."

"That's what I was warning you about," Rosetta explained. "Both of those ladies arrived yesterday on the buses from Sugarcreek. Before she even carried her luggage upstairs, Agnes asked me where to find Lester—and about five minutes later, Elverta did the same thing. Can you imagine how

Lester must've felt when they both found him taking a rare afternoon off at his tiny home?"

"Oh, my. Poor Lester," Christine murmured.

"He's asked for our help—which is why I didn't tell Agnes he's been working over at the new bulk store," Rosetta continued earnestly. "He has no intention of marrying either one of those gals, but he doesn't know how to get them out of his hair, either. If we can convince them to head back to Ohio on Friday with the other wedding guests, we'll be doing him a huge favor."

"But if they insist on staying, there's not much we can do about it," Mattie remarked. "If they keep paying room rent—"

"Oh, they've both paid ahead," Rosetta put in. "And they both chose smaller rooms, figuring they'd be moving into a nice new house when they've married Lester."

"Sounds like a recipe for disaster," Christine said. "I'll alert Monroe to the situation—"

"The way those gals are talking—and seeking Lester out—I'm sure everyone at Promise Lodge will soon get wind of their intentions," Mattie put in. "Maybe our best plan is to stay out of it, so the situation will run its course faster. We can hope Elverta and Agnes will be on their best behavior for the weddings, what with so many of their friends and neighbors here to witness what they're up to."

"I hope you're right," Rosetta said with a sigh. "Won't be long before we find out, *jah*?"

Chapter 4

"It's been a real joy to have breakfast with the bride." Lester gazed fondly at Gloria, who sat across the table from him, surrounded by the rest of their family. He'd watched this pretty young woman grow up along with his own two daughters, who'd married the previous year, yet it was still hard for him to believe that his niece was old enough to get married. "Your big day's finally here, and I wish you and Cyrus all the happiness your hearts can hold, honey."

Gloria flashed him a nervous smile. She'd only eaten a few bites of her muffin and fruit, and she was shifting the remainder of her food around on her plate. "*Denki*, Uncle Lester," she said. "Once I get past exchanging the vows—probably repeating them all wrong—I'll feel a whole lot better."

"Every bride worries about that," her sister, Mary Kate, put in. "But the ceremony's over in a flash, and suddenly you're married—and starving because you were too nervous to eat your breakfast," she added, tapping Gloria's plate with her fork. "Better get some more food in your stomach so you don't keel over in front of everybody."

"You'll do just fine, sweetie," Preacher Marlin Kurtz assured Gloria from his seat at the head of the table. Marlin had married her mother, Frances Lehman, several months after her *dat*, Bishop Floyd, had passed from complications of a stroke the previous spring. Kurtz had been the bedrock foundation of this family ever since . . . even though there'd been a time when Lester had made a big fuss—and a big fool of himself—by insisting that *he* should be the man taking care of Frances.

"And I promise not to preach on the topic of wives submitting to their husbands," Marlin teased as he rose from the table. "There are plenty of other relevant scripture passages that bless a couple with God's wisdom. I'll be off now to meet with Bishop Monroe and the other preachers about our morning's sermons. See you all soon."

Frances glanced at the kitchen clock. "*Jah*, we should be finishing up and making our way to the lodge soon. We can't be late on this special day—and you're going to be the best little man, and the quietest, all during church and the wedding while you're sitting with me, *jah*, David?"

Mary Kate's toddler waved his spoon above his head, laughing. "*Jah*, Mammi!" he crowed, kicking in his high chair.

His *dat*, tall, blond Roman Schwartz, loosened the chair's wooden tray with a warning look. "I'll be in the front row of the men's side, able to see everything you do and hear every peep you make," he warned as he lifted his energetic boy. "Let's get you outside to run off some steam before we head over for church."

Lester chuckled. David was all boy—and thankfully for all of them, Roman had been present at David's birth and loved him as though he was the child's natural father. Mary Kate had fallen victim to an English stranger who'd forced himself upon her—her pregnancy had been the main reason Floyd had moved the Lehman family to Promise Lodge, to escape the stigma and emotional trauma the church district in Sugarcreek might've subjected them to.

After washing down the last bite of his muffin with his coffee, Lester glanced at Frances and his nieces. "I suppose by now you've chatted with Agnes Plank?" he asked, sorry he had to bring up the subject.

"She came by for a minute yesterday, *jah*," Frances replied as she began stacking the dirty dishes. "No doubt in any of our minds why she really came to Promise Lodge, though. Right, girls?"

Gloria rolled her eyes. "Apparently she's been making her plans—for *you*, Uncle Lester—ever since Aunt Delores passed. And when she saw mention of the wedding in my *Budget* letter a while back, she was the first to call us and say she was coming," Gloria replied. "Before we could even invite her."

"Your days as a free man are numbered," Mary Kate teased as she, too, cleared the table.

Lester closed his eyes, embarrassed that Agnes had been making her intentions known to so many folks for so long. "And did Elverta Horst invite herself, as well, after she saw the newspaper column?"

Frances's eyes widened. "Elverta? *We* certainly didn't invite her—I don't even know where she lives," she replied. "Floyd and I hadn't been married long when you started dating her. I recall his having a few brotherly pep talks with you, warning you against—"

"Seems Elverta considers me the one who got away, and she's here to remedy that," Lester put in quickly. "Just wanted to tell you, in case you see me caught between two biddy hens causing a big *flap* later today."

Lester paused to consider his words and decided to just lay out his true feelings. Frances had seen him at his worst, after all, last fall when he was so relentlessly insisting that she should marry *him* instead of Marlin Kurtz. She'd forgiven his lack of judgment and proper decorum, chalking them up to grief for his deceased wife, and he was grateful that he and Frances were on good terms again.

"I did *not* ask for their company, and I've already told them I don't intend to marry again, so they should head on back to Ohio on Friday," he clarified. "But they're both hearing what they want to, rather than listening to anything *I* have to say."

"Poor Uncle Lester," Gloria said as she slipped an arm around him.

"I'm not surprised," Mary Kate put in as she, too, gave him a hug. "You're one of the nicest fellows we know—and cute, too—so it's no wonder you're such a heartthrob. And it's only a matter of time before the bishop or the preachers will be suggesting you should take another wife—"

"Monroe and the preachers here know when to encourage a man and when to leave him alone," Lester insisted. "And for that, I'm grateful."

After she'd placed their dishes in a sink filled with water, Frances held his gaze fondly. "I'll keep you in my prayers, Lester, and we'll hope Agnes and Elverta get the message. I don't know those women very well, but I can't imagine you'd be happy with either one of them. Agnes, bless her heart, talks constantly—and she probably talks more now that she's lost her husband. And from what I remember Floyd saying about Elverta, she's not terribly tolerant when folks don't allow her to be the boss."

"That pretty well sums it up. I'll see you all after our Gloria is officially hitched."

Quickly kissing his nieces' cheeks, Lester started for the door. When he stepped out onto the wide front porch of the Kurtz place, the sun was just rising, lighting the eastern horizon with ribbons of pink and peach. It was going to be a glorious springtime day—and it would also be a perfect time for stretching out in the porch swing and just letting the world go by without him.

But it's a perfect day for Gloria's wedding, too, and I'll not let two cackling hens spoil it. Guide my intentions and my tongue today, Lord. I'm going to need all the patience I can muster.

Lester walked toward the main road that led past Roman and Mary Kate's place, as well as the Peterscheim home and the newer road that went up the hill to where Allen and Phoebe Troyer now lived. Looking down the hill toward the lodge, he saw clusters of wedding guests gathering outside—some of them coming out of the cabins where they'd been staying.

As he caught sight of several longtime friends from Sugarcreek, Lester waved and walked faster. He hadn't seen these folks since he'd buried Delores and his son, Sam, a year ago. And maybe if he remained surrounded by the men, and went inside with them for church, he could avoid dealing with Agnes and Elverta until after the wedding.

"Hey there, Homer! And Walter, it's so *gut* to see you," Lester called out as he approached fellows who'd lived down the road from his farm in Sugarcreek. "Mighty nice of you to make the long bus ride and celebrate Gloria's big day with us."

Walter stuck out his sturdy hand and pumped Lester's. "Wouldn't have missed it for the world, Lester."

"It's a fine sight, looking at all these nice houses you and Floyd dressed up with your siding and windows," Homer said, gesturing up the road. "And it's even better to see *you* again, Lester, at a wedding rather than a funeral. You look well—and happy."

"*Jah*, we Lehmans have done all right here. You'll be hearing Frances's new husband, Marlin Kurtz, give the wedding sermon and—"

"Lester! Lester, I've been looking *everywhere* for you!" A familiar female voice carried over the crowd's quiet conversations.

Lester closed his eyes, again praying for patience. When Agnes slipped her arm through his, he was aware that his former neighbors now had something interesting to speculate about.

"Don't you just *love* weddings?" Agnes continued in a rush. "And the weather's going to be perfect for all the festivities, and—oh, hello, Homer and Walter—after you and I sit together and have our nice wedding lunch, Lester, maybe you can take me for a ride around Promise Lodge so I can see this wonderful place I'll soon call home!"

Lester had barely opened his mouth to make some sort of reply when Elverta made her way through the guests that were waiting to go inside.

"I don't think Lester will be driving you around anywhere, Mrs. Plank, because he'll be sitting with *me* at the wedding dinner. And then we'll be spending the afternoon together," Elverta insisted. "Right, Lester?"

"No, I haven't made plans with either one of you," Lester countered. "I've tried to tell you that I'm not getting married again—"

"Your bishop will soon be setting you straight about that! It's God's will that a man should take a wife," Elverta said. She stood straight and tall beside him, grasping his other arm.

"You think you mean that, but you don't, Lester," Agnes said with a sympathetic shake of her head. "It's been a year now since Delores passed, and you've had time to heal—"

"Which is why he belongs with *me* again," Elverta

butted in. She scowled at Agnes before turning to Lester, holding his gaze with her gray eyes. "Maybe the best plan, since neither of us seems likely to back down, is for you to sit with *both* of us at the meal, Lester. You'll soon see that I'm better suited to be your life's companion—your true love."

"Well!" Agnes gasped. "*I'm* not rude enough to make such a remark! But if we're both there with you at the meal, I can at least keep an eye on *her*. Elverta's trying to take control of your life, Lester. *I* would never do such a thing, because I love and respect you too much!"

Lester glanced toward the front door of the lodge, relieved to see that the women were lining up by age to go inside for the church service. "Better take your places, ladies," he said tersely.

"I'll see you later, Lester," Elverta stated, giving his arm a final squeeze. "You coming, Mrs. Plank?"

"After you, Miss Horst," Agnes replied icily. "You're *older*, you know."

As they left, Lester sighed harshly. "Never saw this coming, fellows," he muttered with a shake of his head. "I have no idea how to convince them to leave me alone."

"You have my prayers and sympathy," Homer said.

"Mine too," Walter put in as they started toward the door to line up with the other men.

Their words were sincere enough, but Lester couldn't miss the way his two friends appeared ready to burst out laughing.

At least those women can't pester me during church and the ceremony. Maybe after hearing the sermons and watching Gloria and Cyrus tie the knot, I'll have a better idea about how to shut them down. Send me a sign, Lord. Throw me a rope, will You?

Lester filed into the large meeting room, where the men's pew benches had been set up facing the women's seats. He focused on the *Ausbund* as the congregation sang the first hymn, while in another room, their leaders conferred about the morning's Scriptures and who would preach. After Bishop Monroe had led Amos Troyer, Eli Peterscheim, and Marlin Kurtz down the center aisle to the preachers' bench positioned against the wall, the worship service began.

"We welcome our guests who celebrate with us this morning, especially the folks who've come from Ohio—the Lehman family and their friends from Sugarcreek, and the Helmuths from around Zanesville," the bishop said in his resonant voice. "We're glad you're joining us! We look forward to worshiping God with you, and then together we'll witness the uniting of Gloria and Cyrus as man and wife."

Monroe Burkholder had a way of filling a room with his optimism, and folks around the crowded room were nodding with hopeful expressions on their faces. After Bishop Monroe had helped him through his grief last year, Lester felt a tremendous respect for him—and he figured if he remained focused on their inspiring leader, his gaze wouldn't wander to Elverta or Agnes, seated across the room from him.

As the hymns, prayers, and Preacher Marlin's Scripture reading led to the first sermon, however, Lester shifted on the hard, wooden bench—and he couldn't miss the way Elverta was gazing intently at him from between the two women who sat in front of her. Lester focused on Preacher Amos, who was taking his place in the space between the men and the women, looking out over the crowd with a confident smile.

"What a joy it is to be celebrating a wedding today and another one tomorrow—which means you folks will sit through a total of *six sermons* before we preachers are finished with you!" he teased.

Laughter erupted around the room. The folks from Ohio smiled, pleased to know that the religious leaders of Promise Lodge had a sense of humor.

"We're blessed to have a bishop and three preachers in our little district, because Eli Peterscheim and I were already serving when Preacher Marlin Kurtz moved here," Amos explained. "Marlin acts as our deacon, but on this special occasion when his stepdaughter Gloria is our bride, he'll be preaching, as well. We four men have agreed that Paul's much-loved thirteenth chapter from First Corinthians will serve as our text on both days. We've each chosen phrases from Paul's letter to preach about so we won't repeat one another—or, Lord forbid, disagree with one another."

After another burst of laughter faded away, Preacher Amos bowed his head to begin with a moment of silent prayer.

A dry cough came from the women's side. Another cough followed, and then another, until the noise became so annoying that Lester glanced over—and sighed when he realized it was Agnes, trying for his attention. As Amos drew a breath to begin his sermon, she wiggled her fingers at Lester in a little wave.

Lester closed his eyes again, humiliated. Surely the men seated around him were aware of Agnes's ploy.

He wondered how he was going to make it through the second, longer sermon and another hymn and a kneeling prayer—and then get through the wedding service, as well—while enduring the two women's shenanigans.

Didn't they realize how adolescent and unbecoming their behavior was?

"As Deacon Marlin read today's passage from the King James version of First Corinthians, many of us could say some of the familiar phrases right along with him—and in our minds, most of us replace the old-fashioned word *charity* with the word *love*," Preacher Amos began. "Most of us are also tuned in to what love *is*, such as patient and kind. But it's also wise to recall Paul's thoughts about what love is *not*."

The compactly built clergyman paused, glancing around the crowded room. "For my sermon today, I'm going to paraphrase parts of verses four and five: love isn't envious or boastful or rude. And love doesn't insist on its own way."

Lester blinked. Hadn't Preacher Amos just nailed Agnes's and Elverta's behavior? They were certainly becoming rude—and in her own way, each woman was boasting of her own merits and insisting that her plan for him was the best . . . regardless of what *he* was telling them he wanted.

Of course, Elverta and Agnes were probably each thinking about how arrogant and pushy her rival was rather than seeing such traits in herself. Still, Lester appreciated the way Amos was addressing the issue. He focused on the preacher's words to file them away as potential ammunition for future verbal skirmishes. As the sermon went on for the next half an hour, Lester listened but—as often happened during church—his attention wandered after a while.

Rather than looking at Agnes or Elverta to gauge their reactions to the sermon, Lester gazed at Gloria, who was seated on the front bench on the women's side. She looked so grown up in her royal blue wedding dress and crisp white apron that his heart swelled with love for her. Not so long ago she'd been a flighty, boy-crazy, moody girl trying to force affection into her life, but now that she'd settled on Cyrus Helmuth, she'd become a woman with a purpose. Lester was so proud of the weekly columns Gloria wrote for *The Budget*—the newspaper read by Plain folks all over the Americas!—and the way she'd taken over as manager of the lodge apartments at Rosetta's request.

As Bishop Monroe rose to deliver the second, longer sermon later in the service, someone on the women's side cleared her throat in such a loud, prolonged way that most folks in the room looked to see who it was.

Lester recognized the sound immediately. Throat clearing had been one of Elverta's more annoying ways to get attention even when she'd been a young woman.

The bishop flashed Lester a quick, knowing smile. "'Though I speak with the tongues of men and of angels, and have not charity, I am become as sounding brass, or a tinkling cymbal,'" Monroe quoted, filling the room with his low, resonant voice. "A newer translation I once heard at an English friend's funeral substituted *noisy gong* and *clashing* cymbal, and those terms have stayed with me. But the gist of Paul's message is the same, my friends," he said as he met the eyes of folks in the crowd. "If our words to each other are not tempered by love, we don't truly communicate. We only make noise and create chaos."

Lester closed his eyes, again recognizing his situation in the sermon. Didn't *make noise and create chaos* sum up what Agnes and Elverta were doing? As Bishop Monroe continued to preach, Lester nodded now and then. He spent the rest of the service with his head bowed, as though deep in prayer—still listening for the words that would jump out at him as a possible solution to his problem.

When Gloria and Cyrus rose to stand before the bishop, flanked by their *newehockers*, Laura Hershberger and

Jonathan Helmuth, Lester told himself he would *not* let distractions from across the room ruin the wedding for him. The young couple's earnest expressions took him back to the day about twenty-five years ago when he and Delores had exchanged their vows.

There'll never be another woman like my Delores, bless her soul. I have to find a way to end the foolishness Agnes and Elverta are kicking up—preferably before they do something we'll all regret.

Chapter 5

"It gives me great pleasure to introduce Mr. and Mrs. Cyrus Helmuth!" Bishop Monroe proclaimed.

The congregation rose, applauding and talking happily among themselves. Lester pivoted on the end of the pew bench and stayed low, quickly making his way toward the back of the men's side. It had occurred to him during Gloria's wedding that perhaps God had arranged for him to be sitting where he could make such an escape, so he took full advantage of the opportunity. While men sidled down the rows into the aisles and the center of the room, blocking Agnes and Elverta, Lester hurried down the back hallway between the meeting room and the kitchen.

The heavenly aroma of roasted chickens and savory cornbread stuffing made him inhale deeply—and realize how hungry he was—but Lester didn't stop to chat with whomever might be working in the warm, fragrant kitchen. Through the mudroom and out the back door he went, determined to elude Agnes and Elverta before they once again cornered him and insisted—

He almost smacked the screen door into a tall, broad-shouldered young woman who was leaning against the side of the lodge. Her eyes widened, but otherwise she stayed stock-still as she studied him.

"Well, well. If it isn't the resident chick magnet, making his escape."

Lester was too stunned to speak. Who was *this*? If he'd met her before, he would've remembered the low timbre of her voice and her sparkling brown eyes.

"Stand your ground, Lester. Those two women are way too old for you."

Lester almost blurted out that he was way too old for *her*, but a subtle spark of male ego told him not to say that yet. This dark-haired creature's cinnamon-colored cape dress was too casual for a wedding; her apron was smeared with grease, and she smelled like a roasted chicken. Even though she was slouched against the building, her velvety brown eyes were level with his as she continued to assess him.

How did she know who he was? Lester had no idea—

"I'm Marlene Fisher, by the way," she said as she extended her hand. "I just moved in yesterday afternoon, so I don't know a soul who came for today's wedding. I've been carving chickens and watching the ovens so Ruby and Beulah could attend Gloria's ceremony."

Lester took her hand, aware of its sturdy strength. He probably held it a little too long, but it felt like such a lifeline, he didn't want to let it go.

Marlene's easy smile intrigued him as she continued. "Why don't you do us both a favor and show me around the Promise Lodge property? I could use a little fresh air—how about you?"

This creature surely had to be an angel sent by God. Otherwise, how would she have known his name—or exactly what he needed at this moment?

"Best idea I've heard for days," Lester murmured as he gestured toward the road. "But I have to ask how you know me, and how you know about those, um, two other women."

Marlene's laughter floated ahead of them on the breeze.

"They're staying in rooms on either side of my apartment," she said. "They were having such a heated discussion in the hallway after supper last night, I stuck my head out to be sure they weren't drawing blood. Let's just say your name came up."

Lester exhaled harshly. "You must think I'm a—"

"When I saw Elverta and Agnes cutting through that crowd of men to lay claim to you this morning," Marlene put in, "it was clear that you hadn't asked for such attention, and that you didn't deserve to be humiliated that way, either. And *denki* for the work you did on my apartment, by the way," she added matter-of-factly. "Irene told me you replaced my windows and helped transform the loft of a Clydesdale barn into my twin brother's apartment, too. We really appreciate it."

What a breath of fresh air, to hear a woman thank him for his efforts. As they reached the road that gradually wound its way up the hill past several of his friends' homes, Lester suddenly felt the sunshine warming his face. He sensed this day wouldn't have to be a constant struggle, after all.

"You're welcome. A little more than a year ago, I was a newcomer here, too, so I'm happy to help you and your brother settle in," he said. "The house across the way belongs to Roman Schwartz and his wife, Mary Kate, who's the bride's sister. Roman is Mattie's son—and Mattie's married to Preacher Amos Troyer, and they live in the next place up the road."

"Longtime friends from Coldstream," Marlene remarked with a nod. "Mattie and her sisters caused quite a stir when they up and left our district so suddenly. They've been a godsend—a true inspiration—to my brother, Mose, and me.

After our *dat* passed last fall, we decided it was time for us to leave, as well."

"I'm sorry," Lester murmured. "About your *dat*, that is—not sorry you came here. Which way would you like to walk? If we go up the road, we eventually come to Bishop Monroe's place, and to Preacher Marlin's original home and barrel factory. If we cross and walk past Christine Burkholder's dairy barn and the little building where the Kuhn sisters make their cheese, we'll soon be at Rainbow Lake."

"It's a great day for a closer look at the lake. I've seen it from my window—even saw a fish jump up and splash back down!"

"*Jah*, we keep it stocked. It's a nice place for picnics and other group gatherings," Lester said as they fell into step. "You know everything else about me, so you've probably heard that I live in the blue tiny home beside the dock."

When Marlene laughed, lightly touching his arm, Lester's insides sparkled the same way her eyes did. "*Jah*, when your lady friends were squabbling out in the hall, the topic of your tiny home came up, too—as totally unsuitable. Mose and I are facing the daunting job of emptying our farmhouse of three generations' worth of stuff, so I admire a man who can prioritize his belongings to live such a simple, organized life."

Lester felt gratified by Marlene's easy praise, and rather amazed by her insight, too. "The house on the hill overlooking the lake is where Allen Troyer and his new wife, Phoebe, live," he remarked, gesturing upward. "Allen's now building tiny homes for a living. Judging from all the orders he's taking, he must be onto something."

Marlene's expression waxed nostalgic. "Back in the day I had such a crush on Allen, even though I was a few years ahead of him in school. I'm glad he's made his peace with his preacher *dat* and come here to settle down with Phoebe."

"You never married?" Lester asked—and then immediately regretted nosing into her personal business. "I mean, you've remodeled a lodge apartment, so I assume—"

"It's all right, Lester." She smiled gently at him. "Mose and I are twins—the only kids in our family—and we agreed to stay home to look after our mother when she developed signs of dementia in her early fifties. Mamm started wandering a lot," Marlene continued in a faraway voice, "so Mose and I kept constant watch while I managed the household and he earned our living as a farrier. I had no time or inclination to take a husband, you see—because after she passed a couple of summers ago, we still had Dat."

He nodded gently. "And what happened with your *dat*?"

"He made wood pallets for several years—until a series of strokes last summer and fall finally took him from us. With what he was going through, it was a blessing that he passed after Thanksgiving."

Lester gave her a few moments to let go of some painful memories that clouded her eyes. "Dementia is so cruel," he murmured. "Your *mamm* left you a long time before she actually passed. And after helplessly watching my brother Floyd slide downhill from one stroke to another, losing his control—his *self*—I'm sorry you and Mose had to go through that, as well. So . . . how are you doing these days, Marlene?"

Her bottomless brown eyes shone with unshed tears, but she bravely blinked them away. "It helps that Mose and I have always been close, and that we believe our parents are at rest in the arms of Jesus," she said softly. "And after all those years of listening for Mamm's footsteps in the night—or Dat's moaning—I've finally gotten to the point I can *sleep*."

As he gazed at Marlene's flawless face, defined by dark brows, long eyelashes, and lush lips, Lester suddenly wanted to give her a reason to stay awake into the wee hours—and his wandering thoughts startled him.

Don't go there! At her age, Marlene sees me as an old goat rather than a young buck.

Lester quickly looked away, sensing they should keep walking. As he continued around Rainbow Lake, he pointed to the place nearest the entry to Promise Lodge. "That's where the Peterscheims live—"

"And who could blame them for leaving Coldstream after the ruckus Isaac Chupp kicked up with their daughter, Deborah?" Marlene said, shaking her head. "Our district was really split about the way Preacher Eli sent her away in disgrace, believing she'd gotten what she asked for when she discovered Isaac and his friends at the Benders' burning barn. Most of the men were equally incensed when she called nine-one-one to report the fire."

Lester nodded as they stepped back onto the road and started up the hill. "That happened before I moved here, but I've heard most of that story. Deborah and Noah Schwartz are quite the happy couple now, with baby Sarah. We were all glad when she and her *dat* made their peace, as well."

Marlene was gazing at the tall, off-white houses they were passing. "So this is Roman's house, and the smaller place up the way is where Preacher Amos and Mattie live—"

"*Jah*, and as we round the bend, you'll see where Preacher Marlin and my sister-in-law, Frances, live with his younger two kids. His married son, Harley, now lives in the house up by the barrel factory, with his wife, Minerva."

"Frances is Gloria's *mamm*, *jah*? Mother of the bride today."

"Right, and she was married to my older brother, Bishop

Floyd, when we all moved here from Ohio," Lester replied. "You're doing very well at keeping everybody straight, for someone who just settled in yesterday."

Marlene waved him off. "Don't forget that the Bender sisters have kept me updated every now and then since they moved here two years ago. And whose place is this?"

He paused, considering how much detail to go into. "Phineas and Annabelle Beachey live here," he replied softly. "Once upon a time I built that home and then went back to Sugarcreek so I could bring my wife, Delores, here with our furnishings. But she and my son, Sam, were killed in a traffic accident a few days before we'd planned to make the move."

"Oh my," Marlene whispered. She briefly grasped his hand. "I'm sorry, Lester. Now I understand why a tiny home seems preferable to living in a place where your dreams didn't turn out the way you'd planned."

Lester swallowed hard. He'd felt so strong lately, he wasn't prepared for the wave of grief that washed over him when Marlene sympathized in such a heartfelt voice.

She allowed him a few moments to pull himself together before they started walking again. "I feel better knowing that although you surely get lonely living all by yourself—"

"I'm mighty glad to have so much siding and window work," he admitted.

"—you're not desperate enough to pair up with Agnes or Elverta," Marlene continued with a perfectly straight face. "There's hope for you yet, Lester."

A beat went by and then her remark struck Lester as the funniest thing he'd heard in a long time. He laughed—probably louder and longer than her remark called for—but the sound of her laughter mingling with his chased away his blues.

"*Jah*, there's that," he agreed. "I can only imagine what

those two must be thinking and saying by now, knowing
I've stood them up—"

"You can bet they're not sitting anywhere near each
other, however," Marlene put in. "Or if they are, I pity the
other people seated at that table. Let's keep walking, shall
we? We don't need their kind of negativity in our lives."

As they topped the hill, where Bishop Monroe's vast
pastures and two huge red barns came into view, Lester
thought her remark was spot-on, even as he noticed how
she was including herself in it. Again he told himself not to
get his hopes up—not to interpret this highly personal conversation as a prelude to any sort of romantic relationship.

"Ah. There's Mose."

Lester watched as the lone figure standing at the white
plank fence reached over to stroke a curious Clydesdale's
nose. He'd always considered Bishop Monroe a large
man—probably six foot seven or eight—but Mose Fisher
stood even taller and broader, exuding a quiet, controlled
strength even with his back turned. After he'd fed the horse
a carrot, Mose took his time stroking its muzzle and nodding as he spoke to it.

"Bishop Monroe's excited about having a farrier here, as
well as someone to help him manage his breeding stock,"
Lester commented. "A couple of our young boys—Lavern
Peterscheim and Lowell Kurtz—clean the barns and do
some of the training after school lets out in the afternoon,
but Burkholder's business is really booming so he needed
another full-time helper."

"Mose was ecstatic when Bishop Monroe took him on.
He's had some schooling and experience as a veterinary
assistant, so he's in horse heaven."

Marlene's face softened as she gazed at her brother's
back. "I can introduce you to my brother if you'd like. But
please understand," she said in a pensive tone. "When we

were five, Mose was kidnapped. The English police brought him home a couple days later, but he was never the same. He's extremely shy around strangers, and he avoids crowds because he stammers badly when he's nervous."

Lester nodded, listening closely.

"I don't make a big deal of it to Mose, but he's now the main reason I'll never marry," Marlene continued in an urgent murmur. "He'd be lost if I left him to fend for himself, because he'll never work up the courage to date anyone, much less take a wife. I can't do that to him."

Part of Lester admired Marlene for her protective devotion to her twin brother while another part of him wilted a little—even though he'd been telling himself not to get his hopes up about the young woman standing beside him.

"How about if I meet your brother another time?" he suggested gently. "Seems to me he's got it right if he's more comfortable around horses than people. And you're a dear sister to stand by him."

Marlene's face took on a glow as she gazed at Lester. "It's nice of you to see it that way. Bishop Obadiah in Coldstream doesn't share your opinion—which is another reason we've left his district. His insistence that Mose and I find mates reached the point that I can barely tolerate looking at that man anymore."

Lester smiled at the defiant undertone of her words. "You've got plenty of company here at Promise Lodge, amongst other women who've taken their own time about marrying or remarrying. None of them have a *gut* word for Chupp, either."

Nodding, Marlene turned and began walking back down the hill. "I already feel very much at home here," she remarked as a smile eased over her face. "And now that we've gotten some air, I'm ready to tackle a plateful of that wedding food. How about you, Lester?"

"It's been a long time since breakfast," he said, his mind already fast-forwarding to the ruckus that might erupt when two particular women spotted him and Marlene entering the dining room together. "And it's been a real pleasure showing you around and getting to know you, Marlene. *Denki* for giving me a reason to leave the scene when I needed one. I feel fortified and ready to face the, um, *music* now."

"Oh, I suspect those two women's squawking will be anything but musical," Marlene said with a chuckle.

Chapter 6

A s they reached the back door of the lodge, Marlene paused to savor one last quiet moment before they went in. "*Denki* for being a friend, Lester," she said softly. "You're a *gut* listener and easy to talk to. And I stand by what I said when you first came outside: Agnes and Elverta are way too old for you."

Why have I said that again? What if Lester thinks I'm coming on to him when that's the last thing I intended? What's he supposed to think, after I've insisted I'll never marry?

Marlene sighed to herself. *Not that Lester would consider marrying me, if he found out I've broken three engagements.*

When Lester held the door for her, Marlene set aside her convoluted thoughts. She stepped into the mudroom and entered the kitchen with her companion close behind her. The countertops were covered with empty roasters and stacked metal pans that fit into the steam table Ruby and Beulah had set up for serving the buffet-style meal. The savory aroma of roasted chicken and cornbread stuffing still filled the air, along with the yeasty fragrance of the angel biscuits Cyrus had requested. Marlene was suddenly so famished she could've pulled a chunk of chicken from the broth in a nearby roaster, stuffed it between the halves of a biscuit, and crammed it into her mouth.

But a wedding called for more decorum. And she didn't want Lester to think she was a slob.

And I should show those two biddy hens how a woman of purpose behaves.

Was she a woman of purpose? If so, what *was* her purpose now that she no longer had ailing parents to care for? Marlene only knew that when she'd been walking and talking with Lester, she hadn't felt so lost and alone in her grief. And she didn't feel like putting up with any more nonsense from Elverta or Agnes.

"Are you ready for this?" she murmured as they approached the dining room.

"Absolutely," Lester replied. "We're going to fill our plates and find a place to sit like the well-mannered, levelheaded wedding guests we are. But first I'm stopping at the *eck* table to congratulate Gloria and Cyrus."

"Fine idea."

Marlene stood taller and smoothed her apron, aware that her clothing was smeared with grease—but for good reason. She stepped into the crowded dining room and made straight for the raised table in the nearest corner, where Gloria and Cyrus were seated between their *newehockers,* Laura and Jonathan, flanked by Mary Kate and Roman Schwartz, who held little David on his lap. Their dinner plates were empty, and they were cutting into their pie. When Gloria spotted Marlene and Lester, she shot up out of her chair to extend both her hands.

"It was so sweet of you to manage the kitchen so Ruby and Beulah could come to the wedding!" she exclaimed before addressing her tablemates. "If you haven't met her yet, Mary Kate and Roman, this is Marlene Fisher, who moved into her apartment just yesterday."

"We've heard you were coming," Mary Kate put in, while her handsome husband waved. "Welcome to Promise Lodge—and to the way we do weddings here!"

"And we'll see you again tomorrow when Jonathan and I tie the knot," Laura put in happily.

Marlene's heart felt light as she spoke with these bright young women, and her soul thrummed at the endearing sight of Lester stepping behind the raised *eck* table so he could embrace his niece. The closeness she sensed in the Lehman family reinforced her belief that this man deserved far better than anything his two middle-aged pursuers had to offer him—even if she wasn't counting on being a part of his future herself.

"It's the first day of forever for you kids, and I wish you all the best," Lester said. He lightly kissed Gloria's cheek and pumped the hand that handsome Cyrus offered him. As he stepped off the dais and onto the floor, he jauntily offered his arm to Marlene. "Shall we get some of that fine-looking lunch and find a place to—"

"Lester Lehman, you have your nerve!" Elverta's voice rose brusquely above the crowd's conversations. "You promised to sit with me for lunch!"

"Lester! So there you are!" Agnes was awkwardly making her way between the tables and the folks who stood in the aisle chatting with friends. "I never figured you for a man who'd leave a lady in the lurch—"

When Marlene would've slipped her hand from the crook of Lester's elbow, he subtly pressed it against his side and flashed her a quick wink. His face was carefully composed in a smile that told her he was ready to face the two women he'd eluded earlier. As Agnes and Elverta made their way from opposite sides of the room, Marlene rather enjoyed the daggers in their gazes as they scowled at her.

Elverta reached them first, but Agnes was still talking, breathless from the effort of coming through the crowd.

"—especially after I rode the bus all the way from Ohio to be with you!" she blurted out.

When Elverta opened her mouth to continue her rant, Lester raised his hand for silence.

"When you ladies made the trip to Missouri, did it never occur to you that I might be seeing somebody else?" he asked in a low voice.

Both women glared at Marlene. She pressed her lips together to keep from laughing at their curdled expressions.

"You just moved in!" Elverta accused. "You can't tell me you and Lester have been—"

"I'm not believing this for a minute, Lester!" Agnes clucked. "Delores has told me all along that you've been lonely and—"

"But think about it," Lester put in, silencing them with a gaze that brooked no argument. "I've not heard from either one of you since I moved to Promise Lodge a year ago. Not a phone call, not a letter. You apparently got bees in your bonnets and took it upon yourselves to change my life whether I wanted you to or not. What am I supposed to think about that?"

Agnes's expression softened. "I wanted to surprise you," she murmured. "I was just going by what your dear, departed—"

"Oh, leave Delores out of this!" Elverta snapped. "The fact that you're hearing *voices* should clue Lester in about your mental state. As for me, I came unannounced because I wanted to see Promise Lodge for myself, and I knew that the bond you and I shared as young adults, Lester, was a love intended to last a lifetime. All these years I've remained alone, my heart's been telling me that if you became a free man again, you'd want no one else but me."

By now Frances Lehman Kurtz had approached and a few other folks had stopped their conversations to follow the little drama playing out near the *eck* table. As Frances slipped her hand through Lester's other arm, Marlene noticed the playful smile on his sister-in-law's face.

"Matter of fact, ladies, Lester and I were having *intense* discussions about marriage last fall, after Floyd passed," Frances said, playfully holding Lester's gaze. "He proposed to me more than once—"

"*Jah*, I did," Lester chimed in, following Frances's lead. "I've always been a family man who takes his responsibilities seriously."

"So you see," Frances continued before Agnes or Elverta could interrupt, "Lester *has* been seeing other women. Truth be told, I was just as surprised as he was that you ladies came to Gloria's wedding—because I've not heard him mention either of your names since Delores passed, and because, well . . . neither Gloria nor I invited you," she finished softly.

For an awkward moment, the two ladies were silent.

Lester cleared his throat. "Weddings are a wonderful time for family and friends to get together, especially after a branch of the family has relocated," he said quickly. "But you came for the wrong reason, if you assume I'll go blithely along with your plans for my future."

Marlene admired the restraint Lester was showing. He and Frances were working together to put Agnes and Elverta in their place without making a spectacle of them— even though they'd been drawing the wrong kind of attention to Lester ever since they'd arrived. The two ladies suddenly seemed to realize that everyone nearby was listening attentively, speculating about how they would respond now that the Lehmans had set the record straight.

"Well, then," Elverta muttered under her breath. "Since

I've already eaten my dinner, I'm going outside for some fresh air."

As the middle-aged *maidel* strode stiffly down the big dining room's side aisle, Agnes struggled to control her emotions. "*Jah*, maybe coming here unannounced—and uninvited—wasn't the smartest thing I've ever done," she murmured, "but my heart's in the right place. You can't fault me for trying, and for having your best interests in mind, Lester."

With a wounded little smile, Agnes made her way toward the kitchen.

Lester exhaled in relief. "*Denki* for speaking on my behalf," he murmured. "I'm sure those two haven't given up, but we've put them off for now."

"Happy to help, dear," Frances said, rising to her toes to kiss his cheek. "How could I leave you at their mercy when you did indeed look after me in my time of need? Enjoy your dinner, you two. It's a wonderful meal to celebrate Gloria's finding the man God intended for her, at long last."

Marlene was aware that the guests around them were nodding their encouragement to Lester as they returned to their own conversations—but they were also watching the way he was behaving with *her*. Lester was dressed in his best black church trousers and vest with a white shirt that set off his well-trimmed dark hair and beard, while she was wearing a faded old dress under a smeared apron.

Who am I kidding? These people have known Lester for a long time—some of them since he lived in Ohio—and they see him treating me as more than a casual acquaintance. If they heard the gossip from Coldstream about the three men I've backed out on, they'd warn him away from me.

As Lester led her toward the steam tables, he kept his voice low. "I put you in a tricky spot back there, Marlene, and I appreciate the way you stood by me. Your presence was

probably more powerful because you didn't say anything
to Agnes or Elverta—but you never dropped your eye contact, either. If I made you uncomfortable," he added, "I
apologize."

She chuckled. "Oh, not to worry. I enjoyed the way you
put them in their place by pointing out their lack of contact
for the past year—and Frances's bit about not inviting them
was the frosting on the cake. But I *am* curious," she said as
she picked up a warm plate at the head of the steam table.

"About what, dear?"

Dear. He was doing it again, using an endearment—
even if it was the one older folks often used with someone
younger, and not in a romantic way.

Marlene helped herself to a slice of roasted chicken
breast and a crispy thigh, hoping her question wouldn't feel
intrusive. "Did you really propose to Frances? More than
once?"

Lester smiled sheepishly as they took helpings of creamed
celery, mashed potatoes, and cornbread stuffing. "I made a
first-class fool of myself, assuming Frances would go along
with my plans for marriage—much the same way Elverta
and Agnes are now approaching *me*," he added. "After my
brother Floyd died, she was strapped for cash, so as the man
of the Lehman family, I believed it was my responsibility to
take care of her."

The lines around his eyes crinkled with humor as he
continued. "I also saw Frances as the answer to my daily
meal and laundry problems, so marriage seemed the convenient thing to do," he said with a shake of his head.
"But Frances informed me she'd be no man's *convenience*,
and she reported my behavior to Bishop Monroe and the
preachers."

Bless him, Lester wasn't sparing his pride as he retold
a very personal part of his history. Marlene knew many

Amish men who wouldn't have admitted such behavior. "It's nice to see that you and Frances have mended your fences."

"Frances is a fine woman, and she did the right thing by telling me to take a hike. Nobody's happier than I am, now that she's made a new life with Preacher Marlin," Lester said emphatically. "She—and the others here—were gracious enough to consider my erratic behavior as a phase of my grieving Delores, Sam, and my brother. I owe these folks a huge debt of gratitude, Marlene. You've come to the right place if you're looking for friends who stick with you through thick and thin."

She nodded, delighted that Lester was gesturing toward a couple of empty seats at a table near the corner. After a busy morning in the kitchen and her informative stroll around Promise Lodge—and the most recent spat between Elverta and Agnes—she was ready to devour a plateful of food.

And—even if he *was* too old for her—Marlene wanted to spend as much time with debonair Lester Lehman as she could before she returned to the kitchen to help wash a mountain of dirty dishes.

Chapter 7

A loud, insistent knock at his front door made Lester sigh. It wasn't yet six-thirty on Thursday morning, and already the day's commotion was starting.

"Lester, open up! I know you're in there—I can smell your coffee!" Elverta commanded. "We really must talk. I've come to apologize."

Such a summons didn't inspire him to hurry to the door. The Helmuth family was hosting a breakfast gathering over at their large home by the nursery so the lodge ladies could reset the dining room for Laura and Jonathan's wedding meal, but instead of attending it, Lester had made toast with peanut butter and jelly. He'd hoped to avoid the two women from Ohio so he'd be in the proper frame of mind for worship, but there was no putting off his visitor. If he didn't respond, Elverta Horst was bold enough to try the door and discover it was unlocked.

When Lester stepped into his open doorway, his uninvited guest stood a few feet away, shading her eyes from the rays of the sunrise. He couldn't help noticing that the sunlight brought out the dry skin and fine wrinkles on a thin face that never appeared very happy. Elverta's steely-gray hair was pulled back so tightly that maybe she *couldn't* smile—but he kept that observation to himself.

"And *gut* morning to you, too, Elverta," Lester said cordially. "I hope you slept well?"

She waved off his conversational niceties. "How was I supposed to sleep?" she countered. "I kept seeing you falling all over that girl who is your *daughters'* age. Really, Lester! A fine man like you can attract a woman *so* much more suitable and appropriate."

Lester crossed his arms, leaning against the door frame. "And this is your apology?"

"Of course not! I'm sorry I lowered myself to that ridiculous confrontation with Agnes at the wedding meal yesterday," she replied. "She's really no match for me—or for you, either, Lester."

Feeling no need to defend himself, he kept quiet. He hoped Elverta would take the hint and leave sooner that way.

"Aren't you going to ask me in so we can discuss these matters?" she asked after a few moments.

Lester's eyebrows rose. "*That* wouldn't be appropriate, and you know it. Besides, you can't stand my tiny home. Why would I invite you in?"

"Because I headed straight over here for a few moments of private conversation before I'd even taken time for my coffee—and before *she* got the idea to come!" Elverta blurted out. "Surely after all the years we've known each other, it wouldn't be wrong for me to—"

"Maybe you'd be better company if you'd had your coffee first," Lester pointed out in the most patient tone he could muster. "Elverta, listen to yourself! You haven't said a single word that makes me want to have a private conversation with you—much less consider a long-term relationship."

She blinked. "My *gut*ness, Lester, but you've changed! Back when we were engaged—"

"I *have* changed," he agreed. "After all, we're a quarter

of a century older than we were when I was seeing you. And we were not engaged, Elverta," Lester added more sternly. "That's what you were expecting, but I realized even then that we wouldn't make a *gut* match. That part hasn't changed."

He didn't enjoy speaking so bluntly—sounding so negative—but he saw no reason to toss this woman even a scrap of hope.

Elverta's face fell. She clasped her hands primly in front of her stiff white apron. "I see."

"Do you?" Lester asked quickly. "Then maybe you'll realize it's best for you to leave. There's no nice way to say this, Elverta: I'm not going to marry you. Go on back home to Ohio."

"I see," she repeated softly. "Fine, then. Break my heart."

As she walked across the grass, leaving a trail where her steps disturbed the dew that sparkled in the sunlight, Lester wished he felt better about their conversation. But he'd done the right thing.

He *hoped* Elverta would believe him, and that she'd board the bus tomorrow morning. Yet something told him this situation wasn't nearly over.

Rosetta grabbed the hem of a yellow tablecloth and walked to the far end of a table with it, while Mattie shook it out from the other end.

"This room looks so pretty in pastels!" she said as they quickly positioned the long length of fabric between them. "What a blessing that Laura and Gloria agreed on which linens to use beforehand—and that Laura was willing to depart from tradition."

"*Jah*, even if every woman at Promise Lodge had taken

a white tablecloth home last night to launder it, we'd have been hard-pressed to get them all back in time," Mattie remarked. "Luckily for us, these linens have remained in *gut* shape while they were stashed away in the cupboards for so many years. Washing and ironing them has made them look new again."

"Oh, I like this shade of lavender!" Marlene said as she and Irene Wickey placed a tablecloth on the table beside the one Rosetta and Mattie had just finished. "And with the other cloths being pink and green and yellow, it'll seem like we're sitting in a springtime garden—or an Easter basket!"

As the four of them laughed, Rosetta was delighted that her niece's wedding day was off to such a fine start. In the meeting room across from the lobby, Bishop Monroe and Preachers Amos and Eli were straightening the pew benches and hymnals for the morning's worship service. Thanks to the Kuhn sisters doing some of the meal preparation ahead of time, the aromas of glazed ham and sweet potato casserole were already wafting from the kitchen. All the pieces were falling into place for a glorious celebration to be shared with more than one hundred guests from Coldstream and Ohio.

"We should use these colors again for the common meal on Easter Sunday," Rosetta suggested. "It's almost time to plan our Easter Monday games and activities—ah! *Gut* morning, Agnes," she called out as their guest reached the bottom of the curved lobby stairway. "Going over for breakfast at the Helmuths' place?"

Agnes shook her head dolefully. "I'll just find a little something in the kitchen, or—"

"You're missing out on quite a spread," Mattie put in to encourage her. "They have two or three kinds of breakfast casseroles and sausages and biscuits and a big bowl of fruit salad. Everybody's welcome, you know."

Agnes shrugged, stopping in the dining room doorway. "I'd rather not meet up with you-know-who this early in the morning," she confessed, looking around to be sure her nemesis wasn't present.

Rosetta sighed to herself. If she and her helpers were to finish setting up the dining room before church, this wasn't the time to have a pep talk about giving up on Lester and going home. "Well, the coffee's on. But you'll have to ask Ruby and Beulah what they might have around, as they're focused on the wedding meal, of course—not figuring anyone would eat breakfast here this morning."

"I'll get by," the little widow murmured in a pathetic tone.

As she tottered along the side aisle with her head hung low, Rosetta wondered if Lester's guest was feeling embarrassed about the spat she and Elverta had started during yesterday's dinner. Or maybe Lester had taken Agnes aside and told her she didn't stand a chance with him.

Agnes hadn't quite reached the kitchen door before Elverta entered the lobby from outside and slammed the front door behind her.

Rosetta raised her eyebrows, meeting the gazes of her sister and helpers. This was no time for a lecture on proper treatment of lodge property either, but she was determined to keep the situation between the two women under control. "Is everything all right, Elverta?" she asked loudly.

The *maidel* peered into the dining room. Her face was pale, and she didn't appear to be in the mood for anything as festive as a wedding. "Oh. Didn't realize anyone would be in here."

Mattie straightened to her full height, letting her tablecloth drop onto the table. "You look upset, Elverta. Is there something we can help you with?" she asked in a purposeful tone. "Did something go wrong over at the Helmuths' breakfast?"

"I wasn't *at* the Helmuth place. I was visiting—"

Elverta's immediate change of expression told Rosetta that she'd spotted Agnes on the far side of the dining room. Exhaling loudly, Lester's other lady friend started down the center aisle of the dining room like a hawk with a sparrow in sight. Agnes's eyes widened, and she appeared too startled to move.

"You might as well go home, Mrs. Plank," Elverta started in archly. "*I've* just been to Lester's place, and—"

"Why would he want to hitch up with a prickly old pear like you?" Agnes demanded, planting her fist on her ample hip. "That'll never happen, *Miss* Horst!"

"Puh! At least I'm not a mousy little motormouth like— at least I'm not *fat*!" Elverta cried out triumphantly.

"That's enough!" Rosetta called out.

"You two are *not* going to carry on this way and spoil Laura's day," Mattie chimed in sternly. She started toward the pair, probably intending to corner them for a lecture.

"I don't know what it's going to take to settle this squabbling," Rosetta continued earnestly, "but if it means insisting you stay in your rooms rather than attending the wedding—"

"What's going on, ladies?" Bishop Monroe asked in his booming voice.

The dining room went quiet. By now Beulah and Ruby had come to the kitchen doorway, frowning as they dried their hands with towels. Rosetta stepped out of the way as Preachers Amos and Eli took their places on either side of the bishop in the arched entryway, clearly disturbed by the raised voices they'd heard.

Agnes whimpered. Elverta remained silent, her eyes wide as she took in the trio of church leaders.

Bishop Monroe cleared his throat. "How about if you two come in for a word of prayer and counsel?" he asked, nodding his head toward the meeting room. "On this day when we'll praise God and witness the sacrament of marriage— the exchange of holy, permanent vows—I want *every* participant to be in the proper frame of mind. Shall we?"

After a moment of silence fraught with tension, Agnes started up the side aisle and Elverta walked through the center of the room, cautiously passing Mattie. They reminded Rosetta of errant schoolgirls who'd been called on the carpet by the teacher—and truth be told, their behavior had seemed more adolescent than adult.

"*Denki*, Monroe," she whispered before the two ladies came within earshot.

The bishop nodded before extending his arm to direct Elverta and Agnes toward the meeting room. When the men had followed the guilty parties across the lobby, Rosetta sighed.

"Well, that took some of the wind out of my sails," she said ruefully. "Let's hope our guests have learned their lesson—and now, let's get these tables set. We've been planning for happiness, and we want to give Laura and Jonathan the best wedding day ever!"

Chapter 8

W hile other ladies set drinking glasses and silverware on the dining tables, Marlene focused on the steam table where the food would be served. After stacking fifty white plates on the end, she carefully positioned her metal cart underneath the table's edge before going back into the kitchen.

"All right, we have the first round of plates ready, and another hundred and fifty plates are within easy reach for a helper," she said. "I'll be happy to take charge of that during the meal, if you'd like me to."

Beulah smiled, wiping her hands on her purple paisley-print apron. "What a blessing you are, Marlene! You've just moved in, and you've jumped in to help as though you've always lived here."

"You're a keeper!" Ruby chimed in as she lifted the lid from a roaster filled with two long, boneless hams. "These are coming along just fine. I'm so glad the kids wanted ham today, because I love the way pineapple slices and maraschino cherries dress them up."

"You ladies amaze me, cooking two huge wedding dinners one right after the other," Marlene remarked. "And what a gift to the brides' families, that they don't have to organize all the food and tables and chairs at their homes."

Beulah shrugged modestly. "My sister and I love to feed people," she said. "Folks here are *gut* about paying for the food they want us to fix, and we always have lots of helpers—"

"And it's such a joy to see Gloria and Laura marrying fine young brothers who intend to stay here at Promise Lodge and keep their family business going," Ruby put in as she put the roaster of hams back into the oven. "This community has grown so much since we came here, with families of all ages and a new generation coming—"

The shrill ring of a telephone startled Marlene. The homes here had traditional white phone shanties at the roadside, so she hadn't expected a phone to be inside a building—even if a mixture of Old Order Amish and Mennonites lived in the apartments.

Beulah bustled over to answer it. After listening for a moment, she pressed the receiver to her chest and looked at Marlene. "I think it's your brother, asking for you. I'm not sure I understood what he said."

"He's very shy with folks he doesn't know," Marlene explained as she quickly passed the worktables and counter-tops covered with pans and utensils. She took the phone and spoke gently into it. "Mose? *Gut* morning—are you all right?"

"I am now," her brother replied with a chuckle. "I—I'm in the b-barn on the b-bishop's phone, and I wasn't sure how to reach you. There's a mare about to foal—with twins—so I'm going to skip the wedding today and stay with her."

Marlene frowned. "But our friends from Coldstream have arrived on their buses—"

"Too many people!" Mose insisted. "It's better if I stay here with the mare. I didn't want you to worry about where

I am, so I called. You be sure to have a *gut* time for the both of us, all right?"

His mind was made up, so Marlene accepted his decision. Still, it saddened her that her reclusive brother felt so uncomfortable in a crowd—especially because he'd known many of today's wedding guests for years. "You're going to miss out on some fine-looking glazed ham and yams, and Ruby's chocolate cake—"

"Maybe there'll be some wedding food left this evening after the Coldstream folks go home, or after the Ohio people leave on the bus," he said. "You can tell me all about the wedding when we head back to the farm tomorrow to clean out the house, *jah*?"

"All right," Marlene agreed. "I hope everything goes smoothly with your mare. I'm sure Bishop Monroe will be glad you're with her while he's in church all morning."

"*Jah*, I talked to him about it before he left for the lodge. He's a *gut* guy, Marlene. We came to the right place."

As she replaced the wall phone's receiver, Marlene smiled at the Kuhn sisters. "When we were five, my brother was kidnapped—gone for a couple of days before the police returned him home," she explained. "He's still very shy around strangers, and he'll do just about anything to avoid a crowd, so he's staying with a Clydesdale mare today to help her birth her twins."

"What a conscientious man," Beulah said. "I'm sure Bishop Monroe's glad to have Mose watching out for his horses."

"I have a feeling a picnic hamper of wedding food will be waiting for your brother this afternoon, whenever you'd care to take it to the barn," Ruby put in, winking at Marlene. "A big man like Mose needs to keep his strength up, handling those Clydesdales."

"How kind you are!" Marlene said, blinking back tears

of gratitude. "I feel like we've moved into a place where we've latched onto two new *mamms*."

Touched by her remark, the Kuhn sisters looked at one another with tremulous smiles. Beulah glanced up at the clock, and then through the window above the sink. "We'll no doubt have a few ladies coming in to check things over any minute now. I think a bunch of folks are coming back from breakfast, because church starts in about ten minutes."

"Have a *gut* morning, ladies, and I'll see you later to help at the steam table," Marlene said as she started toward the dining room.

Indeed, some of the guests were making their way inside to use the restrooms, and she greeted some of her Coldstream friends who were admiring the pretty pastel tablecloths. Most of them had come on rented buses this morning because the trip took nearly three hours in a horse-drawn vehicle—and because they could do their livestock chores before they left, and they'd be home in time to feed their animals again this evening.

On such a beautiful day, the women were forming their line outside before they filed in to sit on the pew benches. Marlene walked past some of the older ladies waiting on the lodge's wide front porch, exchanging greetings with them as she stepped down into the yard. Someone took hold of her sleeve from behind.

Marlene turned and went still. Elverta's expression suggested she'd been sucking lemons for breakfast.

"You're new here, so I should inform you that Lester has *daughters* your age," she muttered disapprovingly. "I'm telling you this for your own *gut*, because men tend to forget about such details when they've caught the scent of a female in heat."

The *maidel* walked away before Marlene could make a rational reply—or a comeback.

Why had Elverta chosen this moment to inform her of such a fact? As Marlene mulled it over, she recalled that Lester had mentioned the son he'd lost in a traffic accident, so it came as no big surprise that he might have additional children, except . . .

Elverta's trying to shame me—just as she ruthlessly accused Agnes of being chatty and overweight. Lester and I are merely friends, so why would it matter to me if his girls are my age?

Yet, deep down, it did matter. As Marlene found two of her longtime friends from Coldstream, Essie and Linda Ropp, to sit with, she wondered if Lester would ever get around to telling her more about his family—

And there he was, dapper and happy in his best clothes as he crossed the lawn.

He doesn't look nearly old enough to be my dat. Why, his hair's as black as his vest and trousers, and from here, I see no sign of any gray. Then again, he proposed to Frances, so maybe I've miscalculated his age.

When Lester smiled at her, Marlene felt better instantly. He came right over, unconcerned about the women who were lining up around her—and watching closely as he reached for her hand. She spotted a few gray hairs at his temples, but he still didn't look *old*.

"It's *gut* to see you, Marlene," Lester said, squeezing her hand before releasing it. "I hope we can catch up to each other after the ceremony? Maybe sit together for the meal?"

Her face fell. "I'd love to, Lester, but I'll be helping at the steam table—"

"I'm not surprised. You're the kind of woman who does what needs to be done without waiting to be asked," he remarked with a nod. "And you're no doubt visiting with your friends from Coldstream today. I'll see you later then."

With a nod to the women around her, Lester strode

toward the other side of the lodge building, where the men were starting to file inside.

Linda elbowed her. "That's the guy you came into the dining room with yesterday," she remarked knowingly. "He seems very nice—"

"And he's *cute*," Essie put in, widening her eyes. "I felt bad for both of you when those two biddy hens made such a fuss in front of the *eck* table."

The line of women shifted forward to enter the lodge, so Marlene and her friends fell silent to prepare their hearts and minds for worship. Their closest friends knew that she and Mose had moved to Promise Lodge earlier this week, but she wondered if other folks from Coldstream had seen the flyers for their upcoming household auction—which she and Mose had kept quiet about, just as they'd sold the farm without advertising it. She and her brother were hoping to minimize the fuss their church leaders would make about them moving away from the district.

Had Bishop Obadiah Chupp come to Laura Hershberger's wedding? As Marlene took her seat between Linda and Essie, she cautiously glanced between the older women's heads. On the men's side, the groom, Jonathan Helmuth, and his *newehockers* sat on the front pew bench. The second row was where the oldest of the men were sitting, and as Marlene quickly checked their white-bearded faces, her heart thudded.

Bishop Obadiah wasn't among them.

Marlene relaxed and felt extremely grateful, even as she asked God to forgive her negative thoughts concerning the bishop He'd chosen for the Coldstream community. Perhaps the Bender sisters had it right: Obadiah and Isaac had caused enough trouble at Promise Lodge—and had gotten their comeuppance—so the Chupp family had chosen not to be here today. She hoped a few other men had chosen to stay home, as well.

The congregation opened their *Ausbunds* and began singing the opening hymn while Bishop Monroe and the preachers met in another room to decide who would preach the day's sermons. As one of the men from Promise Lodge sang out the first phrase to set the pitch and the tempo, Marlene wondered if Mose would ever do that again. Her brother, although flustered and halting when he spoke to anyone who wasn't a family member, had a beautiful baritone voice that effortlessly filled a room when he sang.

As Marlene glanced up from her *Ausbund*, however, she forgot all about hymn singing. She'd once courted Ervin Yoder, who was now sitting directly across from her and staring right at her. He had the hounded, hangdog air of a man who had too many children—which made Marlene glad she hadn't married him. Two fellows seated farther down that same pew bench were gazing at her, as well.

Marlene's throat went dry. Yost Mullet and his cousin Jake were eyeing her so speculatively—so purposefully— that she suddenly wished Mose had come to the service. Had the Mullets seen the sale flyers, perhaps? Or did they have something else on their minds? All three of the fellows who'd caught her eye had wives now, but at various times in the past they'd all been courting *her*—and she had been the one to break the engagements.

Over the years, the men's resentment had eased as they'd moved on and started families with other women. Marlene considered their wives good friends, because she'd known them all her life. Yet as she looked down at her *Ausbund* again, struggling to find her place in the verse they were singing, her tightening insides warned her to listen to her intuition.

But what if I'm being silly? Reading too much into the Mullets' furtive gazes?

As Bishop Monroe, Preachers Amos and Eli, and Deacon Marlin entered the room to begin the worship service, Marlene focused on these men instead of the cousins from Coldstream. The bishop's welcome was warm, and Marlin Kurtz's reading of the familiar thirteenth chapter of First Corinthians reminded her that this day—her life—should be about *love* rather than worries from the past.

"Perhaps the best-known verse from our Scripture lesson today—the one we often see on wooden gift store plaques— has become so familiar that we gloss over it," Preacher Amos began. "Yet earlier this morning, I was reminded that we need to consider this verse very seriously as we witness another wonderful exchange of vows. Paul's words have been translated into many editions of the Bible, but his meaning remains the same: love is *kind*. And love is patient, my friends."

Marlene admired the way Preacher Amos had referred to the latest exchange of insults between Agnes and Elverta without saying their names. She wondered if those two ladies, seated apart in a row ahead of her, felt the sting of guilt that always accompanied a sermon when the preacher seemed to be pointing his finger at—

She made the mistake of letting her gaze wander across the room.

Yost was still staring at her. He raised a dark, disapproving eyebrow as though he *knew* something, and he showed no inclination to drop his gaze.

Flustered, Marlene looked down at her lap for the rest of Preacher Amos's thought-provoking sermon. It was foolish to feel rattled by Yost's behavior—hadn't he always been cocky and domineering? And hadn't he and Jake constantly tried to take more liberties during their courtships than the Old Order—or Marlene—believed were appropriate?

Though she tried to pay attention to the remainder of the service, she felt too vulnerable to focus on matters of faith. Marlene wanted to enjoy watching her longtime friend Laura Hershberger exchange vows with Jonathan Helmuth, but all she could think about was getting *out* of this meeting room and *away* from any possible contact with the Mullet cousins. Even though she'd been seated across from Ervin Yoder and the Mullets during church for *years* after breaking up with them, this morning they seemed to be sitting in judgment, still finding her guilty of her sins against them.

"Let's all congratulate Mr. and Mrs. Jonathan Helmuth!" Bishop Monroe finally announced. "It's a happy day for all of us!"

When everyone stood up, filling the huge room with applause, Marlene quickly excused herself and left the pew bench. Down the center aisle she strode, before the other women could step out and block her progress. They would probably assume she was helping with the meal or had to use the restroom, but Marlene's first responsibility was to Ruby and Beulah. As she jogged through the beautiful dining room, where the sunlight made the pastel tablecloths glow, she prayed the two Mennonite sisters wouldn't ask too many questions or feel let down.

"Ladies, something's come up and I won't be able to help at the steam table," she said as she entered the huge kitchen.

The Kuhns looked up from the pans of fragrant glazed ham slices they were arranging, appearing curious but not overly concerned. "We've got plenty of help, Marlene," Beulah assured her. "Go on and do whatever you need to do."

"*Jah*—and whenever you'd like to take Mose's dinner to the barn, the picnic basket's packed and waiting in the mudroom, sweetie," Ruby put in kindly. "If you need anything, just let us know."

"*Denki* so much! You ladies are the best," Marlene said without stopping. "I'll take it over to him right now, while the food's still warm."

She headed for the mudroom and grabbed the picnic basket. At least, if anyone quizzed her, she had a reasonable excuse for not being in the dining room when the wedding party and the guests started through the buffet line. Marlene felt horrible about ducking out, but with nearly two hundred people wanting to congratulate Laura and Jonathan, her friend probably wouldn't realize she was absent from the festivities anyway.

As she walked quickly up the road that led toward the Burkholder place and the big red Clydesdale barns, Marlene tried to calm her runaway imagination. She would be perfectly safe among so many friends at the wedding meal—and why would Yost and Jake have any reason to confront her, anyway? They had wives and homes and kids now, and *years* had gone by since she'd told each of those men she wasn't going to marry him.

Maybe they got hold of a flyer about our household auction. But that's no reason to panic, because a lot of these guests will be seeing those soon.

Still, she needed the calming effect of her twin brother's company—she would feel better after she told him about how the Mullets had behaved during church.

And wouldn't it be nice to share Mose's picnic lunch? And perhaps see two newborn Clydesdales?

Chapter 9

"Lester, may I have a word?"

Seeing Beulah approach the steam table with a full pan of sliced ham, Lester immediately removed the nearly empty pan so she could replace it. "Absolutely," he replied over the noise of people's conversations. "And if you have any more of those heavy pans to carry, let me do it for you, all right?"

With the deft moves that came from years of experience, the woman in the bright pink polka dot dress placed her pan in its slot and replaced the serving tongs. When Beulah backed away so the guests could continue through the line, she nodded toward the kitchen.

As Lester followed her, he inhaled the salty-sweet aromas of the glazed ham and the big pan of marshmallow-topped yam casserole that Ruby was setting on the countertop. It amazed him, the way these sisters had orchestrated, cooked, and served a big meal the day before, yet they appeared delighted to be doing it all over again today. When he reached the back of the kitchen, where Beulah pointed for him to set his pan, she turned with a hint of concern on her kindly face.

"Maybe I worry too much—and maybe it's really none of my beeswax," she said in a low voice, "but when Marlene passed through here about ten minutes ago, she seemed hell-bent for leather about leaving. Do you know anything about that?"

Lester shook his head. "She appeared preoccupied when I glanced at her during church, but I have no idea why."

"Well, she took out of here with a picnic basket for her brother, Mose, who's spent the morning helping one of Bishop Monroe's mares birth twins," Ruby put in as she stepped over to join the conversation. "But she definitely didn't have horses on her mind when she excused herself from helping with the steam table—"

"And we wondered if maybe you'd like to mosey over that way," Beulah continued with a knowing smile, "because maybe you have a couple of reasons not to be in the dining room right now, either."

"We packed you some dinner," Ruby added as she reached under the counter, "because who knows how long you might want to enjoy the fresh air and sunshine rather than being trapped with two women who picked another fight first thing this morning."

Lester groaned softly. "I don't even want to know what they were bickering about this time," he murmured as he accepted the insulated bag Ruby handed him. "*Denki* for my dinner—and for giving me a mission."

As he exited through the mudroom, Lester shook his head. After observing how subdued and worried Marlene had appeared during her friend Laura's wedding ceremony, he'd intended to catch up to her during the meal to be sure she was all right. He'd also prepared himself to face whatever foolishness Agnes and Elverta laid on him today, because it was better to deal with their confrontations than to continue ducking out. He wanted to be very sure they both boarded the buses back to Ohio tomorrow morning, after all.

And yet the Kuhn sisters' suggestion seemed like the right path to follow. If they were concerned about Marlene's sudden departure, he was, too. Lester walked quickly across the lawn behind the lodge and onto the road leading toward the bishop's barns. He prepared himself to meet Marlene's mountain of a brother, Mose—and to feel like a third wheel if the twin siblings were already eating the picnic Ruby had sent.

As he approached the white plank fence that enclosed Bishop Monroe's large pasture, however, he spotted Marlene coming through the walk-out door of one of the barns. Lester paused at the gate to watch her. As she stopped in the grassy green pasture and lifted her face to catch the sunlight, it struck him—again—that she was a very attractive woman. Before he waved at her, he reminded himself—again—that he had no business entertaining romantic thoughts about her, even if the Kuhn sisters seemed to be pointing him in that direction.

For the moment, however, Lester allowed himself to enjoy the picture she made, standing fearlessly in the pasture as a few curious Clydesdales stopped grazing to approach her. When Marlene extended her arm, speaking gentle words Lester could only imagine from his distant position, the huge horses' ears perked up. They cautiously stretched their necks toward her upturned palm, and one by one, they nuzzled it.

Any woman who can stand so close to such massive animals—three of them, no less— isn't skittish or easily frightened. So what spooked Marlene during church? Why did she bolt after the wedding rather than help at the steam table as she'd planned?

When she started up the gentle rise toward the gate, leaving the horses behind, Lester opened the heavy latch to step in and wave at her. The way Marlene's face lit up made him glad he'd come.

"Lester!" she said as she topped the hill. "I wasn't expecting to see you. Figured you'd be filling a plate by now—"

"The Kuhn sisters packed me a lunch and suggested I check on you," he said, holding up the insulated bag. "Is everything all right, Marlene? You looked like you were a million miles away during church and the wedding—kind of worried, considering that you'd been looking forward to Laura's ceremony."

Her resigned smile told him he'd pegged her correctly.

"I felt bad, letting Ruby and Beulah down," she hedged as she stopped a few feet in front of him. "But they'd packed a lunch for Mose and told me to run along rather than worry about helping them. So they also set *you* up with a meal?" she teased lightly. "Why do I get the feeling they're playing matchmaker and giving you a reason to avoid Agnes and Elverta again?"

Rather than answer that question, Lester gestured toward a picnic table on the side lawn of the Burkholder home. "Maybe you've already eaten with your brother, but I'd be glad—"

"Nope. Silly me, I should've known better than to interrupt Mose while he was helping a mare with her birthing." Marlene stepped out of the pasture, waiting while Lester fastened the gate. "He reminded me that my presence would upset her—because I'm a stranger—and at that moment the first of her twin foals started sliding out."

"Ah. Always a miraculous sight—as long as the process is going the way it's supposed to," Lester remarked as they started for the table in the shade.

"Mose was anticipating complications—which also gave him a reason not to brave the big crowd at the wedding," she explained with a sad smile. "But the mare's in very capable hands, and she and her foals will have the best of care. That's the most important thing, ain't so? So I left his picnic basket for him—and here I am. With you."

Why did Marlene's words make his stomach flutter in that indescribable way?

As she slid onto the picnic table's bench, Marlene warned herself about sounding too chummy—too interested in Lester. And although she was touched by the Kuhn sisters' concern for her, she didn't feel ready to bare her soul to Lester about her reasons for fleeing after the wedding. With Elverta and Agnes causing so much commotion, the poor man didn't deserve to have another needy female vying for his attention.

So she would focus the conversation on something other than herself.

"My word, Ruby packed enough food in your bag to last you for days!" Marlene said as Lester placed foil-wrapped packages on the table between them. "As heavy as Mose's picnic basket felt, I suspect she did the same thing for him."

"They're generous, kindhearted ladies," Lester agreed as he removed utensils wrapped in napkins as well as two plates. "And as you can see, they intended for you to share this feast with me. Go ahead—open some of these packets. After being cooped up in church all morning, I'm ready for some *gut* food. And *gut* company."

Marlene caught a wistful edge in Lester's voice, and she again felt sorry that he was dealing with two impossibly insistent women. "Let's see, we've got some of that fabulous ham with pineapple slices and cherries . . . and here's some fresh bread," she said lightly. "Seems like a sign that I should make a sandwich!"

Lester laughed with her, his face creasing with mirth.

"This container's full of that ooey-gooey sweet potato casserole, and we have slaw, too."

"Wonderful! Slaw makes a sandwich really crunchy and special—better than lettuce, don't you think?" Marlene glanced up to see that Lester was watching her closely as she spooned some of the salad onto her ham before she placed a second slice of bread on top.

"I've never sampled that combination," he admitted, "but if you think it's tasty, I'll give it a shot. Life's too short not to try new things."

Now that she felt safely removed from the two men—and two women—who could disrupt their picnic lunch, Marlene was ravenous. She took a huge bite of her sandwich. The salty ham and creamy-sweet cabbage hit the spot, and Lester's expression told her he was glad he'd trusted her judgment.

"*Gut, jah?*" she asked before biting into her sandwich again.

Lester nodded, chewing with his eyes closed to savor his food. Once again Marlene was aware of how handsome he was, how fit and strong he appeared even in wedding clothes that were basic and rather boxy, like every other Amish man's church vest and trousers.

"Any particular reason you left the festivities? It's not like you to skip out after you'd told the Kuhns you'd help them."

Marlene blinked. Lester's question brought her out of a little reverie about him that she wasn't even aware she'd indulged in. "I, um, saw some folks from Coldstream I hadn't thought about encountering," she answered, hoping he would leave it at that.

His dark eyebrows rose as he spooned some yam casserole onto his plate. "Was it the bishop or his son? I haven't heard many *gut* things about those fellows from the folks who've moved away from that district."

"No, Rosetta didn't think the Chupp family would come, and I haven't seen them. It was just—well, I probably misinterpreted the expressions on their faces when I saw them from across the room," Marlene added quickly. "Some folks are just keen on pushing your buttons, you know?"

"Oh, I have firsthand experience with that," Lester replied with a laugh. He polished off his sandwich and then reached for another slice of bread. As he folded it around a piece of ham and spooned slaw into the opening, he seemed to be considering his next words carefully.

"I really don't want to hear what Agnes and Elverta were squabbling about this morning, but I suspect Elverta started it," he said softly. "She hollered at me as the sun was coming up, saying she had an apology—but it was a trumped-up excuse to plead her case again and to bad-mouth Agnes. She was in a raw mood when I sent her away."

"When she came into the lodge and slammed the door, Rosetta called her on it," Marlene recounted as she helped herself to the yam casserole. "And then, when Elverta spotted Agnes in the dining room, they got into such a heated name-calling spree that Bishop Monroe overheard them. He and the preachers invited them into the meeting room for prayer and a counseling session."

Lester shook his head, sighing. "I've told them both, plain as day, that I'm not interested. But they don't want to hear that—and I don't want to spend any more of our time talking about it," he added apologetically. "It's exasperating. And embarrassing."

Marlene nodded, hoping that if she let Lester keep talking, he wouldn't ask any more about her own worrisome situation. She eyed the two pieces of pie he'd unwrapped.

"What's your preference, Lester? Raisin sour cream or apple with crumbly topping?"

"You can choose—"

"But this is *your* lunch," she insisted, "and the Kuhns packed it with you in mind. So you pick."

Lester looked at the pie and picked up his knife. "How about if I cut them down the middle and we can share them? I'd hate to think I grabbed the piece you really wanted but were too polite to choose."

"The perfect solution."

Lester laughed out loud. "At least I've pleased *somebody* today! I'm beginning to wonder if there's even an *im*perfect solution where Agnes and Elverta are concerned. They don't seem inclined to give up on me and go home."

Marlene nodded. "Sorry they're putting you through this, Lester."

"*Jah*, what are the chances that two women from opposite sides of Sugarcreek would each get it in her head that I'd be a happy man if only I'd marry her?" he mused aloud.

"It's not as romantic as it might seem, having two people determined to—well, but you know all about that," Marlene finished quickly. Lester was such a good listener, so easy to be with, that she almost hadn't caught herself before she told him about the Mullets.

"You got that right," Lester said as he placed a section of each pie slice on her plate before taking his own. "Back in the day, I thought I was pretty hot stuff to be seeing an older woman—because Elverta's got five or six years on me. I'm not sure, but I think Agnes is in her mid-fifties. At this stage of the game, though, age is more about attitude than arithmetic."

He looked up to hold her gaze, his fork poised over his pie. "You were right when you said those gals are too old for me. You're a wise woman, Marlene, and you've given me a lot to think about."

Her eyes widened, and she couldn't swallow her bite of pie. What had Lester meant by such remarks? For a man who'd met her just yesterday, he sounded awfully . . . *interested*. Otherwise, why would he be talking about age and attitude?

"Hmm. My folks used to warn me about being a smart-*aleck* rather than telling me I was smart," she murmured.

Lester chuckled. "My family—Frances and Gloria, anyway—were regularly telling *me* what a fool I was not so long ago, when I insisted I should marry Frances. We all go through phases, ain't so?"

He paused with his fork suspended over his pie, looking directly into her eyes. "I'm grateful that you're willing to listen, even when I'm running off at the mouth about Agnes and Elverta after I said I didn't intend to," he murmured. "You're patient and kind, Marlene. Amos was preaching about *you* today, dear."

Marlene's throat tightened with emotion. She couldn't recall a man ever paying her such compliments, and she liked it—even if emotionally, Lester was getting a little too close for comfort. She had been reminded today why she should not encourage him. Why would a nice guy like Lester be interested in a three-time loser? Her reputation for breaking engagements wasn't something she was proud of—even if, in the end, she'd made the right decision each time.

"You don't know me as well as you think," she murmured. She stood up, leaving the last few bites of her pie on her plate. "*Denki* for sharing your lunch, Lester. I should be washing dishes, since I backed out on helping at the steam table."

As she hurried down the road toward the lodge, Marlene

sensed Lester was staring after her, wondering what he'd said to offend her.

But it was just as well. Sticking to her vow to never marry seemed better than falling for Lester only to disappoint him, the way she'd done with three previous men. Scrubbing greasy pans in the back of the lodge kitchen would keep her out of the Mullets' sight—and after helping the Kuhns and the other women clean up, she could slip upstairs to her apartment.

After all, hadn't she had her new place remodeled exactly the way she wanted it because she intended to spend the rest of her life there?

Chapter 10

On Friday morning Lester was once again grateful to have physical work at the new bulk store to keep him busy. Because Bishop Monroe was looking after his Clydesdales and Preacher Amos was tilling Mattie's plots so she could start planting her early vegetables, Dale Kraybill was the only other person on the premises—and that suited Lester fine. After they'd exchanged greetings and briefly discussed the day's plans, the storekeeper headed to the warehouse area to unpack the shipments he'd received earlier in the week.

"Holler if you need another set of hands, Lester," Dale called out from the doorway. "Some of those refrigerator and freezer units you'll be installing are awfully big for one fellow to handle."

"But you were smart and bought them with wheels," Lester reminded him as he opened his large toolbox. "Same goes for you, far as asking for help. I don't want to come into the warehouse and find you smashed against the floor because one of those shipping crates fell on you. They're stacked pretty high."

"That's what forklifts are for!" Kraybill shot back with a chuckle. "See you when we take a break—or when Irene gets here. We'll be organizing the display for her Promise

Lodge Pies today. And if Rosetta or the Kuhns come in to talk about their displays, please let me know."

"Will do."

As he walked toward the grocery section of the store, Lester considered his strategy. It would be best to handle the taller freezers and refrigerators along the wall first, while he was fresh, and then tackle the waist-high units. Allen Troyer, who'd become a licensed electrician before he'd joined the Amish church, had already installed the wiring and electrical connections, and Bishop Monroe and Preacher Amos had uncrated the units when they'd been working on Tuesday. Lester would roll these appliances into place, attach the doors and handles, and then plug them in to be sure they worked properly.

It was exciting to position the big wall units and hear the thrum of electricity as each unit lit up and began to cool. The white freezers with their clear glass doors looked clean and modern compared to the Old Order bulk stores Lester was used to, where older gas appliances and ceiling lights made a store's interior somewhat darker. Dale Kraybill belonged to a progressive Mennonite fellowship, and he was a friendly, outgoing fellow, so Lester predicted that he'd do a brisk business with English and Plain customers alike.

After installing the first two wall freezers, Lester didn't have to concentrate quite so intently . . . so his thoughts wandered. His encounters with Agnes and Elverta after yesterday's wedding festivities had left him even more frustrated than before: he had the idea that these women were now more interested in irritating each other—each making sure the other one didn't hook him—than they were in a romantic relationship.

He'd watched the buses roll out early this morning, heading for Ohio. The four newlyweds were heading east to collect wedding presents from Lehman and Helmuth families who hadn't attended the weddings, but he was pretty sure neither Elverta nor Agnes was on board.

Shaking his head, Lester wheeled the last three wall freezers into place. He was even *more* frustrated about Marlene's sudden departure yesterday, before she'd finished her pie. He'd thought their conversation was going so well. Her lovely face had appeared relaxed and empathetic as he'd aired his grievances about Agnes and Elverta.

But something had been gnawing at her—something she didn't feel comfortable sharing. Marlene hadn't specified whom she'd spotted, but her expression during church suggested that men were involved—because that was the direction she'd been facing. It got him nowhere, speculating further about her difficult situation with the folks from Coldstream, so Lester focused on the installation process again. It wasn't as though he or Marlene were leaving Promise Lodge, so sooner or later maybe she'd tell him what had spooked her.

A flash of sunlight moving across the wall alerted him that someone was entering the store. "Hi, Irene!" he called out from the waist-high unit he was installing. "Dale's out back, in the warehouse. If you'd like me to fetch him—"

"I can go," she put in cheerfully. "You're hip-deep in your work—and don't those freezers and refrigerators look nice! This store's such a wonderful-*gut* addition to our settlement—"

"And the pies you and Phoebe bake will be a huge draw, too," Dale said as he pushed through the warehouse's swinging door. "That's why I think we should display them right up front, where folks will see them when they first come in."

Lester smiled to himself and went back to his work. Watching Irene and Dale talk so animatedly, with their faces aglow—even though they were discussing shelving—he suspected Dale's bachelor state might not be as permanent as the storekeeper believed it was. Kraybill was quick to say that he didn't need a wife after all these years of doing things exactly the way he wanted to, but didn't a man sometimes *want* something he didn't really need?

If I'm honest, I'll admit I want Marlene for a lot of different reasons—but I sure don't need the adjustments I'd have to make if she became a permanent part of my life.

Lester shook his head. Had it only been a few days ago that he'd been stretched out in his chaise lounge on the dock, delighted because he felt so good about life in his tiny home? And how comfortable he'd become with his solitary life? Even if Elverta and Agnes hadn't turned him on his ear with their pesky marriage propositions, he'd still have to decide how he felt about Marlene.

He hadn't seen her coming. Hadn't anticipated the return of *yearning* for a woman's company.

The sound of more voices alerted him to Rosetta's arrival with Ruby and Beulah. Dale steered the sisters toward the units Lester was working on while he escorted Rosetta to where household items—and her goat milk soap—would soon be displayed.

The silvery-haired Kuhn sisters grinned at Lester, as excited as schoolgirls.

"Oh, these refrigerator cases are really something!" Ruby said as she gripped the handle of the unit closest to her. "Look at the way these doors slide across to keep the contents cooler—much more sensible than those open-topped refrigerators at the grocery store."

"And we won't need to wear our coats every time we're back here," Beulah put in with a nod. She gazed around eagerly. "Won't be long before this place opens. You men have come a long way this week, Lester."

"We have," he agreed. "It's going to be quite a busy place, I expect."

"And I predict that you ladies will sell so much of your cheese here, you might have to expand your little factory!" Dale put in as he and Rosetta joined them.

"Oh no—that's not going to happen," Beulah countered emphatically. "We get just enough milk from Christine's Holsteins to make just enough cheese to keep us as busy as we care to be. Why mess with success?"

"*Jah*, if we expanded our little factory, we'd have to invest a chunk of change in additional equipment," Ruby put in. "And besides that, if we took on all that extra work, we wouldn't have time for such things as cooking wedding dinners—or even making the meals for the renters in the lodge and cabins."

"All work and no play would make Ruby and Beulah a couple of dull, tired girls, too," Beulah added, smiling sweetly at Dale. "But we appreciate your confidence in our products. And you're right—we're going to sell a *lot* of cheese here, because you're in a prime location."

Lester was chortling at the way Kraybill had focused first on one Kuhn and then the other, as though he was following a volleyball across a net during a fast-paced game. Like a lot of sisters, Ruby and Beulah spoke in tandem, instinctively following each other's thought process and finishing each other's sentences.

"You've made some excellent points," Dale remarked. "I'm planning to place your cheeses near the front of this refrigerated section, along with a sign saying they're made next door by local Mennonite residents. Will that be all right?"

"*Jah*, you betcha," Ruby replied. "And when I've bottled my fresh honey, you can have some of that to sell, if you'd like it. My little bees would be tickled to know that lots of new customers will be enjoying what they've made from the clover and the orchard blossoms at Promise Lodge."

"Your store will put Promise Lodge on the map for a lot of folks in this region of Missouri, Dale," Rosetta put in. "We're delighted you've come here—ain't so, Irene?"

Irene's smile was yet another telltale sign that she and the storekeeper shared a closer relationship than they admitted. "Our gain is Cloverdale's loss. The bulk store there will still be in business, but it won't be the same without *you*, Dale."

Kraybill waved her off as he started toward the front of the store. "Shall we make that list of baking supplies and pie pans you and Phoebe need?" he asked her over his shoulder. "I'd best do it now, before I get busy in the warehouse again."

Lester picked up his tools and moved to the spot where the last three floor refrigerators would be installed. Rosetta took a moment to look at one of the units, testing the way the door on the top opened and closed.

"Won't be long before your work's finished here, Lester," she remarked. "Do you know where your next job will be?"

He shrugged as he picked up his pneumatic drill. "With the weather turning warmer, I might take a little time off to—"

Another flash of light made him glance toward the door, and his heart sank. Agnes and Elverta stepped inside, gazing around before they greeted Dale and Irene, who stood at the front counter.

"On second thought, maybe your Truman could let me know if he's got some work?" Lester said under his breath.

Rosetta gazed speculatively at the women before turning to speak with Lester again. "After the chat I had with those two, I sincerely hoped they'd be leaving this morning," she murmured. "Mind if I stick around? It's interesting that they came here *together*."

"Be my guest." Lester positioned his drill, hoping the noise would dissuade the two women from coming over.

"And yes, I'll have Truman call you," Rosetta added. "He's redoing the landscaping around an older apartment complex on the other side of Cloverdale. Who knows? Maybe those buildings could use some of your siding and windows."

With a nod, Lester began driving the screws to attach the handles to the cases' sliding doors. He should've known that the racket of his drill would attract Agnes and Elverta rather than repel them.

"So *this* is where you've been keeping yourself!" Agnes called out as she approached him, with Elverta close behind her. "My word, this is going to be such a fine store! Now the Promise Lodge community will really be self-sufficient, ain't so?"

"It's a wonderful new addition," Rosetta agreed as Lester finished with one of the door handles. "I have to wonder, however, why you're both still here."

Lester held off on starting the next handle, curious about how the women would respond to Rosetta's rather purposeful remark. Even though she no longer lived at the lodge, Rosetta had to be as tired of their squabbling as he was. She was standing in as property manager while Gloria was away, so she was probably trying to prevent future problems.

Elverta glanced at Agnes, clearing her throat. "Well, we *are* both paid ahead on our room rent," she pointed out. "And we realize we don't blend together any better than oil and water. But we've declared a truce."

Lester blinked. This was the last thing he'd expected to hear. "And what does that mean?" he asked cautiously.

Agnes smiled endearingly at him. "We know our disagreements have embarrassed you, Lester, and they fly against the principles of brotherly—or sisterly—love the Old Order faith is based upon, so we—"

"We hope you—and Rosetta—can forgive us," Elverta interjected softly.

"—have agreed to set aside our differences and become better residents here in the Promise Lodge community," Agnes continued, clasping her pudgy hands at her waist. "It was actually young Marlene who very kindly pointed out the error of our ways last night—"

"Reminded us that we'd attract more bees with honey than with vinegar," Elverta put in with a tentative smile.

"—and suggested that we should focus on all we have in common, rather than assuming we could never become friends," Agnes admitted. When she finally paused for a breath, Elverta took up the cause from her own perspective.

"Lester, we've been inconsiderate and intrusive, assuming you'd drop everything to take up with either one of us," the *maidel* said. "So for now, Agnes and I have decided to follow Marlene's advice—"

"Such a kindhearted soul she is—even if she's way too young for you," Agnes put in with a sweet smile.

"—and focus on getting settled here as residents rather than as potential wives. Promise Lodge is a lovely place to live, after all. Does that about cover it, Agnes?" Elverta asked.

"*Jah*, I believe it does. I think we should go back to the lodge now so Lester can get on with his work."

Both ladies gazed adoringly at Lester before heading to the front door. It took a few moments for him to corral his thoughts, which had been racing like Thoroughbreds while the two women presented their case.

Rosetta cleared her throat. "What do you think of *that*, Lester?" she asked as she watched the women leave.

"I—I don't know *what* to think. Maybe it's rude and pessimistic on my part, but I have to wonder how long this truce will last."

"*Jah*, me too."

"Aside from that, you could've knocked me over with a feather when they talked about becoming friends," he continued, shaking his head in amazement. "And I was surprised that Marlene helped them see the light."

"Maybe it's a case of self-preservation. Her apartment is between their rooms, and I suspect their catfights were getting on her nerves," Rosetta remarked with a chuckle. "She and Mose are heading to Coldstream today to clear out the house before their auction, so it'll be a while before you can ask her about that."

As Rosetta excused herself to speak with Dale again, Lester had more questions than answers about the dark-haired Miss Fisher with the sparkling brown eyes.

Did Marlene have an ulterior motive for suggesting that Agnes and Elverta become friends, rather than urging them to return to Ohio? Considering the way she'd taken his side in this situation, Lester found it hard to believe that she wanted those two biddies to continue clucking over him.

And why hadn't she mentioned going to Coldstream to clean out the Fisher farmhouse? Lester would've been happy to help her and Mose, knowing what a huge—and sometimes gut-wrenching—task that could be.

Maybe they prefer to walk that emotional road as brother and sister, without outside help.

Shaking his head, Lester positioned his drill to finish attaching the last door handles.

Maybe it's like Marlene said when she left me at the table yesterday—I don't know her as well as I think I do. I've assumed she has feelings for me, just as I've become intrigued with her. I've got to adjust my assumptions.

And now that Agnes and Elverta might be here for the long haul, I have to devise a stronger strategy. There'll be no escaping them now.

Chapter 11

On Saturday morning after breakfast, Marlene stepped into the upstairs bedroom where her parents had spent their entire married life. She decided to clear out their clothing first, because Mamm and Dat hadn't owned many clothes—and because most of their garments were too threadbare to put in the sale. Mose was out in the barn, sorting through farm and gardening equipment, which was a task just as daunting as the one she faced in the house.

With each trash bag she filled, she sighed deeply. Cleaning out the house wouldn't be as difficult now if she'd gone through Mamm's belongings after her mother had passed a couple of years ago, but Dat had wanted everything left just the way it was after he'd lost the love of his life. As Marlene finished emptying the chest of drawers, she didn't find a single thing to keep as a memento of either parent—partly because she and Mose were quite a lot larger than Mamm or Dat. Their parents had shriveled up in their final years, and the memory of seeing their gaunt bodies dressed in white, lying in their plain pine caskets, made her cry.

"Pull yourself together—the sale's two weeks from today," Marlene urged herself as she dragged the bulging trash bags into the hallway. "You'll never get through all these rooms if you cave in now."

The small room next to her parents' bedroom was where her mother's sewing machine sat. The closet was crammed with her mother's yarn, bins of fabric, an old set of dishes and silverware, worn-out shoes—and probably items Marlene didn't even know about. Mamm had been a pack rat in the best of times, and after her dementia had gotten worse, it was anyone's guess what she might have stuck into a box and stashed away.

Marlene opened the window for some fresh air while she handled the dusty boxes. She was inside the closet, bringing down a couple of boxes from the top shelf, when the old floorboards creaked behind her.

"Ah, Mose! If you could reach this—"

"Hey there, Marlene."

She turned and froze in the closet doorway. Yost and Jake Mullet had entered the small room. Their smiles looked dangerously taut.

"What're you doing here?" she demanded. "You had no business coming upstairs—"

"Well, there *is* this business of you Fishers selling your property without telling us it was for sale," Jake said brusquely.

"Not very neighborly," Yost put in, assessing her with his calculating gaze. "Considering that Jake's and my farms adjoin your back boundary, we're very disappointed that you didn't give us a chance to bid on it."

Marlene swallowed hard. What could she say to sidetrack these unwelcome guests? The Mullets had either seen a flyer for the auction, or they'd read about it in the county newspaper—which all their friends in Coldstream would eventually do. "We have a family member who's wanted this place for years—"

"And seeing you at the wedding on Thursday also reminded me of how disappointed I was back when you broke our engagement, Marlene," Yost continued in an edgier tone. "I didn't like it much that *you* were the one who left."

"Same here," Jake chimed in as he took a step toward her. "So now that you're moving away, we've come to settle that score. We've had a few years to compare notes about the way you ditched us—"

"And now we've got a plan." Yost's laugh filled the room with his meanness rather than mirth.

Marlene's joints turned to jelly. Was that liquor she smelled as she edged away from the closet door? She was tall and strong for a woman, but she didn't stand a chance against two irate men with a vendetta—especially if they trapped her in the closet. The window was open, but if Mose was in the back of the barn, he wouldn't hear her yelling for him. She told herself to remain calm—to try to talk these two predators out of getting their revenge in ways she didn't want to imagine.

"You both have wives and families now," she reminded them in the loudest, steadiest voice she could muster. "Why would you shatter their happiness by doing something foolish to me? When people hear about what you did—"

"Oh, you'll be too embarrassed to talk about it," Jake muttered, stepping closer. His eyes didn't look entirely focused, and his breathing was fast and shallow.

"Not that anybody would believe your word over ours," Yost added, sidestepping to block her path toward the hallway. "The gossip mill ran full tilt after you jilted me, Marlene, and folks took *my* side, you know."

"After you broke up with Yost, I thought you'd finally come to your senses when you started seeing *me*," Jake said with a disjointed laugh. "And whatever you thought you saw in Ervin Yoder, I was certain *I* could've made you a whole lot happier."

Marlene sensed these men had been drinking for a while

to work up their bravado—and to egg each other on. Despite their addled state, she tried to reason with them, hoping to distract them from their dishonorable intentions.

"If you hurt me," she said loudly, "Mose will never let you get away with—"

Yost's laughter sounded like the braying of a donkey. "That simpleminded brother of yours won't be able to stammer out any sort of—"

"You don't talk about *my* brother that way!" Marlene cried out.

Fueled by her sudden anger, she grabbed Mamm's wooden silverware case from the closet shelf and pitched it at Jake's face before hurling an open box of old work boots at Yost. It enraged them, but all those flying boots and utensils made the men stumble. She'd bought herself enough time to get closer to the door—

But not out of the room.

Yost and Jake recovered quickly, and as they came at her, the staccato tattoo of boots on the stairway alerted Marlene that Mose had somehow known she was in trouble. "Get away from me!" she cried out. "Don't think for a minute that you can—"

"Oh, I'm beyond thinking, honey," Yost muttered.

"*Jah*, we're in action mode now," Jake boasted.

"If you keep this up, you'll be sorry," she warned them, holding their focus so they wouldn't know when her brother made it to the door. "It's a small town, and when everyone at church hears—"

Yost let out another laugh as he clutched at her apron. The fabric made a sickening sound as it tore, and when Jake grabbed hold of her dress sleeve, Marlene couldn't help screaming—

Mose crossed the room in a couple of strides and grabbed both Mullets by the backs of their suspenders. He yanked them away from Marlene and flung them against the wall before they knew what had happened to them. As Jake recovered and came at him, Mose punched him solidly in the nose. The *crunch* of breaking bone filled the room, and as Jake covered his face with his hands, Yost ran at Mose with his head down, like a battering ram.

"Hey! You don't go hitting my cuh—"

Mose caught Yost's head in one broad hand and struck him with the other. "And you d-don't g-go attacking m-my sssister!" he bellowed. "Get out of my house! C-come here again, and I'll rep-port you to the p-police!"

Grabbing each man by a shoulder, Mose steered them roughly out of the room and down the stairs.

Marlene fell back against the wall and slid down to the floor in a heap. She could hear the Mullets protesting and yelling threats at her brother, but as their voices rose in the yard and got farther away, a bubble of fear and pain enveloped her. Yost and Jake hadn't hurt her, but they'd come so close—had frightened her so badly—that all she could do was breathe in and out through her mouth, rapidly and mindlessly.

A short while later she was vaguely aware that Mose had returned, and that he was lowering himself to the floor to pull her onto his lap.

"Marlene . . . Marlene," he murmured over and over as he rocked her gently in his arms, "They're gone. They won't do this ever again. I'm so sorry I didn't get here sooner—"

She burst into tears and buried her face against his chest. He smelled sweaty and dusty like a barn, but the familiar scent of him, along with his low voice and repeated phrases of comfort, eventually settled her runaway pulse.

"Oh, Mose," she whimpered. "I've never been so scared in my life."

"What did they say? Why were they here?" he asked, shaking his head in confusion.

Marlene took a deep breath, collecting her thoughts. "When I spotted them at Laura's wedding on Thursday, I got this—this funny feeling about the way they were looking at me," she replied in a shaken voice. "That's why I came out to see you at the barn—"

"But I was busy with the mare," Mose recalled with a sigh. "You should've told me—"

"I thought maybe I was just imagining they had a reason for staring at me," she hastened to explain. "But when they got here today, they were mad because we didn't let them make an offer on the farm before we sold it."

"Why would I want them to have this land, this house?" he asked with a scowl. "I was so relieved when you broke off your engagements to both of them—never really understood what you saw in those Mullets."

"*Jah*, well I'm *really* glad I didn't marry either one of them now," Marlene said as she wiped her eyes with the back of her hand. "I didn't realize they were so mean, so violent—"

"*Jah*, deep down you did—or maybe God whispered it in your ear back then, when you broke up with them," her brother suggested. He let out a long sigh. "So now *I* have taken a violent turn that sinks me right down to their level. I should probably prepare myself for a visit from Bishop Obadiah and a demand for my confession."

Marlene inhaled deeply, recalling the blood she'd seen running down Jake's face and the crunch she'd heard— probably when his nose broke. "Both of those fellows will need some patching up. They'll probably have black eyes for a long while—"

"They deserved worse," Mose muttered.

"—but do you think either one of them will admit what

happened today—or what they planned?" she asked in a whisper. "They can't very well say that they attacked me without having to go before the congregation for a kneeling confession."

"That's *their* problem, ain't so?"

A nervous laugh escaped her. "Or maybe they'll make up some tall tale about *you* coming after *them*, twisting things around so the bishop will think you were the one at fault, Mose," she muttered. "After all, Bishop Obadiah won't be pleased when he finds out we've moved to Promise Lodge—especially because we didn't tell him."

"That's *his* problem. We've done the right thing."

When Marlene envisioned Chupp's scowling face, she climbed off her brother's lap and stood up. She hoped Mose wouldn't notice how badly her legs were shaking. Her torn apron was hanging loose around her waist, and the sleeve Jake had grabbed was gaping open at the shoulder seam.

"Are you gonna be all right, Marlene?" her twin whispered as he rose from the floor. "If you'd rather I worked here in the house, I can. Plenty of stuff to carry up from the basement."

"I—I'll be fine," she insisted in a thin voice. "Those fellows know better than to come back—and sorting through boxes will settle me down. Really, it's all right if you work in the barn."

Mose's expression told her he didn't quite believe her, but he nodded. "I'll be back in about an hour for lunch—if you're sure you'll be all right."

"Go," Marlene said firmly, pointing toward the door. "You've rescued me once today, and I can't thank you enough. But that's all behind us now."

He gazed at her for several seconds before heading downstairs.

The air left her lungs with a *whoosh* as she fell back

against the wall again. The mess of old boots and silverware on the floor was a reminder that it would take the two of them days to get ready for the auction on March thirty-first—in just two weeks. After a moment Marlene convinced herself that the sooner she picked up the mess she'd made, the sooner she could return to going through Mamm's boxes in the closet.

But the thought of her mother made her cry again.

Thank God she and Dat *weren't here when this happened.*

Marlene muffled her sobs with her apron so Mose wouldn't hear her through the open window. She told herself her sorting would be easier if she carried the boxes out to the worktable instead of remaining in the closet. She threw the old boots back into their box and then tossed the silverware into its cracked wooden case without arranging the knives, forks, and spoons in their intended slots. As she took the crates and containers from the closet shelves, however, Marlene knew she couldn't continue.

Her sense of security had been shattered.

The Mullets had invaded her home with their malevolent intentions, and even though they hadn't succeeded in their mission, Marlene felt soiled. Humiliated. Jake and Yost hadn't gotten what they'd come for, but they'd momentarily taken control of her and left her feeling helpless and vulnerable—and they would remind her of it with a cocky gaze every time they saw her from here on out.

Feverishly, Marlene carried box after box down the stairs to pile them on the front porch. By the time her brother came to the house for lunch, she was exhausted—and she'd made a decision.

"Mose, I can't stay here tonight," she admitted in a strained voice. "I know we have several days of work ahead of us, but I have to leave. Please, can we go back to Promise Lodge after lunch?"

Her brother assessed her with his deep brown eyes, gently squeezing her shoulder where her sleeve had been torn away. "All right. I can come back by myself."

"Maybe that would be best," Marlene agreed. "I—I hate to say this, but I can't be in this house by myself. Not for a while, anyway."

Mose nodded sadly. "After we eat, we'll load those boxes and some other stuff on the wagon and go. You need time to let the shock wear off."

They ate a hasty lunch. Her brother hefted the boxes onto their big wagon with the tall sides and added a few crates from the barn. As they drove away, Marlene had never felt so defeated. So weak and defenseless.

Unfortunately, after they'd returned to Promise Lodge and stashed the boxes in a lodge storage area, Marlene didn't sleep that night. Every time she nearly drifted off, she saw the Mullets coming at her in that upstairs room, their eyes glimmering with evil intent as they taunted her.

Yost and Jake knew where she lived, after all. And the other ladies in the lodge couldn't fend off the two cousins if they decided to sneak up the stairway in the dead of night.

Chapter 12

Lester tossed some money into the bowl on the sideboard in the lodge dining room, smiling at Dale as the storekeeper added his contribution. The two men didn't pay rent, so it was only fair that they reimbursed the lodge's grocery fund each time they ate there.

"*Gut* to see you here for Sunday dinner, Dale," Lester said as they shook hands. "Always nice to gather around this table to enjoy whatever the Kuhns have cooked up for us."

"*Jah*, I could make my own meals, as I did for years in Cloverdale," Kraybill remarked as he pulled a chair from the table, "but I've gotten spoiled by the variety of foods Ruby and Beulah always put out on visiting Sundays. And it's nice not to have dishes to wash afterward."

"Well worth the money," Lester agreed as he chose the chair beside Dale's.

"Oh, you two fellows are just here to feast your eyes on my sister and me," Ruby teased. She set a large bowl of glazed carrots on the table while Beulah carried two sliced cakes to the sideboard.

"You've got them pegged, sister," Beulah agreed with a laugh. "But then, how could they not be in love with us? If this cinnamon glaze cake—or this coconut pound cake—doesn't bring them to their knees, nothing will."

Lester and Dale laughed along with the sisters, who both wore bright plaid dresses today. It was such a pleasure to engage in friendly banter with the Kuhns and Irene, who was bringing out a large platter of pork chops—and Lester hoped Elverta and Agnes would take their cue from these three lodge residents. If they were serious about calling a truce, perhaps they wouldn't hound him all during dinner.

At the sound of footsteps, Lester watched the two women descending the double lobby staircase, one behind the other instead of choosing opposite sides—which indicated that maybe they were getting along better now. When their eyes lit up at the sight of him, Lester reminded himself to remain patient and kind unless their conversation became bothersome.

"How are you, Lester?" Agnes called out eagerly.

"Are you about finished working over at the new store?" Elverta asked with a nod at Dale. "It's the nicest-looking bulk market I've ever seen."

"*Denki* for saying so," Dale remarked.

"Matter of fact, I *am* finished with all the bulk store's installation work," Lester said as the ladies sat down across from them. "I start a new window and siding project this week, with Rosetta's husband—and Irene's son—Truman Wickey. He's been very persuasive with the owners of several apartment and townhome developments hereabouts, suggesting I replace their old windows or siding."

"It's too bad you don't have more work right here at Promise Lodge," Elverta hinted.

"I don't suppose that'll happen until more folks move in and build homes," Dale pointed out.

At the sound of the front door, Lester looked up to find the two Fishers coming through the lobby to enter the dining room. It was the first time he'd seen the twins together, and their resemblance was striking: they were tall and broad-shouldered, with dark eyes, expressive brows, and thick black hair that set off their olive complexion. Lester noted the way Mose assessed who was already in the dining room. For such a burly fellow, he appeared rather hesitant.

Marlene's expression gave Lester pause, too. She appeared exhausted . . . perhaps worried about something as she lightly took her brother's arm.

"Mose, this is Elverta Horst and Agnes Plank," she began, pointing as she introduced the folks at the table. "And Dale Kraybill owns the new bulk store that opens soon—and Lester Lehman lives in the blue tiny home beside the lake—"

"We're delighted you're joining us for dinner today, Mose," Beulah put in as she arrived with a cheese potato casserole. "Visiting Sundays get a little quiet at the lodge, what with other folks spending time with their families."

"We were tickled to hear about the twin foals you delivered last Thursday," Ruby remarked. She placed a big bowl of green beans on the table and took a seat beside the two ladies from Ohio. "Bishop Monroe grins from ear to ear whenever he talks about them, and it sounds as though more mares will be giving birth soon."

Mose nodded his acknowledgment before following Marlene to the table. Lester was pleased that she'd chosen to sit beside him, while Beulah sat at the end nearest the kitchen and Irene took the chair across from Mose. They all bowed for a moment of silent prayer.

When folks began passing the serving bowls, Lester handed the green beans to Marlene. "Rosetta was telling me you Fishers have been cleaning out your house in Coldstream, preparing for your auction," he remarked. "I had the impression you were to be gone for several days—"

"Decided we'd handled enough dusty old boxes for one visit," she put in quickly.

Her tone told him she was finished discussing that topic. After Lester watched Mose place three pork chops on his plate, he leaned forward to look past Marlene.

"Will you have lots of farm equipment in your sale, Mose? Or mostly household items?" he asked. "Either way, if you'd like some help—"

"We've g-got it covered," he stammered before sticking a large bite of green beans in his mouth.

Lester took that as a hint that Mose felt shy eating among so many strangers. He recalled how emotionally drained he'd felt while he was cleaning out the home he'd shared with Delores and Sam, and decided to let the Fishers eat in peace. They'd probably dealt with as many memories and worn-out pieces of furniture as they could manage at one time.

"I bet a big strapping man like you has the ladies waiting in line, ain't so?" Elverta asked, smiling at Mose. "It's too bad you missed the wedding festivities on Thursday. Plenty of gals to choose from."

Lester blinked, taken aback by her tactless remark. It was no wonder Mose's cheeks reddened as he focused more intently on his food—and beside him, Marlene was scowling, too.

"Cat got your tongue, honey?" Agnes asked coyly. "When Marlene mentioned her brother would be working with the bishop's Clydesdales, I had no idea how big and strong you'd be—but then, it only makes sense that it would take a muscular man to handle those huge horses and—"

"Agnes, can't you let Mose eat his dinner without pestering him?" Lester cut in sharply. "You and Elverta don't know when to quit."

He felt bad about speaking in such a negative way, but

he was embarrassed for Mose. The two women didn't seem to realize how foolish and flirtatious they sounded, as though they'd given up on *him* and were trying for Mose's attention now—even though they were nearly old enough to be his mother.

For a few moments, only the clinking of silverware punctuated the uncomfortable silence. At least Elverta and Agnes had taken the hint and were focused on their food.

Dale cleared his throat. "What activities are you planning for Easter Monday, Beulah?" he asked in a hopeful tone. "I know it's early, but I'll be stocking quite a lot of candy eggs, colorful baskets, and lawn games—and of course I'll be having a sale on white chicken eggs and packages of dye. I'd be happy to let you ladies choose whatever you'll need before I set those items out for display."

Beulah gave him a big smile. "I'm not sure whether Rosetta has anything planned yet, but you've made a lovely offer, Dale—"

"I'm thinking the youngsters will surely color eggs for a hunt," Ruby chimed in. "It would be nice to have some new baskets for that. We'll ask Rosetta and Gloria."

"We could definitely use some new lawn games," Lester said with a nod. "The ones in the shed by the lake have seen better days—they were used for years while this place was a church camp."

As another silence set in, Lester noticed that the Fishers were tucking away their dinner as though they weren't inclined to join the conversation. When Mose had scraped the last cheese and potatoes from his plate, he stood up.

"*D-denki* for the nice d-dinner," he murmured as he leaned toward Ruby.

She blinked in surprise. "Oh, but we have two cakes on the sideboard—"

"If you don't want to stay, Mose, you're welcome to

take some cake back to your apartment," Beulah said to encourage him. "We've got more than enough, dear."

Mose flashed her a self-conscious smile as he shook his head. After he'd passed between the dining room tables and closed the front door behind him, Marlene let out a sigh.

"He doesn't mean to be impolite—and he *loves* your food, ladies," she added apologetically before focusing on Irene. "My brother's very shy around folks he doesn't know. He was kidnapped when we were children—he'd wandered away from our family at a county fair, and an English couple whisked him off before we realized he was missing."

"Oh my, how horrible for him—and for your family," Irene said as she shook her head. "Did Mose ever visit with a counselor or—"

"The schoolteacher gave him some extra help with his speech, but my parents believed that seeing an English counselor would've frightened Mose more than it would've helped him," Marlene explained. "We were just thankful to God that the police found him and returned him to us a couple days later."

"Your *mamm* must've been beside herself," Agnes murmured sadly. "Boys will be boys—and they can skedaddle through a crowd quicker than a wink."

"Yet Mose has become a farrier, and has taken some veterinary training," Lester said, "so he's risen above his fears enough to become a productive adult with some specialized skills most Amish don't have. That says a lot for your brother."

Marlene's grateful smile made Lester glad he'd spoken up. As he studied her face, however, he couldn't miss the puckered crease between her eyebrows. Was she worried about something in Coldstream concerning the upcoming auction or the house? He didn't think he should inquire about such things with so many other folks present.

"Could you help me carry a few boxes from the storeroom to my apartment after dinner, Lester?" she asked him quietly. "I was in such a state when I hauled them out of Mamm's closet yesterday, I didn't realize how heavy some of them were."

"Of course, I will," he replied.

"But let's enjoy our cake first." Marlene smiled at Ruby and Beulah. "Which cake's the best, ladies? I'm not going to ask who made them!"

The Kuhns laughed from opposite ends of the table.

"One's a cinnamon glaze cake," Beulah replied, "and it's so dense and moist, it doesn't need frosting."

"Oh, but if you like coconut, you'll want to try the crazy-*gut* pound cake that's beside the bowls of whipped cream and berries," Ruby insisted. "It's not frosted, either, because it's loaded with butter and cream cheese and coconut—"

"Sold!" Lester blurted out, because he was a sucker for anything with coconut in it. "Can I bring you a slice, Marlene—or two? I'm going to try them both."

"That's a fine idea. A thin slice of both kinds, please," she replied. "A little something to sweeten my weekend."

As he rose from his chair, he caught her remark—as surely as he felt two pairs of eyes fixed upon him from across the table. The cakes were already sliced, so Lester crowded a generous piece of each one onto two plates before he put a dollop of whipped cream and berries on the coconut pound cake. When he'd handed their plates to Marlene, he decided to be polite.

"While I'm here, may I get cake for any of you other ladies?" he asked. "Kraybill, you'll have to fend for yourself."

"Not a problem!" the storekeeper said as he rose from

his chair. "I'll even be a sport and carry the other plates to the table. We're outnumbered, Lester, so we'd better play nice."

Their teasing eased some of the tension in the room. As soon as folks began sampling the cakes, the conversation started up again—because although they looked rather plain, both cakes tasted extraordinary. Marlene closed her eyes in enjoyment and seemed to be feeling better by the time she'd scraped up every last morsel between the tines of her fork.

"Ladies, I'm too full and you've outdone yourselves once again," Lester said as he laid his fork across his plate. "*Denki* for this wonderful meal."

"Ditto," Dale joined in. "After everything I devoured, I certainly won't be rummaging through my fridge looking for supper."

"Happy to cook for you fellows. Join us anytime," Ruby said, rising to collect the plates. "For the record, those were Irene's cake recipes—"

"And you can be sure we'll bake them again!" Beulah crowed as she, too, stood up. "I can't decide which one I like the best."

"You'll just have to keep tasting them so you can decide," Irene teased. "Truth be told, I bake so many pies for the shop each week, I was happy to eat cake that somebody else baked."

"You cooks sit tight," Marlene said, "because as soon as Lester carries some boxes upstairs, I'll be back down to wash the dishes. It's Sunday, and you've done more than your share of work today."

"Count me in on cleanup, Marlene," Dale said, smiling at her. "I'll get everything gathered up by the sink and run the dishwater while you and Lester handle those boxes. Take your time, dear."

"Irene, I believe that's our cue to make like a tree and leave," Beulah said, obviously pleased with the offers of help.

"The recliner's calling my name, so don't get any ideas about sitting there, sister," Ruby teased. "And if I just happen to nod off, it *is* my day of rest, you know."

Lester followed Marlene through the dining room and down the back hall to the large area where folding tables and chairs were stored. The stacks of old boxes made his eyes widen.

"You've got your work cut out for you," he murmured as he and Marlene each grabbed a box. "Will some of this stuff go back to Coldstream for the sale? And let *me* carry these, honey—they look awfully heavy."

She didn't answer him—and she didn't set down her box, either. "A lot of our parents' things are so worn out, I don't expect much of the stuff in these boxes will go back," she replied as they started up the back staircase from the kitchen. "Let's just say I reached a point yesterday when I couldn't deal with any more sorting."

Lester nodded, fully understanding what she meant. After they'd reached the second floor, he enjoyed the view of the lodge's spacious lobby as he looked over the railing of the open double stairway.

"When I was working on your apartment, I was envious that you ladies have such a beautiful place to live," he remarked. "The old woodwork has been so nicely preserved, and now that the walls have been painted, it feels very homey up here."

The door he was walking past swung open very abruptly.

"Lester, it's totally inappropriate for you to be going into Marlene's apartment," Elverta said sharply. "I was appalled that she even suggested such a thing at dinner—and in front of all those people!"

Before Lester could respond, the doorway on the other side of Marlene's corner apartment flew open, as well. "Men are *not* allowed up here, Lester!" Agnes announced archly. "Both Rosetta and Gloria, the manager, have stressed to us that only the female residents are to be walking these halls."

Marlene rolled her eyes before setting her box down to open her door. "Who do you suppose remodeled these apartments and did the painting in your rooms?" she countered. "And who carries the furniture upstairs or down every time a resident moves in or out?"

"*Jah*, as a rule, I'm not allowed here," Lester acknowledged with all the patience he could muster. "And as for Marlene asking for my help *in front of all those people*—not a one of them batted an eye, did they?"

"Well!" Elverta put in with a huff. "I intend to stand right here and watch you carry—"

"And *I* will go into Marlene's apartment to be sure there's no hanky-panky—"

"Agnes, you'll do no such thing!" Beulah retorted as she and her sister proceeded up the open staircase from the lobby. When they reached the second floor, they scowled at both of the ladies from Ohio. "And Elverta, you can mind your own beeswax, too. *Gut* grief!"

"*Jah*, we all had fair warning Lester would be coming up here to help Marlene," Ruby chimed in, "so if his presence bothers you gals, stay in your rooms. It's as simple as that. I thought we were all adults here."

Frowning sourly, Agnes and Elverta both stepped back into their apartments. The loud closing of their doors echoed in the open stairwell.

With a sigh, Marlene carried her box into her apartment. She dropped it against the wall near the window, glancing at Lester as he remained in the doorway. "If I'd been worried about your intentions, dear man, I'd have asked my brother to carry these boxes," she said softly. "You have to take everything Agnes and Elverta say with a grain of salt."

Dear man. Lester felt his pulse rev up, and it wasn't from the exertion of carrying a heavy box up a flight of stairs. "I could hardly believe my ears when they came to Dale's store on Friday, saying they'd declared a truce," he remarked as he set his box on top of the one she'd carried. "But in some ways, they're no easier to be around now than when they were scrapping like cats."

Marlene laughed softly. "I really appreciate the way you stood up for my brother at dinner, Lester," she whispered. "I couldn't believe the way those two biddy hens were carrying on until you shut them down."

Lester shrugged. "They needed to be taken down a couple of pegs."

She nodded her agreement. "If we bring up two more boxes apiece, that should keep me busy for the next day or so. But if you have other things you need to do—"

"Happy to help," Lester insisted. "I don't envy you the task of clearing out your lifelong home, Marlene. And as I told Mose, if you want me to come to Coldstream to help you, just say the word."

He glanced toward the wall between Marlene's apartment and Agnes's room. "Truth be told, my hours at the complex where Truman Wickey's working are pretty flexible," he admitted in a low voice. "Long as I'm finished by the first of May, the manager will be happy."

Nodding, Marlene headed out into the hallway again. By the time they'd carried up four more boxes, she'd gotten quieter. Lester didn't need more of a hint: he'd finished the favor she'd asked of him, so it was time to be out of her apartment—much as he would've enjoyed staying to chat with her.

"Well, I'll see you around, Marlene—"

She held up her hand, closing her door carefully so it didn't make a sound. "Lester, can I ask another favor?" she whispered.

His runaway heartbeat betrayed what he *hoped* she was going to ask—but of course, such anticipation was inappropriate. "Of course, you can," Lester murmured. He could picture the possibility that Agnes had a drinking glass and her ear against the wall, eavesdropping on them.

"Could you please install a dead bolt lock on my door? Well, maybe two of them?"

His mouth dropped open. "Have I done something to frighten you, Marlene?" he blurted out. After all, there had to be a reason she'd looked so tired and worried all morning.

Her dark eyes widened as she shook her head emphatically.

Lester frowned, pointing in either direction to indicate the residents of the two adjoining rooms. "Have they been sneaking into your room while you're out?" he whispered.

"I—I don't—it's not that." Marlene turned slightly, closing her eyes against something that was causing her great pain.

Lester wanted to point out that none of the other lodge ladies had locks on their doors, because they felt perfectly safe and secure. But he kept his comments and questions to himself. He sensed Marlene didn't want to share whatever was weighing so heavily upon her heart, and that was her right, after all.

"I can do that," he said. "Do you want them this afternoon, or—"

"Tomorrow's fine. You probably don't have any spare

locks lying around—and it *is* Sunday," she added. "*Denki*, Lester. I'll sleep a lot better at night."

As he took his leave, Lester pondered Marlene's unusual request. It was a pretty afternoon and the hardware store in Forest Grove, a few miles down the road, was open because it was owned by enterprising English rather than by Plain folks. He hitched up his rig and headed to town with a lot on his mind.

What had happened in Coldstream to convince Marlene she needed two dead bolt locks? Or had the Fishers installed such security measures years ago after Mose had been kidnapped, to prevent their handsome son from being snatched again? For all Lester knew, Marlene's family had also begun locking doors when her mother had taken to wandering off because of her dementia.

There could be any number of reasons she wants those locks. It's an easy favor to grant if she'll sleep better, so just leave it be.

But his mind was still spinning around Marlene's little mystery when he arrived in Forest Grove. If Marlene felt insecure at Promise Lodge, Lester believed it was his place to ensure her safety—and her emotional well-being.

Chapter 13

About an hour after Lester had left, Marlene draped the wet flour sack towels over the backs of the kitchen chairs. "Dale, it was so nice of you to help with the dishes," she said as the storekeeper was leaving. "Have a *gut* week!"

"I'll be busy getting all the stock on the shelves so I'm ready for the store's grand opening next Saturday," he said happily. "And if you'd be inclined—after you and Mose have held your auction and settled everything in Coldstream—I'd be delighted if you'd like to work for me. Will you consider it?"

Marlene's jaw dropped. She hadn't thought about what she might do once her parents' affairs were in order—but she would need *something* to occupy her time, wouldn't she? It would only take about half an hour to clean her new apartment, which left days on end when she would no longer be caring for a full-sized house or an aging parent.

"I will," she murmured. "I haven't thought much beyond the auction—and I appreciate your suggestion."

With a nod, the storekeeper started home. Marlene passed through the dining room, straightening a few chairs on her way to the lodge's big front porch. It was a sunny spring day, and it wouldn't be appropriate to sort through the contents of those boxes this afternoon; sitting in the fresh air seemed like a fine idea. Through the kitchen window she'd seen Lester leaving, probably heading to town to buy her locks. The other lodge residents were upstairs, and she was looking forward to some quiet time on the porch swing.

She hadn't been in the swing long before Mose came around the side of the lodge. His smile told her he was relieved to see her without anyone else around.

"Will you come with me to speak with Preacher Amos?" he asked softly, easing onto the swing beside her. "I need to confess about striking the two Mullets yesterday. I'm thinking he'll understand the situation better than Bishop Monroe."

Her brother's request came as no surprise. Ordinarily, Mose was mild-mannered and gentle, but in the heat of a difficult moment he'd lashed out with his physical strength—and sooner or later, the church leaders in Coldstream would find out about it.

"*Jah*, of course I'll go with you," she replied. "Best to get this matter off your chest, ain't so? And maybe Amos will have some words of wisdom for us. Truth be told, I hardly slept a wink last night, remembering our run-in with those fellows."

"Me neither," he admitted. "And . . . and we know the Mullets won't just drop the matter, either. Even if what they did was wrong."

For a few moments they lingered in the pleasant breeze, drifting lazily back and forth as the swing creaked under their weight. When Mose stood up, Marlene went along with him. They crossed the lawn together, passing some of the tilled plots that awaited Mattie Troyer's vegetable seeds. Across the road, some of Christine Burkholder's black-and-white Holsteins stood at the barnyard fence watching Marlene and her brother walk past.

"On a totally different subject," Marlene said as they strolled, "what would you think if I worked at the new bulk store? After the auction and the house stuff are all settled, of course. You can't look around Promise Lodge without seeing the businesses our friends from Coldstream have started here—work that has given them all something useful to do."

Mose's dark eyebrows rose in thought. "You'd probably be *gut* at storekeeping," he remarked. "You're organized and friendly and—well, I wondered what you might take on now that you're not looking after our parents. If that's what you'd like to do, why not?"

Why not, indeed? As Marlene and her brother reached the property where Preacher Amos and Mattie lived, she brightened at the thought of a new experience. And for the first time in her life, she'd be paid for the work she did! She didn't anticipate needing a lot of money, as their profits from the auction and selling the farm would be their nest egg. Some of that money would go toward paying her rent, although Mose's barn apartment was considered part of his pay.

It was nice to have an opportunity to think about. Working in a new store would be fun! And Marlene sensed that Dale would be a fair, pleasant man to work for.

Mose stepped onto the Troyers' porch, and after a moment's hesitation he knocked on the door. His expression had tightened at the thought of discussing what he'd done yesterday. Marlene admired her brother for volunteering to confess—and Preacher Amos would stand with them if the church leaders in Coldstream became upset about whatever story they got from the Mullets.

Mattie smiled through the glass of the front door as she opened it. "What a nice surprise to see you Fishers! It's a fine time for a visit, as Amos's girls and their husbands left for home just a bit ago to put the babies down for a nap."

"Let me see if I remember what's happened with Amos's twins," Marlene ventured as she and her brother stepped into the front room. "Bernice and Barbara are married to the redheaded Helmuth brothers, and both couples live in that double house near the nursery. If I recall from spotting them in the crowd before Laura's wedding ceremony, they each have a baby."

"You got it right! You've had a lot of people's lives to figure out since you moved here," Mattie said with a chuckle.

Mose cleared his throat nervously. "I um, was wondering if we c-could speak with P-preacher Amos," he murmured. "It's kind of p-private."

"He's just gone to the barn to do the livestock chores," Mattie said, gesturing for them to follow her toward the kitchen. "Shall I holler for him, or—"

"We'll g-go on out there," Mose replied. "*Denki*, Mattie. It's *g-gut* to see you. I was d-delivering twin f-foals on Thursday, so I m-missed visiting with you and the other f-folks at the wedding."

"Amos will be pleased you've come," she put in, turning to smile at them. "We're so glad you kids live at Promise Lodge now. Here you go. Have a *gut* visit."

Marlene smiled as Mattie held the back door open for them. She recalled the furor Amos had kicked up when he sold his Coldstream farm to join Mattie and her two sisters as they started the Promise Lodge community a couple of years ago.

"Seems to me Amos and Mattie have made quite a nice life for themselves," she remarked as she walked alongside her brother. "Their home here isn't as big as most of the others, but it's fresh and new."

"Amos has much nicer outbuildings here, too," Mose

remarked as the preacher stepped out of the rustic red barn and into the fenced corral area. He waved and called out, "P-preacher Amos, might we b-bend your ear for a b-bit? Something's c-come up."

"Always happy to talk with you folks," the wiry church leader replied. His hair and beard had more silver in them these days, but his smile was as warm and genuine as it had always been. "How's your work going at the Coldstream farm? I was surprised you didn't stay longer—but then, maybe you've got everything whipped into shape for your sale, eh?"

"Oh, we have a long way to go," Marlene said as they stopped a few feet in front of Amos. She looked at her brother. "Do you want to tell it, Mose, or shall I start?"

Mose's breath left him in a rush, along with his words. "I—I have a c-confession to make, P-preacher Amos, because the M-mullets—J-jake and Yost—c-cornered Marlene upstairs to attack her on S-saturday and I punched them. B-both of them."

Amos's eyes widened. "Maybe we'd better sit down behind the barn and sort this out," he suggested gently. "That's where I go when I need to pray on things, or when I want to enjoy the peaceful woods and the wildlife."

Nodding, Mose followed the preacher through the shadowed barn. Marlene came behind them, glancing at a couple of buggy horses munching their evening meal. She sensed her brother felt better already, now that he'd blurted out the confession he'd shared with no one else—and *she* was relieved, knowing Preacher Amos would listen without judging them and without raising his voice in condemnation about what Mose had done.

As he exited through a back door, Amos gestured toward two benches arranged against the barn's exterior wall.

Marlene chose the second bench, allowing her brother to sit beside the preacher.

"What a beautiful spot," she murmured. "I can see why you come here, Amos. It's not hard to imagine God Himself walking amongst these old trees, especially now that the redbuds and dogwoods are starting to bloom."

"He and I chat here fairly often," Amos replied with a nod. He focused on Mose then, turning sideways so he could also see Marlene. "So tell me about this visit from the Mullets—why they were there and what went on. You *look* fine, Marlene, but I hope you weren't harmed in ways and places I can't see."

"I'm fine," she quickly assured him. "I suffered quite a scare, though. Mose got there just in time to yank Yost and Jake away before they um, cornered me in Mamm's upstairs storage room."

As the memories of Saturday's confrontation haunted her yet again, Marlene inhaled deeply to steady her nerves.

Amos frowned. "Why were they there?" he asked gently. "Does this have anything to do with your broken engagements—even though they happened several years ago?"

Marlene sighed. "They were upset because we sold the farm without offering it to either of them first," she muttered. "I was so glad your cousin Myron wanted the property, Amos—"

"Well, he's a cousin several times removed, but he's tickled to have an affordable place to start out." Amos scratched his beard, thinking. "I guess I don't understand why the Mullets felt compelled to take out their frustrations on *you*, dear."

"They f-figured out I was in the b-barn, so they w-went upstairs, thinking I'd never know about it," Mose put in bitterly. "Luckily, Marlene's w-window was open. I just had this f-feeling she was in t-trouble, right b-before I heard her holler."

"You're right about the engagement issue," Marlene admitted with a shake of her head. "I have a feeling they fueled each other's need to get their licks in—they were staring at me all during Laura's wedding on Thursday. And I smelled liquor on their breath Saturday, too."

She paused to regain control of her emotions. Talking about her Saturday morning encounter brought back all the turmoil and shame she'd suffered during her terrifying encounter with the Mullets.

"I—I threw boxes of stuff at them, trying to get away," Marlene recounted in a tight whisper. "But if Mose hadn't gotten upstairs in time, things would've turned out . . . much worse. As it was, only my apron and the sleeve of my dress were torn—and my nerves got pretty frazzled."

The preacher's eyes widened as his expression grew very somber. "So when Mose got up the stairs, he grabbed them?"

"B-by their suspenders," Mose said with a nod. "B-but when they came at me, I . . . I lost all sense of c-control. I *hit* them, Preacher Amos. Really hard."

"I'm pretty sure Jake's got a broken nose. Both men will have serious black eyes," Marlene put in.

"And—and now that I've c-confessed to you, I'll do whatever y-you say I should, P-preacher Amos," her brother said in a dejected voice. "I p-probably should've g-gone to B-bishop Obadiah, b-but he's going to be p-plenty upset when he hears we've s-sold the farm."

"We didn't tell him," Marlene explained. "He'll see the flyers for the auction, no doubt— I suspect that's where Jake and Yost learned about us leaving. We just didn't want to listen to Chupp's sermon about leaving his district, you know?"

"Oh, I know all about that, *jah*." Amos let out a long, lingering sigh. "Shall we offer up a word of prayer? You have indeed confessed, Mose—of your own free will—and that's what our faith requires of us. But the devil's in the details. Shall we bow our heads?"

Marlene closed her eyes, grateful for their longtime friend's patience.

"Our Father and our God, we ask Your presence with us as we discern Your will for our lives," the minister began softly. "Guide us along the path You would have us follow. Open our minds and our hearts to the proper, faithful way You want us to handle this difficult situation—and hold Mose and Marlene in the palm of Your hand during this time of trial as they bid *gut*-bye to their lifelong home in Coldstream. We ask all these things in the name of Your Son, Jesus Christ. Amen."

"Amen," Marlene murmured. She raised her head, waiting for Preacher Amos to speak first. He was a man who habitually waited on the Lord rather than rushing into answers.

Mose sighed softly, smiling at her. They had done the right thing, coming here. Already he appeared more relaxed, ready to put his faith and his life into God's hands—and to listen to Amos's counsel.

After a few more minutes of gazing toward the trees, which swayed gently in the late-afternoon breeze, Amos looked at them. "You have confessed your moment of violence, Mose, and I believe you're sincerely sorry that you struck the Mullets. In my opinion, this matter needs no discussion outside our circle of three and God—although the most beneficial step would be for you to apologize to Jake and Yost."

Mose nodded as though he'd anticipated this suggestion.

"Perhaps if you take the lead on this apology, the Mullets

will follow suit and apologize for the way they treated Marlene. And perhaps not," Preacher Amos added with a rueful smile. "But at least you'll be right with God, Mose, and you will have acknowledged your wrongdoing to the men you struck. Then comes the *forgiveness* part, when—hopefully—you both can soften your hearts and reconcile with Yost and his cousin.

"And Marlene," the preacher continued in a pensive tone, "on a practical note, maybe you shouldn't mend the apron and dress they tore. Take them to the house in Coldstream—until after the auction, anyway—as evidence of the Mullets' regrettable intentions, in case Bishop Obadiah confronts you. Because I suspect he will."

"*Jah*, me too," she mumbled. "Too many folks—including their wives—will be asking how they got black eyes and a broken nose. Whatever story they've concocted will get around to the bishop, and I bet he'll be ready for us the next time we go to Coldstream."

Amos nodded. "What if some of us went with you?" he asked. "Anyone could understand why you wouldn't want to work in the house alone again, Marlene. And with a bunch of us there to help, we'll have you ready for your sale a lot faster."

Marlene's jaw dropped. "Oh, but I couldn't ask you folks to—"

"You didn't ask, dear. I offered," Preacher Amos pointed out with a smile. "I'm thinking that if Mattie and I, and Christine and Monroe, and Rosetta and Truman were there—because Truman could drive us and save a lot of road time—Bishop Obadiah would see our support for you and Mose."

He chuckled softly, as though recalling a humorous situation. "Chupp already knows that when the Bender sisters unite for a cause, he won't get by with half truths or assumptions about who was at fault," Amos pointed out. "And he knows that *I* will stand by you, as well, because Mose has confessed to me."

"Having another b-bishop along would be a *gut* idea— and B-bishop Monroe would want to know how this situation is c-coming along," Mose agreed, nodding at Amos. "We would appreciate the help, too. Many hands make light work—and everyone you mentioned has been through this same ordeal."

"It's a very generous offer," Marlene agreed. "Once you figure out when everyone wants to go, let us know."

"Will it be all right if I share your story with them, Marlene? Mose's confession is confidential, but the others need to know what has happened so we'll all be on the same page when the Mullets—or Chupp—stop by your place while we're working," Amos pointed out.

Marlene sighed, but she nodded. Folks would have to know about her ordeal to help her get past it.

"Sure, you'll have to tell them," Mose replied. "We really appreciate anybody who's willing to rally around us this way."

"*Denki* for your help, Amos," Marlene put in gratefully. "We knew we could count on you to handle this tricky situation in a fair, faith-based way."

After she and Mose took their leave of the Troyers, Marlene headed for the lodge and Mose returned to his loft apartment in the Clydesdale barn. When she went to bed that evening, she slept a little better. And for that, she was grateful.

Chapter 14

Monday morning after breakfast, Lester walked over to the lodge with his toolbox. As he stepped up onto the big front porch, he was glad he'd tucked Marlene's locks inside it, so they weren't visible: Elverta and Agnes had stationed themselves in wicker chairs on either side of the door. They didn't appear to be chatting with each other, but they weren't bickering, either.

"Lester, what a fine surprise!" Agnes crowed, letting her knitting needles fall idle into her lap. "It's a lovely spring morning and you've already made my day just by showing up."

"Not going to the bulk store or another job site?" Elverta quizzed him as she looked over the top of *The Budget*. "I figured you'd be long gone by this hour, hard at work."

Lester stopped at the top of the porch stairs, considering his responses carefully. He didn't feel the need to inform these ladies of his schedule, and intuition told him that no matter what they'd said, they'd been awaiting his arrival—or hoping for it, anyway.

Had Marlene told them he was coming, and why? He decided to keep her request for locks confidential for now.

"Oh, I'm a working man," he replied vaguely. "But being my own boss means I can keep a flexible schedule—"

"So let's go for a walk today!" Agnes blurted out. "I've picked out a couple of potential places for us to build a home—"

"Oh, *I* did that the day I arrived," Elverta pointed out in a superior tone. "And truth be told, I'd be delighted if we built a house right there beside the lake."

"—and the lots I've chosen have beautiful views, but they're relatively small," Agnes continued euphorically, "because I don't figure we need a lot of farmland or property—but of course, you already have a tract of land, so that's where I'd be happy to live, Lester. Anywhere *you* are is where I'd like to call home, so if you'd rather—"

Lester held up his hand. He paused, reconsidering what seemed to be their favorite topic of discussion. "Just so you know, I sold all my land when the Beacheys bought my house," he stated. "And Allen Troyer's been letting me live in the tiny home out of the kindness of his heart ever since. So these days, I own nothing but a few kitchen utensils and clothes."

Both women went silent. They stared at him as though he'd sprouted a second head. Apparently it had never occurred to them that a man his age would be content to live without any physical property.

And if that makes me look like a poor choice for a husband in their eyes, so much the better!

Lester used their moment of silence to turn the tables. "I haven't heard either of you mention selling your farms in Ohio, so I'm guessing you still own them, *jah*?"

Elverta and Agnes eyed one another cautiously, as though neither wanted to be the first to reveal her circumstances.

"I still have my plot of ground with my house on it,"

Elverta finally admitted. "I didn't want to sell before I came out here, thinking you might be tired of living alone in Missouri and ready to move back to Ohio—with *me*."

"Oh, but *I* still own a farm!" Agnes put in triumphantly. "You'd be quite at home there with *me*, Lester—or I could sell it and provide a nice cash contribution toward our new house here at Promise Lodge."

Lester had grown weary of the conversation, but he tried to sound patient. "Well, at least you both have homes to return to when you finally realize I'm not going to hitch up with either one of you," he pointed out firmly. "And now if you'll excuse me, I have a repair project—and I don't need your opinions or supervision while I work, *denki*."

As he entered the lodge, he heard the two women expressing their chagrin.

"Well, *that's* a fine how-do-you-do!"

"Puh! He's got no call to sound so—so sanctimonious!"

"We were being so nice to each other, and he didn't even notice!"

Lester quickly made his way up the double staircase to the upper floor. He'd asked Ruby to slip his note under Marlene's door last night, so Marlene was expecting his visit. She opened her door before he could knock, and he wondered if she'd watched him walk over—which meant she might've overheard his porch conversation through her open window.

Marlene's tight expression made him forget all about Agnes and Elverta, however. "Everything all right, dear?" he asked as she gestured for him to enter her apartment.

Her smile seemed nostalgic as she closed her door behind him. "*Jah*, mostly. Sometimes when you're rummaging around in old boxes, you find things you don't expect."

Lester nodded. "You realize I have to work with your

door closed part of the time, *jah*? If you'd rather step out while I—"

"I don't care who knows you're in here, Lester," she whispered with a conspiratorial chuckle. "It'll give a certain two hens something else to cluck about, ain't so?"

He nodded, pleased to hear her teasing. When he set his toolbox on a small table near the door, he could see that Marlene had opened a few of the boxes they'd carried up on Sunday. Their contents sat in piles around her main room— a set of old dishes, some worn rag rugs, a small box containing spools of thread and other sewing notions. Housewares, mostly, and none of them appeared to be worth putting in a household auction.

Marlene had returned to the box she'd been sorting through. She seemed calmer than she had on Sunday, and quite content to have him there in her apartment as they worked on their separate projects.

Lester reminded himself that no matter how comfortable she appeared with him, however, they were alone behind a closed door—and temptation could easily come knocking no matter how honorable their intentions were. He was a man, after all, and Marlene was an extremely attractive woman.

"Before I start installing these locks, are you sure you still want them?" he asked, keeping the conversation safe and businesslike.

"*Jah*, please," she replied emphatically. "And *denki* for doing this for me, Lester. What do I owe you for the locks and your time?"

"Not a thing. Rather than two dead bolts, though, I got you a dead bolt plus a chain slide lock," he explained as he held them up. "That way, you can open the door to look out into the hallway, but you'll still have a chain to keep someone from pushing the door open."

Marlene nodded. "That's probably better. After I thought about it, I realized that having two dead bolts—and probably two locks of any sort—would be overkill," she admitted softly.

Lester smiled at her observation. "You haven't told me why you feel you need them—and that's your business," he added quickly. "But just to reassure myself, I'm going to ask this again: have I done or said anything to frighten you, Marlene?"

"Absolutely not!" she blurted, looking up from her cardboard box. "I could've asked Preacher Amos or—well, any of the other men to install my locks if I felt uneasy about your being here."

"Does it bother you that I'm forty-five?"

Where did that come from? And where will I go with it now? Not the smartest thing I've ever asked a woman—because what if she says yes?

Marlene's eyes had widened slightly, but she didn't seem the least bit rattled by his question. "Truth be told, I thought you were younger, Lester. Not that it matters," she said with a shrug. "I'm thirty-five, although some days—like now, as I sort through my mother's things—I feel as hopelessly old and tired as most of her stuff looks."

"Grief does that to you," Lester said gently.

As he removed the locks from their packaging, he wondered what else he could say to comfort her. He hadn't known her parents—and he wasn't keen on repeating the old platitudes about time and healing that he'd grown so weary of after Delores and Sam passed—so he chose the tools he was going to use.

"If we're asking personal questions, Lester, does it bother you that I never plan to marry?"

He blinked, wishing he weren't so drawn in by the soulful

gaze of her dark eyes . . . eyes he wouldn't mind looking into for years to come.

"*Jah*, it does," he murmured. "You told me a while back you wouldn't marry because you didn't want to leave Mose to fend for himself. Now that you're both at Promise Lodge, however, you wouldn't be abandoning him if you found a husband. Life is long, Marlene," he added plaintively. "I hate to think about you spending the rest of yours alone, sweetheart. I've lived by myself a year now, and although I've gotten pretty *gut* at it, it's not a lifestyle I recommend."

Fearing he sounded like a lonely old codger making a play, Lester refocused on his tools. With his tape measure, he determined the correct placement of the dead bolt about seven inches above the doorknob and marked it with his pencil. He opened the door so he could mark the same spot on the outside of it, relieved that Agnes and Elverta had remained downstairs. Once he started up his battery-operated hole saw, he figured its noise would attract the attention of any residents who happened to be upstairs.

But no one peeked out of her apartment. As he bored the hole for the dead bolt's latch in the side of the door, it occurred to Lester that with both Kuhn sisters in the kitchen and Irene making her Monday pies out in the little white shed near the dairy barn, he and Marlene were alone upstairs.

As his thoughts strayed to the attractive young woman who worked across the room, Lester reminded himself that the two biddies who lived on either side of her might appear at any moment. He quickly fit the latch bolt into the side of the door and screwed in its metal plate, telling himself he'd better finish this job quickly, before his willpower abandoned him. Marlene was gentle and kind, not to mention nicely proportioned. More than once he'd imagined what her body might look like after he'd lovingly removed her clothes—

"Oh! Oh, Mamm, I had no idea you'd kept—"

When Marlene started sobbing as though her heart might break, Lester's best intentions flew out her window. How could he steel himself against wayward male thoughts when she was crying like a little girl who'd lost her only friend— or her mother? He set his screwdriver on the table and strode over to her, wrapping his arms around her shaking shoulders.

"Sometimes a *gut* cry is the only way to deal with such a profound loss," Lester murmured, swaying gently with her. As an afterthought, he asked, "Is it all right if I hold you, Marlene? If you'd rather be alone, I'll go. I can finish installing—"

"Stay," she whimpered, hanging onto him as though she might collapse. "I feel so silly, bursting into tears about—"

"You're not silly," he insisted softly. He tucked Marlene's head against his shoulder, still rocking her. "You're sad because you miss your *mamm*. And considering that she wasn't in her right mind for quite a long time, you miss your *mamm* the way she was when you were a child and *she* was the one holding you when you cried."

For several minutes Marlene remained in his arms, soaking his shirt with her tears until she regained control of her emotions. When she finally eased away with a loud sniffle, her pink-rimmed eyes and tear-streaked face touched something deep inside him.

I know exactly how desolate she feels. And this is the most inappropriate time in the world to kiss her—

Somehow, he bussed her cheek rather than kissing her lush mouth the way he longed to.

Marlene, however, cupped Lester's jaw and pressed her lips firmly against his.

He was so surprised, the lovely moment passed before he could fully enjoy it. She broke away with a soft gasp and stepped self-consciously out of his embrace. "I'm sorry," she rasped. "I shouldn't have—"

"Oh, but you did. And *I'm* not sorry at all."

Lester remained where she'd left him, mere steps away. His lips—his entire body—thrummed in ways he hadn't felt for far too long, but he swallowed hard. Tried to concentrate on what she was lifting out of the box to show him.

"Mamm made these cloth dolls for me when I was a wee girl," Marlene said softly. She cradled them against her chest, closing her eyes. "She sewed me other dolls, but these two—Sally and Simon—were always my favorites. I played with them so much, she had to keep patching their bodies, or restuffing them, or making them new clothes.

"But she never threw them away or insisted that I play with my other dolls," Marlene added in a faraway voice. "Mamm understood that these two were my best friends— that they were *real* to me—so she kept washing them and stitching them together again when their seams gave way."

She inhaled deeply, as though the dolls' scent reminded her of those precious moments with her mother. "As she worked on Simon and Sally, Mamm would remind me that God didn't intend for anyone to be cast aside or thrown away," Marlene continued softly. "She said that even when people needed fixing or they'd done something horribly wrong, we should repair them—or our relationship with them—and we needed to forgive them as Jesus taught us. Seventy times seven times."

Marlene let out a sigh that whispered of her mother's lingering love. She focused on Lester. "After Mose was kidnapped, our family prayed for the couple who snatched him away. We offered our forgiveness, even if God was the only one who knew we'd attempted reconciliation," she continued softly. "And we believed—of course—that my brother deserved every bit of fixing and encouragement we could give him."

Lester swallowed hard because a lump had formed in his throat. "Your *mamm* was a wise woman," he whispered. "I—I'm glad you found your dolls, Marlene. What a wonderful gift she kept back for you, knowing that someday you'd recall her love and her lessons exactly when you needed to feel her presence again."

Smiling through her tears, Marlene nodded. "Look at them," she said, shaking her head. "They're dirty, and they're lumpy from being crammed into Mamm's box, but their smudged faces bring back some of the best days of my life."

Lester sincerely hoped he could change that idea by showing Marlene that her best days might lie ahead of her. She was still a young woman, after all.

"And the dolls also remind me that I have a boatload of praying and forgiving to do right now."

His eyebrows rose but he decided not to quiz Marlene about that statement. If she wanted him to know who needed her forgiveness and why, it was best to let her explain it in her own good time.

Lester finished installing the dead bolt and soon had the chain slide lock attached to the inside of her apartment door, as well. He sensed it was best to leave Marlene to her unpacking, and to the wistful memories her dolls had dredged up, so he said goodbye and headed downstairs. When he thought about the impulsive way she'd grabbed him, his heart soared with hopefulness.

Marlene kissed me! And she didn't just peck the air near my face—she laid me a gut *one across the lips!*

He was still smiling when he crossed the lodge's unoccupied front porch. He waved at Rosetta, who was coming across the lawn.

"Lester, you look like you just won first prize at the county fair!" she called out.

"You might say that, *jah*," he agreed. Then, because Rosetta owned the lodge building—and because he was concerned about Marlene's emotional state—he decided to say something about the task he'd just completed.

"I'm not sure why, but Marlene asked me to install two locks on her apartment door," Lester said softly. "She doesn't suspect that anyone's been coming in while she's gone—"

"Well, that's a *gut* thing," Rosetta murmured.

"—but she wants to sleep better at night," he finished. "I have no idea what's caused her to say that. Just thought you'd want to know."

Nodding, she thought for a moment. "*Denki* for sharing that, Lester—and for taking care of her request without making any fuss that might upset the other ladies. If Marlene doesn't feel safe in her apartment, I need to find out why."

He nodded. "She's having a hard time, missing her *mamm* while she unpacks those boxes she brought back from Coldstream. We all need to keep her in our prayers and let her know she made the right choice by coming here."

As he headed for home, Lester sent a few words to God on Marlene's behalf. Then he went back to thinking about that kiss again.

Chapter 15

Later that morning, Marlene shook her head over hundreds of old Christmas cards—judging from the dates on the envelopes, Mamm had stuffed ten or twelve years' worth of holiday greetings into the large box before taping it shut.

Why had her mother kept all those cards? If she'd sealed the box, that meant she hadn't looked at them for years—

"Knock, knock, Marlene. We thought you could use a break."

As she hurried over to her apartment door, she wondered who *we* included. She thought she'd recognized Rosetta's voice—and when she swung the door open out of habit, it caught against a steel chain. As Marlene unhooked the slider, she saw that Christine and Mattie were peering at her over Rosetta's shoulder.

Their gazes told her they were *very* curious about the lock she'd just unfastened.

"Come in! I've opened a box crammed with Christmas cards." Marlene sighed as she motioned them inside. "Until the past couple of days, I had no idea how deeply ingrained my mother's pack rat habits were."

The three women filed into her apartment, taking in the empty boxes and the piles of old items that cluttered her

front room. Back in the day, the Bender sisters had sold
their farms and bought the Promise Lodge property without
asking Bishop Obadiah's permission, so Marlene admired
them immensely. She also knew she might as well get
straight to the point about the shiny new locks on her door.

"As you can see, Lester installed some new hardware
this morning," she murmured.

"He mentioned it to me as he was leaving," Rosetta said
with a nod, "so we thought we'd offer you a picnic lunch
today, out in the fresh air and sunshine—"

"And you can tell us what those locks are all about,"
Christine said kindly.

"I have a hunch it involves something that happened
while you and Mose were in Coldstream for a very short
weekend," Mattie chimed in, gently holding Marlene's
gaze. "Amos doesn't reveal confidential things he hears
from folks in the congregation, but if there's something we
gals can help you with, Marlene, you know we'll do our
best to set it right."

Marlene chuckled ruefully. "I should've known you'd
see through my attempts to deal with the situation myself.
A picnic sounds perfect—a chance to chat in the fresh air,
away from these dusty boxes and other curious ears."

The sisters nodded knowingly. "We thought we'd walk
over to Mattie's backyard," Christine said as the four of
them headed into the hallway. "We'll have lots of sunshine,
it's close by—and no one will be tempted to eavesdrop on
our conversation."

"*Jah*, Beulah tells me that when our two new residents
aren't pestering poor Lester, they're quizzing her and Ruby
about him," Rosetta said as they descended the enclosed
back stairs that led to the kitchen. "They seem to be more
civil toward each other for now, but something tells me
their truce won't last."

"And one of these days, they'll have to either look in on their homes back East, or sell them, ain't so?" Mattie speculated. "Seems very odd for two middle-aged Amish gals to be living with one foot in Missouri and the other in Ohio."

As they passed through the mudroom, Marlene already felt better. Although it would be painful to recount her confrontation with the Mullets yet again, she sensed that in their own way, these women from Coldstream might come up with more effective methods of dealing with the situation than Preacher Amos could. It had taken a lot of focused energy, determination, and faith for Mattie, Christine, and Rosetta to start new lives at Promise Lodge——not to mention deal with Bishop Obadiah's objections when they'd left his church district.

Marlene smiled to herself as they walked across the lawn toward the Troyer place. Yost and Jake had *no idea* what they were in for, now that the Bender sisters were taking her side. When they'd spread an old quilt on the grass behind Mattie's house and unwrapped containers of food they'd carried from her kitchen, Marlene's mouth dropped open.

"My word, I would've been happy with sandwiches and chips, but someone has gone to a lot of trouble!" she exclaimed. "Look at this mac and cheese, and sliced ham, and this layered green salad with the dressing on top. Even if you all pitched in, how did you pull this picnic together in such short order? Lester didn't leave my apartment until a couple hours ago."

Rosetta smiled as she handed around some paper plates. "Bender magic."

"*Jah*, we *gut* fairies just wave our wands," Christine teased.

Mattie shrugged, obviously pleased with Marlene's reaction. "You know how it is. You think you're cooking macaroni for two and you end up with enough for five meals—"

"And ham! No matter how small you think it is when you buy it, it hangs around until you finally have to freeze the rest," Rosetta said.

"And we're doing Monroe a favor, eating some of this salad for lunch," Christine said matter-of-factly. "He'd much rather focus on the meat and potatoes and forget about the rabbit food."

After they'd bowed for a short silent prayer, they loaded their plates. As Marlene savored her first flavorful bites of food, she decided it was best to get right to the point. These women had known her all her life, after all. There was no point in making them wait—and nothing she could say would offend them.

"You were right about us having an incident in Coldstream on Saturday," she began softly. "It started at Laura's wedding on Thursday, when I noticed that Yost and Jake Mullet were watching me from the men's side, with something on their minds. Turns out they were upset because we'd sold the farm without giving them first dibs on it—and, um, they wanted to settle old scores over the engagements I broke."

Christine scowled. "Seriously? That happened years ago."

"And as I recall, it didn't take either of them long to hitch up with somebody else," Rosetta put in. "But we should be quiet and let you tell us what happened, Marlene. If you came back from Coldstream early, feeling you needed two locks on your door, you were traumatized. *Terrified*."

Nodding, Marlene told her story. The three sisters listened closely, their lunch temporarily forgotten when she got to the part where Mose arrived just when Jake and Yost had nearly trapped her. As the painful details poured out, Marlene felt as though she was unpacking a box of poison pellets that would've contaminated her soul—eaten away at her emotional well-being—if she'd kept the truth about the Mullets bottled up inside.

"You must've been frightened out of your mind," Rosetta whispered, gently grasping Marlene's wrist. "We're so glad Mose got there in time—"

"Yost and Jake got exactly what they deserved from him, too," Christine put in tersely. "I was relieved when you broke up with them, Marlene, because our *dat* caught those boys in the chicken yard once, wringing the necks of Mamm's hens with their bare hands and leaving them to die. Now that's just *meanness*."

"When Preacher Eli came to shoe our horses one time, he told Dat that Yost's buggy mare had thrown two shoes probably *weeks* before the vet was finally called to tend her injured hooves," Mattie muttered. She gazed sadly at Marlene. "No wonder you didn't want to work alone in the house after Mose sent the Mullets away."

"But your auction's coming right up—on the thirty-first, *jah*?" Christine asked. "You're going to need some help clearing out the rest of your boxes. I'm thinking we sisters need to organize a work frolic."

"And we need to have Amos and some of the other men along to help Mose with the farm equipment—and in case Yost and Jake decide to visit again," Rosetta chimed in. "Who knows what sort of stories they've told their wives about how they got black eyes and that broken nose?"

Marlene's head was spinning. Her three friends were putting plans into place with an ease and speed that amazed her—as though they organized such efforts all the time. "Preacher Amos suggested the same thing yesterday when Mose confessed to him," she said softly. "I suspect he didn't share the details with you, Mattie—"

"No, but *you* have, so now it's official!" the preacher's wife said with a chuckle.

"Mose will be going to the farm on Thursday to meet with Myron about what equipment he wants to buy," Marlene offered. "I think he's planning to stay and work a day or so, too."

"Amos mentioned that," Mattie said with a nod, "and he's going along—because it's been a while since he's seen Myron, and because he thinks it's best to be prepared in case Bishop Obadiah drops by with questions. We all know that Obadiah rides a pretty high horse when it comes to folks leaving his church district—"

"And although Mose is a big, strong fellow, he'll be no match for the bishop and the Mullets if they team up and demand answers, or if they accuse your brother of unprovoked violence against the Mullets," Christine pointed out.

"*Jah*, there's that," Marlene said with a sigh. "Jake and Yost both have a way of twisting the truth around to support their own stories."

For a few moments they resumed their picnic. Marlene could practically see the cogs turning in the Bender sisters' heads as they chewed their food, so she remained quiet. It was a blessing to be sitting in the sunshine, eating salty-sweet ham with creamy mac and cheese as three lifelong friends considered her predicament.

"I really appreciate how you're helping Mose and me," she murmured. "And those locks on my door? I asked Lester to install them because now that the Mullets know where I live, I could imagine them coming here to—"

"Say no more," Rosetta assured her kindly. "Any one of us would be having the same fears and nightmares if two men with bad intentions had cornered us."

"I think we should let Mose and Amos—and whoever else goes along on Thursday—handle the men's work outdoors,"

Mattie suggested, "and then we women can go along with them sometime after that, to finish inside the house."

"Don't forget that Dale's having his grand opening at the bulk store next Saturday," Christine said with a smile. "We want to be here for that!"

As they all laughed and took a few more bites of food, Marlene recalled another detail that might be helpful. "Not telling you what to do, because Mose and I will be glad for whatever help you give us," she began, "but Amos also suggested that we include Truman, because if he drives, we'll spend less time on the road and more time working."

"That Amos!" Rosetta teased, poking at Mattie's arm. "Seems you married a genius—or at least a master organizer, sister."

"And to think Amos came up with that idea—and the one about a work frolic—without our help," Mattie put in with a laugh. "He's been around us sisters so long, our ways must be rubbing off on him."

Rosetta beamed at Marlene, an expression she recalled from when the two of them had been scholars together in school. "How could Truman possibly resist such an invitation? I'll check with him about going to Coldstream for a day or two next week, and we'll plan accordingly.

"And we'll plan for happiness, Marlene," she added with a nod. "Because we *will* get you through this, and you'll be every bit as delighted as we are that you came to Promise Lodge."

How could she argue with that? Marlene smiled as she gripped the hands the Bender sisters offered her. With the help of her friends—and that surely included Lester— she would put the Mullets and the auction and her grief behind her. Someday her own smile would shine as brightly as the three she saw right now.

Chapter 16

When Lester got home Thursday afternoon after installing twenty new windows at the apartment complex where Truman had gotten him work, he was beat. He waved at Truman as the pickup headed back to the road. He'd pushed himself all day so he could complete the job sooner than he'd agreed, leaving the next several days open—in case Marlene asked him to help with clearing out the farmhouse in Coldstream. He entered his tiny home with a tired sigh, wishing he had room for a big, comfy recliner.

His thoughts wandered to the upholstered chairs he'd seen in Marlene's apartment. It wouldn't be proper for him to go upstairs and pay her a visit, but no one would mind if he collapsed for a while in one of the cushioned wicker chairs on the lodge's front porch—

He spotted a familiar plump figure making her way across the lawn.

Lester groaned. Agnes was carrying a pie in one hand and a gift sack in the other, wearing an expectant smile. His first impulse was to pull down the shades and pretend he wasn't at home, except his visitor had most likely been watching for him from her window, waiting to pounce when he returned from work.

He prepared himself for whatever ploy Agnes might try this time, rubbing his temples as they began to throb with a headache. She'd be knocking on his door any moment—

And then Elverta came out onto the lodge's front porch, looking toward his place. She was holding a small set of binoculars to her eyes. Because he'd worked longer hours at the complex and was dependent on Truman's work schedule for his rides home, Lester had managed to avoid the two women since Sunday dinner—but that meant they'd had nearly four days to revise their strategies and plan their next attacks.

Agnes knocked, three sharp raps on his door. "Lester? I've made you a couple of gifts, honey!"

His headache pounded. There was no way around it: he had to deal with her.

When Lester opened his door, Agnes flashed him a radiant smile from her spot in front of his steps. "Hi, Agnes. How've you been?" he asked, hoping she'd take the hint from his weary greeting and leave soon.

"Fine and dandy!" she crowed, placing her foot on the lower of his two stairs. "I thought I'd bring you this fresh peach pie and a little something I knitted this week. May I come in—just for a moment? I'd really love to see your tiny home, Lester. I've never been inside one, but—"

"Oh, that's not such a *gut* idea."

"—I know you've been busy with your installation job, dear, so I promise I won't stay long," Agnes continued with a wider smile. "If you wanted to come to the lodge for some nice leftovers—still warm—we'd be happy to set you a place at the table, Lester. The Kuhns made several different appetizers tonight, just for something different."

When she took the next step up, she was directly in front of him. Still smiling as she held his gaze, Agnes was standing so close to the door that Lester couldn't shut it without knocking the pie out of her hands and making her tumble backward. He didn't need to look to know that Elverta was making her way over, and he saw no way to prevent the altercation that would erupt when the spinster found him and Agnes together in his small main room. He stepped back and let her in, careful to leave his door wide open.

"Oh, look at this!" the little widow said as she gazed around. "All the miniature kitchen appliances are built in, and there's a little pull-down table—but where do you sleep, Lester? I don't see any sign of a bed—"

When he pointed up, Agnes's eyes widened. "My stars, you're on quite a ledge there. What if you fall out of bed, or walk in your sleep, or—"

"Tiny homes aren't for the feeble or the faint of heart," Lester agreed. He spotted Elverta passing his kitchen window and braced himself.

"And what have we *here*?" she demanded loudly. "Agnes, you know it's absolutely *wrong* to be in Lester's home unchaperoned—especially since it's barely big enough to turn around in!"

Startled—because Elverta was stepping inside to join them—Agnes cried out and dropped the pie. As it hit the floor upside down, Lester climbed the lowest two rungs of his loft ladder, hoping to stay out of the fray.

"Now look what you've done!" Agnes shrieked. "Nobody invited you to—and now there's no way to pick up my pie without—"

"Who are you trying to fool, Agnes?" Elverta asked with a raised eyebrow. "You no more made that pie than I did! You bought it from Irene's pie shop."

"Well, at least I came over with something besides a bad attitude!" Agnes shot back.

"Ladies," Lester said loudly, although he thought that label was a stretch. "Let's not get into a—"

"And what's in this wee little sack?" Elverta snatched it from Agnes's pudgy hand and peered inside. "Is this what you've been knitting all week? If it's supposed to be a pair of socks, why, they're not even big enough for a baby, let alone for Lester!"

"That's none of your beeswax!" Agnes cried out, grabbing for the gift bag.

Elverta, however, stuck the bag behind her and backed up against the doorway. "What am I to tell the others about your little visit today?" she asked archly, sneering at Agnes. "If the bishop hears about this—"

Lester let out an exasperated sigh. "Ladies, let's stop this bickering—"

"You have no reason to tell Bishop Monroe *anything*, Little Miss Tattletale!" Agnes shot back. "After all, if you can give him such an eyewitness report, it means *you* were inside Lester's house, too!"

"*Jah*, to be sure nothing went on that the church leaders need to know about," Elverta retorted. "God's watching you, Agnes."

"Stop!" Lester cried. "Just stop it right now."

His tone of voice finally got their attention. Both women looked at him fearfully, as though they'd never known he could sound so fierce. Lester inhaled deeply, closing his eyes to lessen the headache, which felt like a tornado was spinning in his brain.

"I thought you two had declared a truce. Now that it's obviously worn off, I'm asking—no, I'm *demanding*—that you leave my house," he muttered. "I didn't invite either one of you here. And the last thing I need after a long day of installing windows is a couple of women who have no control over their tongues and no respect for my privacy. Go on, now. *Leave*."

Agnes's face fell, and she looked ready to cry. Elverta

blinked as though she'd had no idea just how tightly wound up she and Agnes had become.

"You heard me," Lester said, motioning toward the door. "Get out of my house and don't come back. There's no polite way to say that, but then, you've both gone way beyond the point of being *polite*."

Agnes sniffled. "But what about my pie? And aren't you going to make Elverta give you that bag—"

"Leave them. Just *go*. Elverta, you're closer to the door, so you step out first," Lester said sharply. "Trust me, Agnes will be right behind you—and this would be a *gut* time to find a ride back to your homes in Ohio."

With a disgusted huff, Elverta gave Agnes a parting scowl and tossed the bag at her before stepping outside.

Agnes looked toward Lester, appearing ready for another attempt at winning him over, but he quickly pointed toward the door.

"Not another word," Lester warned her.

She hung her head and set the bag on the kitchen counter. As she left, he climbed down and shut the door, shaking his head.

Why were the two women still at Promise Lodge? Neither of them was mentally deficient, yet they didn't seem to hear or understand the word *no*. How much longer would he have to endure their aggravating behavior?

Lester let out a long sigh. Why was his main room, with its efficient kitchen on one side and Allen's small, stiff futon on the other side, plenty large enough for a man to spend the winter in, yet suffocatingly small when two ruffled hens had invited themselves in?

Lester peered inside the gift sack and pulled out a couple of socks that were indeed so small, he wasn't even going to try one on. What had possessed Agnes to knit them? She obviously had no clue about the size of a man's foot—even though, as feet went, his weren't all that large. It seemed a shame to throw them away, considering that she'd spent time on them and had bought the yarn. Maybe he'd use them to clean the kitchen and bathroom.

With a sigh, Lester fetched a dustpan. He slipped it under the pie and inverted it, relieved that only a few small spots of filling had leaked out onto the floor. The aromas of peaches, sugar, and cinnamon wafted up from the slits cut into the cracked top crust, reminding him that he was ready to eat after a long day on the job.

Lester dumped the pie into his trash can, however. It was a horrible waste of Irene's wonderful dessert, yet he wasn't in the mood to remove the top crust and eat the rest of it.

He took a can of pork and beans from his cabinet, opened it, and grabbed a spoon. It was a sad excuse for a meal, but he didn't have the energy to prepare anything else.

Marlene glanced out her apartment window and stood stock-still. If Elverta and Agnes were stalking across the lawn, shooting daggerlike glares at one another as they came from the direction of Lester's tiny home, it could only mean one thing. And it hadn't been pretty.

After all Lester had done for her this past week—no questions asked—she could surely find a way to repay his favors. As she left her apartment and quickly descended the back stairway, hoping to avoid the two incoming rivals, she knew exactly what he needed. No matter what had gone wrong, everything felt better after a helping of hot, gooey cheese.

When Marlene reached the kitchen, Beulah was staring into the deep freeze, probably figuring out what to serve for supper the next evening.

"Will it be all right if I take that leftover chili-and-cheese concoction to Lester?" Marlene asked. "Something tells me he could use some consolation and a friendly ear."

Beulah flashed her a knowing smile. "Sweetie, you and Lester are welcome to anything in this kitchen—and *jah*, that hot dip really hit the spot with those corn chips, ain't so? We'll have to do appetizer night more often."

"You've got my vote on that. *Denki*, Beulah," she said as she picked up the warm foil-covered pan on the counter. "Have a *gut* evening. I hope you find something to do besides cooking!"

"And I hope you and Lester will simmer up something wonderful," her friend said with a wink.

After she'd grabbed the fresh, unopened bag of corn chips beside the warm pan of dip, Marlene started out through the mudroom door. She walked quickly, wondering if anyone happened to be looking out their window . . . wondering how she would explain her presence in Lester's tiny home if anyone quizzed her about it. The proper thing would be to knock, offer Lester the chips and dip, and leave—or stay with him, if he suggested they sit out on his dock.

By the time Marlene reached the tiny blue home on the shore of Rainbow Lake, the evening breeze was turning chilly as the sun set. She stood in front of Lester's door for a moment before knocking firmly.

In for a dime, in for a dollar. If I'm going to have to confess, I might as well make it worth my while.

The shade fluttered briefly before the door swung open.

"Marlene, it's *gut* to—those two biddies didn't spout off about what just happened here, did they?"

The lines of Lester's face were etched deeper than usual, and her heart went out to him.

"I purposely avoided meeting up with them—and I really don't want to hear what happened, unless you want to get it off your chest, Lester," she replied, holding up her food. "It's only leftovers, but it's full of chili and cheese and—if you'd rather I just gave it to you and left you alone—"

"Get in here," he murmured with a faint smile. "And for the record, if somebody sees you coming in, so be it. We're adults. And I'm tired of dealing with two women who behave worse than most children I know."

As Marlene stepped inside, her stomach fluttered and her senses went on high alert. She knew exactly what the empty can of beans with the spoon in it meant.

She smiled when she spotted an unexpected appliance. "You have a microwave? If we put this dip in it for a little bit, the cheese will get hot again."

Nodding, Lester removed the foil from the pan and inhaled gratefully. "You're an angel of mercy—a *gut* Samaritan helping a poor old guy who's been clobbered and left for dead on the side of the road," he murmured as he opened the microwave door. "Allen builds these tiny homes for English folks, you know, so they have all the modern conveniences. And since my power's coming from solar panels on the roof, I'm not on the grid. Bishop Monroe doesn't ask whether I use all the gadgets."

"Ah. Bishop Monroe's a kind man."

"And you, my dear, are the kindest, most thoughtful young woman I know. You have no idea how you've saved my day from going down the toilet."

After Lester pushed a button to start the microwave, he pointed to the cabinet at the right of the small built-in sink. "Plates are there, utensils are in the drawer below it. I'll fold down my table, and we'll be in business."

Marlene smiled. It impressed her that he'd steered her toward real plates rather than paper ones—although she wouldn't have complained about disposable dishes. She watched in fascination as he folded his table down from the wall and took a folding chair from its slot alongside the lower counters.

"A place for everything, and everything in its place," she murmured as a *ding* announced that the layered dip was ready.

Lester smiled wearily. "But there is no place here for either Elverta or Agnes, no matter what sort of fantasies they seem to be spinning in their heads," he muttered, gesturing for Marlene to sit down. "I can't figure out how to convince them to head back to Ohio. And now, I'm finished talking about them. This stuff smells fabulous, Marlene. Tell me about it."

"I ate mine by putting corn chips on my plate and then spooning the hot chili and cheese over the top of them, but some folks dipped their chips into it," she said, popping open the bag. "Either way, you're getting a layer of cream cheese, some chili, some melted cheddar, and those olives and diced bell peppers in each bite—and it was all I could do not to polish off the rest of that pan by myself at supper."

"Oh, but I'm glad you didn't!" he said as he quickly put chips on his plate. He took one, dragged it unceremoniously through the dip, and popped it into his mouth. "Mmmm . . . every bit as *gut* as you said it was. Don't let me hog it all—"

"But I've already eaten my supper—"

"Don't let that stop you, dear! You'd be doing me a favor, joining me instead of making my meal a spectator sport."

Marlene laughed out loud, stopping suddenly when Lester held her gaze with dark, sparkling eyes.

He smiled, pausing between chips loaded with dip and dripping yellow cheese. "It's *gut* to hear you laugh, Marlene. I've been concerned about you since you asked me to install those locks," he admitted softly. "Have you found a spot for your dolls?"

Her heart fluttered in her chest. Not many men would care enough to ask such a question about raggedy keepsakes that had no meaning to anyone but her.

"For now, Sally and Simon are sitting in my extra chair. I'm going to wash them—very carefully—and make a few repairs to them after the household auction is behind us," she replied. "I'll have a lot more time then—although Dale has asked if I'd work in the new bulk store."

Lester's eyebrows rose as he scooped more of the dip onto his plate. "And what'd you tell him? I'm sure he'd be happy for your help. Most of our other women have their own businesses—or husbands—keeping them busy, and our young girls are still in school."

His expression was so kind, so encouraging, that she suddenly had her answer—as well as another idea.

"You know, I think I'll take the job," Marlene said. "If I don't have some sort of work to occupy me, I'll go batty. And it might be fun, seeing all the different items Dale has for sale—as well as the folks who come into his store."

She paused, ready to open a little more of herself—ready to trust this gentle man with more of her past. "Mose and Preacher Amos went today to talk with the fellow who bought our farm in Coldstream. If—if it fits your schedule, Lester, I'd be grateful if you'd go with a bunch of us to ready the place for our auction. Not sure yet when we're going," she added as she poured more chips onto her plate. "Depends on when Truman can take time off, so he can drive us."

Lester's smile erased five years and a lot of weariness from his face. "I'd be delighted to go along. I, um, finished my window installations today so I'd have the time free, in case you asked me."

Marlene's hand stopped with a cheese-loaded corn chip inches from her mouth. "That's the sweetest thing anyone's done for me in a long time, Lester," she whispered.

He shrugged, obviously touched by her comment. "Look what you've just done for me, bringing over this food when I needed a cheese fix more than you can imagine," he said softly. "Although you could've shown up empty-handed, and I'd still feel a lot better than I was before you got here. I'll say it again, Marlene—you're an angel. And I'm glad you're *my* angel."

Her mouth went dry. She couldn't stop looking at him. Little red flags shot up in the back of her mind, warning her that Lester was getting too close—too personal—and that it would be best if she left before she did something foolish like kissing him again.

And yet kissing him seemed like the perfect dessert.

After he ate another couple of chips in the small, suddenly silent kitchen, Lester sighed. "Said too much, didn't I? But I meant it, Marlene. I'm excited that you asked me to help with your house clearing, and I intend to keep working away at you, little by little, to change your mind about that marriage issue.

"But if I'm reading you all wrong," Lester added in a purposeful voice, "please say so. I know exactly how exasperating it is to be pestered by someone whose affection you don't want to return."

Marlene's eyes widened. "Oh no, it's not that—"

"*Gut*," Lester said, lightly grasping the hand she'd been gesturing with. "Let's stop there, shall we? We'll give our feelings a little time to simmer, without pushing them. You have a lot on your mind right now."

How was it that he sensed what she needed? Innately

understood her doubts about moving forward in a romantic relationship?

"*Denki*, Lester," she murmured.

"You're welcome." He leaned over the small table and gently brushed her lips with a kiss.

Marlene smiled as a thousand butterflies fluttered in her stomach. Lester's kiss had ended too soon. Then again, he knew exactly how to leave her wanting more.

Chapter 17

As Lester walked over for the bulk store's grand opening on Saturday morning, he was delighted to see several cars in the parking lot and a number of customers entering the front door. It was satisfying to know that he'd played a vital part in getting Dale's store ready for this big day. Several of his Promise Lodge friends would be present to help during this special event—and Lester had agreed to direct folks to the extra parking area over by Helmuth Nursery, if need be. First, though, he wanted to see how things were going inside.

"Preacher Marlin, you've quite a selection of your products here," Lester remarked, gesturing at the various styles of rain barrels and oversized planters made of half barrels. When an English fellow approached from the parking lot, he smiled, gesturing toward his friend.

"We're glad you've come today!" Lester said. "This fellow, Marlin Kurtz, makes these rain barrels and this lawn furniture in his factory right next door. It's *gut* to shop locally, ain't so?"

The man smiled—perhaps at Lester's Amish turn of phrase. "My family's happy to see a bulk store and mercantile-style shop opening here on the county highway," he remarked.

"I've already got my eye on one of these barrels with a potting table and water pump attached."

Nodding, Lester left Marlin and his customer to do their business. Dale also had birdhouses and other garden décor arranged along the front of his building, beneath the over-hang that would protect the items from the weather. As Lester entered the store, the noise level told him that several folks were browsing—and buying. The smile on Dale's face as he ran the cash register indicated that the day was already a big success.

"How about a taste of peach pie?" Phoebe asked as customers came near the small table where she and Irene were standing. "We bake our Promise Lodge Pies right next door! Can't get them any fresher than that."

Lester waved at the ladies. Folks were tasting the bite-sized samples as fast as Irene could cut them—and several were taking fresh pies from the display. A little farther into the grocery section, by the refrigerated cases, Ruby and Beulah were also a popular pair as they offered toothpicks with chunks of their cheese. Rosetta, as well, stood beside a display of her handmade goat milk soaps, happy to talk with ladies who picked up her round and rectangular bars to inhale their fragrances.

When he spotted Marlene, Lester stepped out of the main flow of traffic to observe her before she caught him at it. As he'd foreseen, she moved with graceful efficiency along the crowded aisles to guide an English couple toward the item they'd asked about.

Lester realized that she was head and shoulders taller than the women around her, and as she walked farther down the aisle, he felt his pulse thrumming. Dale had mentioned that Marlene had spent all day Friday with him, learning the store's inventory, and how he wanted her to help with restocking and customer questions. Judging from her confident expression, she'd caught on quickly.

He noticed that Mattie and Christine were helping in the housewares section. Farther back, Lester spotted Preacher Amos where straw hats, suspenders, and other Plain men's clothing was displayed, and Bishop Monroe stood chatting with a couple of men near the wall where rakes, spades, and other outdoor tools were hanging. Some departmental signs were suspended from the ceiling, as well as large, colorful pictures of Easter baskets and colored eggs, which pointed at the shelves where the candies and egg dyes were sold.

Lester saw a lot of smiles and loaded shopping carts as he turned toward the main entrance again, heading outside to help with traffic control. It was a great day for Dale, and for Promise Lodge, as well.

"I'm telling you, *I* saw this package of chocolate-covered haystacks first!" a female voice rang out in the candy aisle. "It's the last bag, and it's *mine!*"

Lester winced. Agnes was here—and he already knew whom she was squabbling with.

"You were fingering the peanut clusters!" Elverta snapped. "I'm buying these haystacks for Lester! It's not as though *you* need to be eating candy, after all."

"And you can keep your opinions to yourself, Miss Know-It-All! This bag is *mine!*"

With a sigh, Lester started toward the two feuding women, but the aisles were jammed—and now folks were gawking to see who was causing the commotion. "Excuse me, folks, please," he muttered repeatedly as he squeezed between their shopping carts.

"If you want a bag of coconut haystacks, ask Dale to get you one," Elverta countered in a strident tone.

"No, *you* ask Dale—"

"Oh, *now* you've done it. Ripped the bag—"

Agnes shrieked, and as Lester made his way between the wide-eyed customers at the end of the candy display, cone-shaped chocolate-covered candies shot up into the air.

"I'm *tired* of you pushing me around, Elverta!"

"Not nearly as tired as I am of *you*, Agnes!"

"Ladies, please!" Dale called out as he hurried between people to regain control of the escalating argument.

But he was too late. Elverta, taller and stronger, grabbed Agnes's shoulders and gave her a hard shove—

And when Agnes landed against a display of pickled vegetables, glass jars flew off the shelves and landed on the hard floor with a dramatic shattering of glass.

"Folks, let's all step to the back of the store—or outside—so nobody gets hurt," Bishop Monroe called out in his strong, resonant voice.

"*Jah*, please—step aside so we can clean up the broken glass," Dale put in loudly. "Sorry for the inconvenience!"

The tangy aroma of vinegar and spices filled the air, along with Agnes's blubbering. "Get your hands off me! Haven't you caused enough trouble—"

"You don't know *half* the meaning of 'trouble' yet!" Elverta shot back.

"Stop this! We're going back to the warehouse," Lester said tersely. He managed to catch hold of Elverta just as Bishop Monroe and Preacher Amos arrived.

"Get moving," Lester said, pinning the spinster's arms to her sides. "Do you have any idea how much damage you've done—"

"She started it!" Elverta put in frantically.

"Not another word, understand me?" he muttered. He carefully steered the surprisingly strong woman through the broken glass, pickled vegetables, and the pungent pond of spiced vinegar covering the floor.

As they passed the customers who'd stepped out of their

way, Lester couldn't recall ever feeling so embarrassed—
or disgusted. Behind them, Bishop Monroe was holding the
same sort of conversation with ruffled, sputtering Agnes.
Preacher Amos had preceded them to the warehouse door
to open it, and as Lester walked Elverta into the cool,
cavernous warehouse, he knew something definitive had
to be done.

"Sit down on this crate and don't move!" he said none
too gently.

"And you can take a seat right over here, Agnes," Monroe
put in. "I don't know what got into you women, but you
owe Dale quite an apology—"

"Not to mention the money you cost him when those
jars of food hit the floor," Preacher Amos chimed in sternly.
"What were you thinking? I've never *seen* a display of such
childish, immature behavior—"

"But we've seen the last of it."

Rosetta had entered the warehouse behind them, along
with her two sisters, and she stopped in front of Agnes and
Elverta. "You've both paid advances on your rent, so I'm
deducting Dale's damages from your deposits before I
refund the rest of your money," she said, crossing her arms
tightly. "Tomorrow's the Sabbath, but I'm hiring a driver to
take you to the bus station in Bethany first thing Monday
morning. From there, you'll have to figure out your own
way back to Ohio."

Agnes's eyes widened and she began to cry. "But—but
you can't just throw us out—"

"I just did," Rosetta informed her. "You two have been
nothing but trouble for Lester since you arrived. He's tried
every way he knows to convince you to go home, so now
I'm making the decision for you."

"We're standing firm with Rosetta," Mattie said in a
no-nonsense voice. "This is our home, and you're flying in

the face of the friendships and businesses we've worked so hard to establish."

"*Jah*, we'll not tolerate residents who disrespect each other and destroy people's property," Christine put in firmly. "It's not the Amish way, and you know it."

The three Bender sisters stood shoulder to shoulder in a semi-circle facing Agnes and Elverta. They hadn't raised their voices, nor had they made any threats, but Lester was glad *he* wasn't the object of their intense scrutiny.

Elverta blinked as though she finally had an inkling of the trouble she and her nemesis had gotten into. "But why do both of us need to go? If you send Agnes back, we'll stop—"

"Nope," Lester put in. "Rosetta's right—and she owns the building you live in. We've all had enough. You wouldn't listen to me, and now I'm glad someone else has stepped in to make you see reason."

As Agnes and Elverta realized the finality of Rosetta's words, they slumped on their crates.

"I'm going back into the store to help clean up that mess, so Dale can run the cash register," Lester said quietly.

"And I'd like to return to my soap display," Rosetta put in with a sigh.

Preacher Amos nodded. "You folks take care of your business and I'll escort these ladies back to the lodge. "It'll be a *gut* time for the three of us to pray together, and to discuss apologies and potential confessions at church tomorrow."

"I'll go with you," Mattie said. "Much as I hate to even consider this thought, I'll stay in the lodge with you ladies after Amos leaves, to be sure you behave yourselves while the Kuhns and Marlene are here at the store working."

As the warehouse door closed behind Lester, he sighed loudly. Who would've ever believed that Mattie would be

staying at the lodge to monitor two middle-aged Amish
women?

*But then, who would believe what a mess Elverta and
Agnes made in Dale's store because they're so caught up in
outdoing one another? It's such a relief that they'll be going
back to Ohio, come Monday.*

When he got to the scene of the mess, Beulah was carrying a plastic bin full of broken glass and pickled vegetables
away as Ruby mopped up the vinegar. Marlene had wheeled
Rosetta's table display of soaps to block one end of the
affected aisle, and she was closing the other end with the
table Irene and Phoebe were using to cut their pie samples.
Most of the customers had stopped gawking and were
politely keeping to other parts of the store, so order would
soon be restored.

Lester caught Marlene's eye. "If you'll tell me where to
find a bucket I can fill with soapy water, along with a clean
mop, I'll wash the floor after Ruby's gotten up the last of
the vinegar," he suggested. "Unfortunately, no matter how
thoroughly we clean it, I suspect we'll be smelling vinegar
in that aisle for a while yet."

"I'll get them for you, Lester." Marlene smiled, shaking
her head. "The aroma of vinegar is nothing compared to
what folks might tell their friends about today's ruckus,"
she murmured ruefully. "I sure hope that catfight won't
keep people away."

Ruby chuckled, looking up at them. "For all we know,
it'll have the opposite effect," she said as her mop swished
rhythmically along the floor. "We might have customers
showing up in hopes of a little extra entertainment."

"Well, it won't happen again," Rosetta stated as she
straightened the soaps on her table. "Agnes and Elverta
will be leaving us first thing Monday morning—and I'm

deducting the cost of the pickled vegetables and candy Dale has lost from the advance rent they've paid us."

"They finally agreed to leave?" Beulah asked as she returned to help her sister.

"I gave them no choice."

"Ah. Well, I'm glad to hear it," Beulah said, gently squeezing Rosetta's shoulder. "The lodge hasn't been a peaceful place to live while they've been here."

By the time Marlene returned with the soapy water and a sponge mop, Ruby had wiped up all the vinegar she could. Lester worked in the aisle then, shaking his head as he thought about how a tiff over a bag of chocolate-covered coconut candies—supposedly intended for *him*—had triggered such a bizarre, mindless encounter between two jealous women.

Ironically, Lester didn't even like haystack candies. They were a staple in most Dutch bulk stores, but in his experience, they were usually dry or stale or just unappetizing. He was secretly glad he hadn't had to act pleased or grateful when Elverta had given him that bag of candy.

When he'd finished cleaning the floor, he and Marlene made room for a folding table near the checkout counter. A lot of Dale's Easter candy and filled baskets would be blocked off until the floor dried, so they moved seasonal merchandise to the spare table. Between checking out customers, Dale asked Marlene to turn on the speaker system and tell customers about the temporary change they'd made.

Her lashes fluttered nervously, but she picked up the microphone.

"Neighbors and friends," she said in strong, clear voice, "we thank you for your patience while we cleaned up our mess. We've arranged our Easter merchandise on a table in the front—so you can still purchase your goodies and stuffed animals and baskets!" she added with a chuckle. "*Denki* for shopping with us today! We wish you a blessed, wonderful-*gut* Easter with your families."

Lester's heart swelled with pride. Marlene's confident announcement—made without any warning or notes— was one more sign of how well suited she was to working with customers. Moments later, people were thronging to the table to select bags of chocolate eggs and jelly beans, chocolate crosses and bunnies, as well as boxes of egg dye and colorful baskets with assorted treats in them.

Waving at Dale—and winking at Marlene—Lester headed outside to check the parking situation. He wasn't surprised to see one of the redheaded Helmuth twins from the nursery—he couldn't tell if it was Sam or Simon—directing drivers toward empty spaces in his business's lot. Lester suspected that the grand opening at Dale's bulk store had attracted a lot of new customers for the nursery, as well: several folks were meandering alongside the greenhouses to view different varieties of blooming ornamental trees and bushes.

Lester walked over to the entry to the Kraybill parking lot, where cars were turning in off the county highway. It gave him a chance to chat with incoming customers as he pointed them toward empty parking slots—and it relaxed him after the drama he'd witnessed between Agnes and Elverta.

Why would two women raise such a fuss—and over an ordinary, everyday man like himself?

They weren't really squabbling about me as a man. They just had it in their minds that Lester Lehman would be lonely—desperate for a companion—and then it became a competition as each vied to fulfill her naïve, selfish fantasy about hitching up with me.

It wasn't a flattering picture. And in the end, it had only served to make both women appear self-centered and pathetic.

"Lester! Come take a late lunch break with me!"

He blinked and looked over to the store's entry. Marlene was there, waving eagerly at him with a bright smile on her face. Bishop Monroe was also leaving the store, adjusting his straw hat in the breeze as he approached Lester.

"Seems you've been summoned," the bishop said with a knowing smile. "How about if I take your place here? And if you haven't heard—we'll be going to the Fisher farm first thing Monday morning, soon as Agnes and Elverta have left with their driver. I was glad to hear Marlene saying that she'd asked you to come along."

Lester's eyes widened, but he didn't ask any questions. "Happy to help," he remarked. "*Denki* for letting me know."

As he set off across the paved lot, carefully walking between the cars, his heart felt as free as the robins and cardinals that were singing above him in the trees. Maybe, if a wonderful woman like Marlene was inviting him to share lunch with her, he wasn't such an ordinary, everyday man after all.

And he didn't feel the least bit lonely or desperate, either.

Chapter 18

At church the next morning, Marlene wasn't surprised that Bishop Monroe and Preacher Amos chose to preach the two sermons in a way that indirectly discussed Agnes's and Elverta's behavior in the bulk store without naming their names.

"As Deacon Marlin read this morning's Scripture lesson from the fifth chapter of Galatians," the bishop said during the second sermon, "we're reminded of the behaviors that stem from following our fleshly, human inclinations—instead of turning to 'the fruit of the Spirit'."

He stepped back to pick up a flat wooden object he'd stashed behind his spot on the preachers' bench. "When I was at the grand opening of Dale's bulk store yesterday, I found a plaque that seemed so appropriate, I bought it to post here in the lodge, where we'll all see it whenever we're here."

Bishop Monroe held up the wooden sign, slowly turning it so all in the congregation could see the words. "Our King James Bible uses old-fashioned words for some of these character traits, but their modern synonyms on this plaque make the point faster: 'love, joy, peace, patience, kindness, generosity, faithfulness, gentleness, and self-control,'" he read aloud, emphasizing each word for effect.

Marlene smiled to herself. Was it her imagination, or had Bishop Monroe said *self-control* a little more loudly than the other words? Across the room on the men's side, she saw Lester smiling as though he'd noticed that, too.

Bishop Monroe set the plaque aside, refocusing on his listeners. "When Paul writes this letter to the church in Galatia, he points out that all of these desirable attributes are reflections of Jesus's command to love our neighbors as we love ourselves. It's the Golden Rule restated, isn't it?"

Marlene nodded, and Agnes and Elverta—seated a couple rows ahead of her—were doing the same, even though they were looking down at their laps. Whatever Preacher Amos had said to them after he'd escorted them away from Dale's store must've had the desired effect, for they looked like little girls who'd been sternly scolded by their *dat*. Aware that everyone at Promise Lodge had heard about their fight—and their eviction—the two women appeared suitably subdued and humbled.

"As we prepare to walk with Christ on His path toward the cross," the bishop continued in his resonant, eloquent voice, "I hope we'll all pay special attention to how we show the fruits of the Spirit in our daily lives, and that we'll strive to live up to the words He spoke to His disciples in the upper room. It's John thirteen, verse thirty-four, that says, 'A new commandment I give unto you, That ye love one another, as I have loved you.' So simple, yet sometimes so difficult."

As the service came to a close, Marlene felt uplifted. The bishop's words weren't aimed only at Elverta and Agnes. The part about loving others as Jesus loved her was a sharp reminder that even though the Mullet cousins had treated her badly, she was still supposed to love them. And forgive them. It was a challenge she'd have to work on—perhaps as soon as the next day when she went to Coldstream.

It was no challenge, however, to feel buoyant when Lester came to her in the crowd as folks were getting up after the service. His smile made Marlene so happy, she felt like a puppy wiggling all over and wagging its tail.

"Looks like you survived your first day of working at the store with flying colors," he said as they stepped out of the stream of women headed for the kitchen. "But I bet you've got tired feet."

"I've got tired *everything*," Marlene shot back with a chuckle. "But Dale was ecstatic about his grand opening, so it was worth the effort. He's a nice man to work for."

"He handled the mayhem between Agnes and Elverta very calmly, I thought," Lester remarked after a moment. "A lesser man might've marched them out the front door while reading them the riot act and telling them to never come back."

Marlene nodded. "Dale has seen a lot in his many years as a storekeeper. He told me about a few incidents in his Cloverdale store that made this one look pretty tame—but it was still a shame it happened," she added. "You're right about that pickled-vinegar smell. I suspect it's going to haunt us for a while."

When she looked to one side, she noticed Elverta watching them from a few feet away. The *maidel* still appeared subdued as she approached a few moments later.

"Wonder if I could have a word with Lester?" she asked under the buzz of the other conversations around them. "It won't take long."

Marlene smiled cautiously. "Sure. I'll go help the other ladies set out the common meal. See you later, Lester."

"*Jah*, that's the plan," he said firmly. "I'm hoping you and I can eat together—or go for a walk after dessert."

"We'll make it happen," Marlene said as she briefly squeezed his hand. Spending time with Lester sounded a lot more appealing than pondering a strategy for handling Jake and Yost if they stopped by the farm tomorrow.

Lester reminded himself about Bishop Monroe's sermon on the fruits of the Spirit—especially about patience, kindness, and gentleness. He was as lacking in love as the next person when it came to his feelings for Elverta Horst and Agnes Plank of late. He was glad he'd only have to tolerate those ladies for another eighteen hours or so.

"How are you today, Elverta?" he asked softly.

"Well—I'm *sorry*, Lester," she blurted out.

For a moment her face got so puckery, he thought she might burst into tears.

"I—I'm sorry that I came here assuming you'd see things my way and change your entire life for me," she continued in a miserable tone, "and I'm even sorrier that I allowed Agnes to get my goat to the point I went so overboard fussing at her. Can you forgive me?"

Lester was tempted to string her along for a while, but that wouldn't be very loving. "*Jah*, I can do that, Elverta. I hope you'll have a safe trip home tomorrow."

Upon his forgiveness, her face brightened considerably. "But if you've forgiven me, can we start fresh, back at square one?" she asked hopefully. "We could—"

"No, we couldn't," Lester put in firmly. "Rosetta's making your arrangements and refunding the remainder of your rent money, and that's that. We've had this chat before."

Elverta sighed loudly. "I wanted to try one more time while somebody else wasn't here to copy my idea," she said, glancing at the crowd around them. "I guess this is *gut*-bye, then."

"It is, and it's for the best," he agreed.

"You probably won't be there when our driver arrives early tomorrow morning," she hinted.

"No, I won't." Lester almost mentioned the trip to Coldstream but thought better of saying he'd be spending the day at Marlene's farm—even if a lot of other folks were also going.

"All right, Elverta, you've had your turn," Agnes said loudly as she stepped out from behind Lester. "Maybe you should go on over and see if Dale's back from his Mennonite service in Cloverdale, so you can speak with him, as well. Preacher Amos is going to ask him if we apologized, after all."

Elverta's brows furrowed with annoyance, but she walked away.

As Lester turned to look at Agnes, he noticed her pale face and pink-rimmed eyes. He had to wonder if she was also sorry about her unseemly behavior in Dale's store—or if she mostly regretted that things hadn't gone her way over the past couple of weeks.

"*Jah?*" he prompted gently.

"I'm sorry," she blurted out. "And I don't guess there's much point in asking for another chance."

"Apology accepted. And you're right." Lester waited to see if she'd say anything else.

After a few moments, Agnes screwed up her courage. She looked down at the floor. "Would this have turned out any different if Marlene hadn't come to Promise Lodge?" she asked wistfully.

"Nope."

"So you'd rather be alone than be with me? Even though Delores told me to come all the way out here?"

Lester groaned inwardly, reminding himself again of the *patience* Bishop Monroe had preached about. He thanked

God that the hours were ticking down until a driver would head east with these frustrating ladies.

"Some questions are best left unasked, Agnes," he replied, not wanting to fuel any further conversation. "Let's just leave it be, shall we?"

Agnes resembled a whipped dog as she made her way down the aisle of the lodge's big meeting room, which was nearly empty now. After a moment, Lester caught sight of her ascending the staircase from the lobby, probably going to her room rather than joining everyone else for the meal.

Maybe we've got the gut-*byes behind us now. Maybe this whole awkward situation is finally over, and a pleasant afternoon stretches ahead—*

"L-lester? How ab-bout if we ssstep outside for a m-moment?"

When Lester looked up, Marlene's brother was standing to one side of the lobby, watching him intently. As he stood near the stone fireplace in the rustic space that rose two stories to the lodge's beamed ceiling, where a huge chandelier of antlers was suspended, Mose Fisher had a sturdy, rugged appearance that fit right in with the décor. It was another reminder of how *large* he was . . . and how physically powerful. Lester suspected that when Marlene sewed her brother's clothes, she had to make the sleeves and chest a larger size to accommodate his muscles, just as she had to lengthen his pants beyond the standard pattern pieces.

"Sure, Mose," Lester replied as they passed through the door onto the wide front porch. "I'm hoping we can get better acquainted tomorrow when I go along to help you prepare for your household auction."

A few feet across the porch, Mose pivoted. As he leaned closer, his expression left no doubt that this wouldn't be an exchange of social niceties. "Y-you ssseem to be ssspending a lot of t-time with my sssister," he stated, holding Lester's gaze with two very intense dark eyes. "I w-won't sssay this t-twice, Lehman. T-treat Marlene right, or y-you'll be d-dealing with me. Got it?"

Lester blinked. Fisher wasn't threatening him, exactly, but it was clear he didn't trust Lester, either. "I wouldn't dream of mistreating your sister, Mose," he replied as calmly as he could. "I know this is a difficult time—for both of you—so I've offered my help and my friendship. Nothing more."

Mose didn't drop his gaze, but he didn't step back for several seconds, either. "I sssuspect y-you've g-got a l-lot more than *help* on y-your m-mind," he said warily. "Marlene's b-been hurt b-before—n-not m-my place to t-tell her ssstory—b-but if I g-get the ssslightest hint y-you're c-crossing the l-line, n-not respecting her, y-you'll b-be sssorry."

What could he say to that? Lester decided it was best to leave things as Mose wanted them. "I understand," he said quietly. "Feel free to talk with me again if you need to. It's what brothers do."

With a quick nod, Mose stepped around him and went inside.

Lester remained on the porch for a bit, wondering what had brought on Mose's ultimatum. Had he noticed when Marlene and Lester had walked around the grounds to-gether? Or had he seen his sister taking a pan of food and a bag of chips to the tiny house last night?

Or did Mose's words refer to something that had hap-pened at the Fisher farm the previous weekend? Perhaps the reason Marlene had returned to Promise Lodge sooner than everyone had expected—and had asked for two locks to be installed on her apartment door?

Mose is right about one thing: it's Marlene's place to tell that story. Not in my best interest to pry it out of her.

Lester let out the breath he didn't realize he'd been holding while standing before the largest, burliest man he'd ever encountered. It was uncanny and a little unsettling, the way Marlene's lovely facial features had appeared so menacing on Mose while he'd delivered his warning. It was as though Miss Fisher had a fierce, protective grizzly bear for a guardian angel.

But that was all right, wasn't it? Just one more challenge on the path that might lead to becoming more than Marlene's friend someday.

Lester stepped inside, where the buzz of voices filled the dining room. Displays of affection were inappropriate in public, so he fixed a careful smile on his face before approaching the tables where his friends were enjoying their meal.

It wouldn't do for folks to know just how much he wanted to kiss Marlene again today.

Chapter 19

The next morning around six-thirty, Lester saw a plain gray SUV pull up beside the lodge's front porch. As he watched from his kitchen window, Elverta and Agnes came outside carrying their suitcases while the Kuhns and Rosetta followed behind them, remaining on the front porch. After the driver hefted the luggage into the back of the van, he drove the ladies away.

No hugs. No well-wishes, and only a couple of waves goodbye. The three women watched from the porch, as though to be sure the vehicle kept on going down the road to the bus station in Bethany.

Lester allowed sheer relief to wash over him as he finished his coffee. Not wanting to be late, he left a few minutes later to join the rest of the folks going to Coldstream.

"*Gut* morning, Lester!" Rosetta called out as he crossed the lawn. "Looks like a perfect day for our work at the Fisher farm."

"It does," he agreed. "And it's nice to know that by the time we get back here, Agnes and Elverta will probably be on a bus crossing Illinois or Indiana!"

The mood immediately lightened. A short time later a large white van pulled up near the lodge, with CLOVERDALE MENNONITE FELLOWSHIP on its sides in large green letters.

Truman hopped out of the driver's seat and left the door open wide.

"Plenty of room for the coolers and picnic baskets on the back bench seat," he suggested as other folks showed up with these items. The event was taking on a holiday feel, as though the group was driving to the country to enjoy the springtime weather and flowering trees.

"Won't take us long to get to Coldstream—and this church van is just the ticket, as it'll hold fourteen passengers," Truman explained to Lester.

Lester reached for his billfold. "I didn't bring along food, so let me buy the gas," he insisted as he took out some bills.

When Truman tried to wave him off, Lester folded the money and stuck it into his friend's shirt pocket. "*Jah*, you're going to take this. Everyone's doing something to help Marlene and Mose today."

As though on cue, Marlene came out the front door and down the lodge steps. Dressed in older clothing for a day's work, she appeared subdued—but she brightened when she spotted Lester.

"*Denki* for taking time off from your work to join us today," she said. "With this many friends along, the work will go quickly and efficiently—no matter what else might happen while we're there."

Her remark puzzled Lester, but the other folks approaching the van were nodding, so they apparently knew what to expect.

"Ladies first," Bishop Monroe suggested. "That way we men can meet with Mose and plan out what needs to be done outside—and Truman can be in on it while he drives."

Rosetta, Christine, and Mattie all stepped into the van, along with Alma Peterscheim and Frances Kurtz. Lester gestured for Marlene to precede him, and he was immediately followed by Bishop Monroe, Mose, and Preachers

Amos, Eli, and Marlin. As folks settled into the comfortable single seats arranged along each side, Lester realized immediately that even though Marlene was sitting directly behind him, the high seat backs would prevent any conversing with her.

It was just as well: Mose had chosen the seat across from Lester and was sitting sideways with his long legs out in the aisle. Soon Truman was pulling onto the county highway and most of the other men had also turned in their seats so they could chat together. Behind him, the ladies were already talking and laughing in their lighter voices, consulting with Marlene about the number of rooms and storage areas in her home. Lester focused on the male conversation, which covered implements stored in the barns and the stable, as well as a couple of smaller outbuildings.

Lester immediately noticed that Mose's speech was much smoother this morning—probably because he'd grown up with most of this crowd, and he'd been working with Bishop Monroe for a couple of weeks. Along with Lester, the Kurtzes and Truman had never been to Coldstream, so he and Preacher Marlin were following the others' lead, listening closely to what Mose and Amos proposed for auction preparations.

When they passed a road sign for the Coldstream city limits, folks got quieter and began looking around, noting changes on the farms of their former neighbors. Mose was telling Truman where to turn, and soon they pulled off the pavement and onto the Fisher farm. Lester's initial impression was that the house and buildings looked a little tired, probably because Mose and Marlene had focused their attention on their aging parents rather than on maintaining their property.

"Folks, let's be sure we're all on the same page," Preacher Amos said as he stood up in the aisle.

Everyone got quiet, watching him with anticipation.

"Most of you know that a few of us came here with Mose last Thursday to meet with the fellow who's bought this place," Amos began. "Mose and Marlene sold their farm to a distant cousin of mine, and because they wanted to avoid a run-in with Bishop Obadiah, they didn't tell anyone in Coldstream they were selling out. We thought the bishop might pay us a visit on Thursday, but he didn't—and neither did Jake or Yost Mullet, who caused some trouble for the Fishers the weekend before that. Their farms adjoin this one, and the Fishers didn't ask if they wanted to buy the place."

Lester's inner antennae went up. As he counted backward, he realized Preacher Amos was referring to the time the Fishers had returned from Coldstream earlier than expected— right before Marlene had asked him to install those locks.

"Eli and I—and the Fishers—agree that we need to settle this matter rather than let it fester," Amos continued in a voice that thrummed with purpose, "so we've called and left messages with the bishop and the Mullets, telling them we'll be here today. Unless any of you has a better idea, Eli and I—as former preachers here—have agreed to handle whatever might arise if tempers flare again. Are we agreed on that?"

The atmosphere had become decidedly more somber. The other passengers nodded.

Lester sensed that everyone else knew more than he did about the situation with the Mullets, which had apparently gotten ugly—but he didn't feel right asking for specific details. If the local bishop and the Mullets showed up today, he'd piece it together as the conversation went along.

As everyone stood up to exit the van, a glance at Marlene's expression told Lester he'd made the right choice. He would've given anything to wrap her in his arms and relieve the fear that clouded her brown eyes, but with all the women behind her watching them, Lester simply nodded at her.

"We're all here for you, Marlene," he murmured.

He followed the other men down the aisle and off the bus, ready for a day that would be a labor of love.

Marlene tried to block the recurring images of Jake and Yost that ran through her mind as she led the other women into the house. Surely there would be no repeat performance if the two cousins did arrive, considering the number of other folks who were here working with her and Mose today.

It would be just like them not to come by, knowing that Amos and Eli will quiz them about what happened. Then again, if they've convinced Bishop Obadiah that Mose attacked them, all three men might be wound up tighter than tops.

"All right, girls, let's take a room at a time, like we've agreed. It's faster—and a lot more fun that way," Mattie suggested as everyone stepped into the kitchen. "Marlene, do you have any guidance about what goes in the sale and what does not?"

It felt strange to hand over such a decision to her friends, yet that was the only expedient way to be ready for the auction, which was only five days away. "I noticed that the two dumpsters Mose ordered have arrived. We got them because so much of our parents' stuff is too worn-out to sell," she said sadly. "Let's just say when you find items *you* wouldn't keep, they should go in the dumpster. I'll trust your judgment. The boxes I've already sorted through have mostly contained items that should've been pitched years ago. I fully expect to fill those dumpsters."

"If we have questions, we'll just ask you, Marlene," Rosetta put in matter-of-factly.

"Most of us have been through this same situation, sweetie," Frances remarked with a kind smile. "And we'll get you kids through it, too."

They all headed upstairs to the storage area—because Marlene wanted to get that room emptied first and put it behind her. Having five other women pulling out boxes and chatting made the task much less onerous—and if Yost and Jake were foolish enough to sneak upstairs again, the sound of so many voices would keep them at bay.

They settled into a system of pulling out boxes, sorting, and then taking trash downstairs in small, manageable loads. Marlene designated a corner for items she wanted to keep, and they placed auction items on top of the stripped beds for the men to carry down later. In less than half an hour they moved on to the bedrooms, and by lunchtime they had completed the entire upstairs.

"That was amazing!" Marlene said as she and her friends began taking food from the coolers and picnic baskets. "You ladies have made this feel more like a frolic than a chore—"

"Many hands make light work," Christine quipped.

"—and I doubt I could've finished that storeroom and one bedroom by myself today," Marlene continued. "I can't thank you enough for coming up with this fine idea."

"That's what friends are for!" Alma said as they began carrying food to one of the long tables set up alongside the house.

"And besides," Rosetta added with a smile, "it's always more fun to sort through other peoples' old stuff than to deal with your own. *Gut*ness knows our house could use the same sort of going-over, considering how so much of Truman's *mamm's* and grandparents' stuff is still there."

Soon the men emerged from the barn to join them for the meal. Some of the women had warmed casseroles in the oven and produced an assortment of hot dishes with beef, chicken, noodles, and cheese as well as cold fare like potato salad and mixed fruit—and of course several desserts.

"This is quite a spread!" Bishop Monroe said as he surveyed the meal. "Shall we return thanks and dive in?"

They stood together in the welcome sunshine, bowing their heads. Marlene was pleased that Lester had come to stand beside her as Monroe began to speak.

"Lord, we thank You for the energy You give us to do physical work and to help our friends," he prayed, "just as we're grateful for the fellowship that makes preparing for this sale a whole lot easier. Bless this food and the hands that prepared it and give us Your strength for the remainder of the day. Amen."

"Boy, am I ready for this," Lester murmured as he got into line to fill his plate. "But we've made a lot of progress out in the barn. How'd you ladies do this morning?"

"We finished the entire upstairs," Marlene replied. "The basement's next—and who knows what we might unearth down there?"

She spooned chicken and noodles onto her plate, as well as helpings from the other casseroles and salads. Mose had set a couple of long folding tables end to end and enough chairs of various sorts that everyone could sit together.

"Great day for a picnic!" Preacher Marlin remarked. "It's always nice to eat in the open air, even if we still need our jackets."

"After all the dust we were kicking up in the barns, this is perfect," Truman agreed.

As the *clip-clop, clip-clop* of hooves announced the arrival of a buggy, everyone looked toward the road. When

Marlene saw the elderly driver with the scraggly gray beard, her insides tightened with apprehension.

"Well, well, if it isn't our old friend Obadiah," Christine muttered under her breath. "He always did have a knack for showing up just as we sat down to eat."

At the far end of the table, Preacher Amos stood up, waving at their guest. "Obadiah, did you come alone?" he called out. "You're just in time to fill a plate and join us here."

The visiting bishop was scowling as he stepped down from his buggy. He held his comments until he'd walked closer to the end of the table—and until he'd made eye contact with Mose and Marlene.

"What was I to think when I saw flyers for a household auction here this coming Saturday?" he demanded brusquely. "So you Fishers are going to pull the same stunt as Amos and the Bender sisters and steal away like thieves in the night, rather than telling me about it?"

Marlene clasped her hands under the table, knowing that whatever she said would be wrong.

Obadiah didn't seem to notice. He continued his spiel without allowing time for anyone to reply to him. "Yost and Jake Mullet were plenty upset when they came to me with black eyes and a broken nose," he said more loudly. "They were upset—understandably—because you'd already sold your farm without having the common courtesy to offer it to either of them first! And then to have Mose *attack* them for no reason—"

"So the Mullets didn't have the *common courtesy* to come with you today?" Rosetta challenged calmly. "Amos specifically asked you all to be here so we could settle the matter of this so-called attack."

"Those two are probably hunkered down at home recovering, so their friends won't ask how—or why—their faces got messed up," Christine put in before the bishop could get another word in.

"And *I'm* wondering what kind of stories they told their wives," Mattie added without batting an eye. "Because we all know that if they'd left Marlene alone, this so-called *attack* would never have happened."

Marlene blinked, stunned by the three sisters' vehement response to Bishop Obadiah's opening remark—especially because they'd agreed that Amos and Eli would do the talking. When she felt Bishop Obadiah glaring at her, she willed herself to hold his gaze without turning away. After all, the Bender sisters had told her several times that she had nothing to be ashamed of—that she should hold her head high and stand up to whatever her accusers might say.

The bishop placed his fists on his skinny hips, determined to have his say as he focused on her brother. "Mose, you know full well that you outweigh and outpower the Mullets," he blustered. "Before you take leave of our district, you must confess your wrath and violence toward—"

"Mose is way ahead of you," Preacher Amos interrupted. "He has already given me a full confession and has agreed to reconcile with the Mullets—which is why we're all here today supporting the Fishers as they relocate to Promise Lodge."

The bishop waved Amos off. "And Marlene, if you'd listened to me all those times I insisted you take a husband," he continued doggedly, "or if you'd simply offered Yost and Jake a chance to buy your land, you wouldn't be at the very center of this confrontation. After all, you nearly married both of those men! Why *wouldn't* they be upset?"

Marlene's eyes widened fearfully, but she was also getting fed up with the bishop's intimidation tactics. "I'd rather die than allow the Mullets to live in my family's home," she muttered.

Mattie—who'd left Coldstream because Obadiah had condoned her first husband's abuse of her—stood up to emphasize her point. "I don't care what Yost and Jake told you, Bishop. I believe Marlene about who was outnumbered, overpowered, and at the mercy of intruders," she stated firmly. "Two men don't trap a woman in an upstairs bedroom to talk about real estate."

Folks around the table began murmuring among themselves, nodding their agreement with Mattie. Obadiah, however, continued to glare at them indignantly, throwing up his hands.

"This is what happens when the men of the church don't keep the women in their place!" he finally exclaimed. "Seems to me your entire district is on the downhill slide, Burkholder. Even *God* will turn His back on you for the way you've twisted His word and the *Ordnung* to suit your convoluted beliefs."

As Chupp stalked back to his rig, Marlene sank back against her folding chair. Thanks to the stalwart support of their friends, she and Mose had made it through the first round of this ordeal. But it had taken its toll on her.

And what must Lester and these other folks think? Now that they'd heard more about her run-in with the Mullets, as well as the way Mose had manhandled them, would she and her brother still be welcome residents at Promise Lodge?

Lester let out the breath he'd been holding. He was stunned by the exchange that had just taken place.

After moving to Promise Lodge from Ohio, he'd heard

that Mattie and her sisters had left the Coldstream district because of numerous ongoing disagreements with the bishop, but now that he'd witnessed Bishop Obadiah's outrage, he fully understood why the Bender sisters, Amos, the Peterscheims—and now the Fishers—could no longer tolerate Chupp's spiteful, narrow attitude.

A couple of sentences, however, were ringing like bells in his head:

I'd rather die than allow the Mullets to live in my family's home.

Two men don't trap a woman in an upstairs bedroom to talk about real estate.

Lester hadn't heard the full details of that Saturday's encounter, but he didn't need to. It was only normal that Marlene had dated—and probably courted—men, back in the day. Yet why had she *nearly* married Jake and Yost, then changed her mind?

Wasn't a change of mind—and heart—often a gift from God, however? Lester had never been sorry he'd changed his mind about Elverta, after all. Most folks had someone in their past who hadn't turned out to be as wonderful as they'd figured on, after time told the truth.

Smiling gently, Lester turned to the subdued woman seated at his left and murmured, "I had no idea, Marlene. I'm sorry this has happened to you."

She looked down at her lap, as though too ashamed to respond.

"Well, we stated our case, so we've made the first move—and it was the correct first move," Preacher Amos said after Bishop Obadiah's rig had pulled away. He looked down the length of the table to focus first on Mose and then on Marlene. "Forgiveness on either side will be difficult to come by if the Mullets don't show up. But I firmly believe our hearts are in the right place."

"I totally agree, Amos," Bishop Monroe chimed in. "We should all take this matter to God in prayer in the coming days, asking Him to guide our thoughts and to guide the Mullets—and Bishop Obadiah—so their hearts will no longer be hardened against us. Meanwhile, we have a fine meal to enjoy before we return to our work."

Lester sensed Marlene felt too mortified to eat much more of her lunch. She stared at her plate, lost in thought, pushing the chicken and noodles around the other food without much interest. Ravenous as he was after a morning's physical labor and a breakfast of only coffee and toast, Lester made short work of his first plateful and went back for more—as did most of the other men.

He found himself standing next to Preacher Amos at the dessert end of the table, so he took the opportunity to ask a few questions when he wouldn't embarrass Marlene.

"So Yost and Jake cornered Marlene upstairs with the idea of having their way with her? *Both* of them?" he asked quietly.

"*Jah*, it was a nasty business," the preacher muttered. "Mose showed up just in time, but they'd gotten close enough to tear her apron and dress."

Lester's insides tightened. No wonder she'd wanted locks on her door. Any woman caught in such a terrifying situation would have a difficult time letting go of it.

"I was really hoping those fellows would show up today, yet I'm not surprised," Amos continued with a sigh. "If they're pinning the blame on Mose and Marlene, and they've convinced their bishop to believe them, they'll probably never muster the courage to admit the truth— because then, of course, their wives and everyone else would know what they'd been intending when they cornered Marlene. I'm not sure those two have enough backbone to come clean."

"Ah. They'd rather save face than confess."

"I suspect that's the way it'll be, *jah*." Preacher Amos chose a large square of frosted chocolate cake as well as a slice of peach pie. "So our mission will be to support the Fishers during the sale this Saturday, and then to help them move forward into their new life amongst us."

Nodding, Lester picked up a dessert bowl and spooned a large serving of banana pudding into it. With a glance toward Marlene, who still resembled a whipped pup, he also chose a large brownie with sprinkles on it.

When he returned to the table, he placed the brownie on the rim of Marlene's plate. "How about a hit of chocolate?" he whispered. "Or I'll share my banana pudding if that looks better to you. I'd like to help without being a pest about it, sweetheart. We've had our share of pests lately, *jah*?"

Marlene blinked. Then a timid smile spread slowly across her face. "You're a gentle, thoughtful man, Lester Lehman," she whispered as she picked up her brownie. "Nobody was happier for you than I was when that gray SUV pulled away this morning."

He returned her smile. Other folks around them were getting up for more food, so he took advantage of their movement to share one more idea.

"Give yourself some time to get past this incident with the Mullets—and don't think for a minute you deserved it or did anything to bring it on," Lester murmured earnestly. "If you want an ear, let me know. And if you don't, I'll leave it alone."

Her grateful nod gave him the energy to work his hardest all afternoon. By the time Truman drove everyone back that evening, the Fishers were ready for their sale. All they had left to do was load the items they'd decided to keep onto a wagon, so Mose could drive it to Promise Lodge.

It had been a very productive day—and very informative. Lester knew he'd be thinking about what he'd learned for a long time, deciding what to do with that information.

Chapter 20

Saturday, March thirty-first was a cold, overcast day for an auction, but Lester was happy to help the Fishers close the book on their life in Coldstream. Once again Truman drove, and because Preachers Eli and Amos and Allen Troyer were the only other men joining Mose, the items Marlene and her brother wanted to keep would fit into the van when they drove back to Promise Lodge.

"I can understand why Marlene didn't want to come to the sale," Lester remarked as they started down the road. "No matter how eager you might be to have an auction behind you, it's never easy to say *gut*-bye to the home you've known all your life."

Mose nodded, sighing deeply. "That about sssizes it up."

"I'm sure my wife and her sisters are just as happy to remain at Promise Lodge with her," Amos remarked as he peered out at the clouds. "March is going out like a lion, and they'll be cozy at home instead of out in the wind and cold. And truth be told, we don't really need their supervision!"

The fellows chuckled at Amos's observation. Lester suspected the women were just as happy to avoid a potential visit from Bishop Obadiah and the Mullets, but he kept that sentiment to himself. Mose had enough on his mind today without being reminded about the unfinished business that still hung between him and the two men who'd cornered his sister.

The sale started at nine o'clock, and the Mennonite auctioneer, Seth Coblentz, had a capable staff to help him. He'd also provided a lunch wagon where folks could buy coffee, hot sandwiches, and bowls of chicken and corn chowder. The Coblentz crew started near the barns and sold the livestock and basic farming tools first, before moving on to the household items. Lester kept busy—and warmer—by helping the other men shift sale pieces into place so Coblentz could work at a steady pace without having to wait for his next item.

As he carried wooden chairs, boxes of Mason canning jars, and held up braided rugs and table linens so the bidders could see them better, Lester hoped the items would go to folks who would love them as much as the Fisher family had. It was sad to be selling off bits and pieces of a family's life. As usually happened at a sale like this, the items of lesser interest and quality were auctioned first, and the antiques and any pieces that collectors might've come for were saved for the end.

"Next, folks, we have a solid oak table with several leaves and ten matching chairs, and we'll sell them together," Seth called through his microphone. "These pieces have seen the wear and tear of generations, but with a little TLC, the set could be like new again. Who'll start me off with twenty-five hundred?"

The bidding began and the auctioneer's rapid chant rang out over the crowd. As his two assistants hollered *yep!* and pointed to acknowledge the bids as they went higher and higher, Lester suddenly felt compelled to save the kitchen table for Marlene. A lot of stories and memories were ingrained in that table—probably dating back to her grandparents. Surely she'd have a place for it someday, wouldn't she?

Without further thought, he yanked the card with his bidding number from his pocket and waved it at the fellows who were tracking the bids. He hadn't initially intended to buy anything, but he was glad he'd already signed in with the bookkeeper so his bids could be counted. Coblentz nodded and kept up his chant as Lester stepped over to join the crowd.

"Who'll give me four thousand? Four—now five!"

Lester kept nodding, maintaining eye contact with the bid tracker nearest him. Until now, the sale had been rather lackluster, but it seemed the attendees knew a good set of Amish furniture when they saw it.

"Who'll give me give me six thousand? Six—now seven!"

Lester didn't waver. He knew exactly who needed that table, and its price was immaterial to him.

"Folks, we all know that this set—a table, five leaves, and ten chairs—was built to last a lifetime," Coblentz said in an enthusiastic voice. Even though the bidding had been steady to this point, he was sweet-talking the audience— appealing to their emotions as well as to the sense of pride and craftmanship that had gone into making the kitchen set years ago.

"Mose Fisher has told me he can remember his great-grandfather, Isaac Fisher, sitting at the head of this table whittling toys for him," Seth continued with a kindly smile. "He believes Isaac was the one who originally built these pieces, and if you looked it over before the sale, you saw the solid oak—no veneers—and the dovetailing and other details that mark this set as a cut above what you find in furniture stores these days. Now—we've got seven thousand. Who'll make it ten?"

Lester blinked at the huge leap Coblentz had made—but when one of the other bidders raised his card, Lester did, too. As the auctioneer raised the bid another five hundred, it became clear that only two men were still bidding. The other fellow was well-dressed and English, possibly an antique dealer from Kansas City; Lester was even more determined that Marlene should have her family's cherished kitchen table.

"We've got ten five, who'll make it eleven?"

After a moment, the English fellow nodded his head. Swallowing hard, so did Lester.

Coblentz looked at each of them, pausing for effect. "All right then, who'll make it eleven five?"

Lester gazed steadily at the auctioneer and nodded.

Seth glanced at the English fellow, who shook his head. "Sold! Eleven thousand five hundred dollars!" he cried.

The auctioneer smiled at the crowd, which had diminished to a few out-of-towners and some curious locals. "A fine set of furniture and a fine run of bidding. The Fisher family appreciates your interest, and we move on now to a set of maple bedroom furniture."

Lester resumed his duties, holding up the mirror that went with the bed and dresser, until Preacher Amos came up to speak near his ear. "Let the rest of us handle what's left while you settle up with the cashier," he murmured with a little smile. "I can recall moving a perfectly *gut* kitchen table out of your house when you sold it to the Beacheys at Christmas, so there must be love in the air, *jah*?"

As Amos nonchalantly walked away, Lester blinked. Had his motives been *that* obvious?

And what if they are? I just wanted to make Marlene happy, and this seemed like a once-in-a-lifetime way to save part of her family's heritage for her.

After Lester left the cashier's desk, he felt jubilant. After all, a lot of fellows couldn't have written a check for eleven thousand five hundred dollars on the spur of the moment without worrying about where the money would come from. He was a hardworking man who owned a successful window and siding business, and he had a lot to offer a second wife . . . maybe it was time to be thinking in that direction. Now that Agnes and Elverta had gone back home, he wouldn't have to contend with their foolishness, so he could concentrate on winning Marlene.

The aroma of hot Polish sausages lured him over to the lunch wagon, where he bought a long bun heaped with sausage and sauerkraut. As he leaned against the barn, away from the other folks buying food, the first spicy mouthful made him moan. He was hungrier than he'd realized, and it felt good to relax after a long morning's work.

As a tall, broad-shouldered fellow in a heavy barn coat and black felt hat approached him, Lester chewed and swallowed. He and Mose had both been shouldering a lot of loads this morning, but without talking. The brusque warning Marlene's brother had issued during their last chat still rang in his ears, but Lester reminded himself to be polite— to be *kind* to this very shy man who'd just watched the last remnants of life with his parents go to the highest bidders.

Mose nodded before leaning against the barn about two feet away. "Well, that's d-done now," he murmured. "I was k-keeping a loose estimate as the sale p-progressed, and by the time we p-pay C-coblentz, we won't g-get much for all our stuff."

"That's usually the case, unfortunately," Lester put in gently. "It's a crying shame, when everything your family valued turns out to be worth so little in the end."

"I was sssurprised you b-bought the table. *Denki* for hanging in there ssso that d-dealer from Moberly didn't get it," Mose added with a wan smile. "He c-comes to a lot of the sssales in this area. Your p-purchase p-probably amounted t-to half our intake."

Lester hadn't been keeping track, but he wasn't surprised to hear Mose's estimate. He balked for a moment, but decided to confess. It was probably best if this big, burly man heard his intentions straight-out, rather than listening to other folks' opinions. "Truth be told, Mose, I bought that table for Marlene, figuring she'd surely want it for her home one of these days."

Mose's eyes widened.

"But can we keep that as our little secret?" Lester added, turning to face him. "The other guys will speculate about my motive, but I'd rather wait for the right time to tell Marlene I bought it for *her*. Do you think I did the right thing?"

When Mose let out the breath he'd been holding, it sounded almost like a sob. "Marlene was so upset about putting that table in the sale, but she has nowhere to put it, so she let it go," he admitted softly. After a moment, he let out a long sigh. "I owe you an apology for the way I ssspoke to you the other day, Lester. You don't d-deserve the sssame hostility I feel toward the Mullets."

Lester smiled. No matter how Marlene might feel about his buying the table, he'd risen several points in Mose's estimation—and that counted for a lot. "Apology accepted. You had *gut* reason to feel hostile about the way those guys treated your sister. You were protecting her, as any brother worth his salt would do."

Mose's lips curved in a furtive smile. "Bullies are cowards," he said in a faraway voice. "When I struck them, I was avenging my sister, *jah*, but I was also getting in some licks for the way Yost and Jake have treated *me* over the years. I'm not surprised they didn't show up last Monday. And I'm not sorry that I've evened the score."

Lester suspected that the two men who'd stooped so low

as to gang up on a woman had teased Mose mercilessly about his stutter . . . which had smoothed out during the course of their conversation. Did this mean Mose was feeling more comfortable with him?

"Bishop Monroe bought our best wagon on Monday, when everyone was here," Mose continued in a congenial tone. "The table and all those chairs won't fit in the van we've got today, so how about if I bring them to Promise Lodge in that wagon? I can leave as soon as I tend to the final details with Coblentz."

Lester's eyes widened. It was a generous offer—and it saved him the effort of finding a way to transport his purchase. "May I get everything loaded in your wagon and then ride back with you? I appreciate your help, Mose."

"Great. I could use the company."

When he smiled, Mose reminded Lester so much of his attractive sister—but his handshake left no doubt about Mose being all man. Their agreement brought the auction to a satisfying conclusion. Lester hoped the ride to Promise Lodge would mark the beginning of a longtime friendship, as well.

Chapter 21

As Marlene entered the lobby of the lodge on Saturday afternoon, she stopped to inhale the heavenly aromas drifting from the kitchen. After years of being the one who'd done all the cooking for her family, it was such a blessing to walk into her new home after a busy day at Dale's store and know that supper was already in the oven—and the Kuhn sisters and Irene had most likely done some extra baking and food preparation for Sunday's meals, as well.

She walked toward the burst of laughter and heard Rosetta's voice in the mix. The table nearest the kitchen was already set for the evening meal, with a few extra places in case Dale or Lester or Mose joined them. Two pies and a plate of cookies sat on the sideboard. Marlene almost had to pinch herself to realize that she'd made her dream of an entirely new life come true and was already reaping the benefits of new friendships.

From the doorway, she smiled at the sight of Ruby and Beulah moving briskly in their colorful floral-print dresses as they pulled pans of dinner rolls from the oven. Irene's plaid was more subdued. Rosetta still dressed in solid Amish colors, although she'd married a Mennonite and often attended church with Truman and his *mamm* when it was a visiting Sunday at Promise Lodge—something that absolutely would *not* have happened had she and her two sisters remained in Coldstream.

"You ladies make such a picture in this kitchen," Marlene remarked fondly. "Always busy—and always smiling as you work. You're all such a blessing to me."

The four women turned toward her, their faces alight with her compliment. "We've got it *gut* here, and we know it!" Ruby pointed out.

"If you're happy and you know it, wag your tail!" Beulah crowed, and all four women playfully stuck out their backsides and shook them, laughing all the while.

"How was your day at Dale's store?" Irene asked. "As busy as last week at the grand opening?"

Marlene went toward a pan of filled thumbprint cookies and began arranging them in a nearby plastic bin. "Business was steady all day. A little easier because I knew more about what I was doing—and because we didn't have a big mess of pickled vegetables to clean up."

Her friends chuckled. "I suppose Agnes and Elverta made it back home," Ruby said.

"Not a bit surprised that they didn't call to let us know," her sister remarked with a shake of her head. She glanced up from her pan of puffy, golden-brown dinner rolls. "I hope you don't think less of Lester because those two women were here chasing after him, Marlene. I'm sure he did nothing to encourage their attention while he was still living in Ohio and married to Delores."

Marlene blinked. Were the Kuhns nudging her toward a romance with Lester again? It seemed like a good time to sample one of the cookies she was handling, so she closed her eyes and savored the blend of moist peanut butter cookie filled with red plum jelly.

"Oh, but this is a treat," she said in a low, appreciative

voice. "I might just have to have another one—unless you're saving them for a special occasion."

"Eat up! You were on your feet all day, working with customers," Beulah assured her quickly.

"More where those came from," Ruby put in, nodding toward the dining room. "We've already set some out for tonight and figured on having them for tomorrow, as well."

"If *you* don't eat them, someone else will," Rosetta teased as she came over to snatch one for herself.

For a few moments, the five of them focused on their cooking tasks. The kitchen felt cozy and warm, and Marlene counted two other batches of cookies on metal racks on the worktable, as well as two coffee cakes, a couple of pies, and a large casserole of vegetables that had been baked with rice and cheese.

"My word, you ladies were busy today," Marlene remarked. "Looks like you have tomorrow's meals well in hand, and all these goodies baked, as well."

"Cold, blustery weather makes me want to stay in the kitchen," Ruby remarked, "although we mixed up a couple batches of cheese in our little factory early this morning, before we started our cooking."

"*Jah*, I've been wondering how your auction was going, what with folks having to spend the day outside," Beulah said. "Any idea if Mose and Lester might be having supper with us?"

Marlene shrugged. "The auctioneer figured the sale might last until one or two o'clock, but then there's the cleaning and settling up to do afterward—and Mose said something about driving a wagon back for Bishop Monroe. That'll make him pretty late."

"Might've been a tough day for him, watching the last of your parents' belongings go home with other folks," Irene said softly. "I can understand why you didn't want to be there for that."

Marlene smiled despite the wave of nostalgia that made her blink back sudden tears. She was hoping her brother hadn't had to contend with Yost and Jake in addition to handling the last details with the auctioneer—but she chose not to speculate aloud about that topic. She didn't think Irene or the Kuhn sisters knew about her run-in with the Mullets, and she saw no need to worry them with the sordid details.

When Marlene noticed Rosetta's odd expression—and that she'd set aside more than half of the cookie she'd taken—she forgot her personal concerns. "You all right?" she murmured.

Rosetta waved her off. "I'm just tired. I suspect I inhaled a lot of dust when we were cleaning out your house—"

"Oh, I'm sorry," Marlene put in, gently grasping her friend's wrist. "It was so nice of you and your sisters to work so hard at our place—not to mention all the commotion we've had dealing with Bishop Obadiah and Lester's two visitors."

Beulah let out a laugh. "Those two gals' behavior was enough to wear *anybody* out."

"*Jah*, take a load off, Rosetta," Ruby suggested, gesturing toward the dining room. "We can finish the rest of this kitchen stuff."

"I made us mac and cheese and a big salad for tonight's supper, figuring we wouldn't have any men joining us," Beulah remarked. "If they do happen to come in hungry—"

"They'll be happy with whatever you have left," Marlene interrupted with a chuckle. "Don't go fixing something extra after all this other food you've made today!"

"Amen to that," Rosetta put in as she went to the sink to wash her hands. "I saw that big pork roast you got ready for

Sunday dinner, along with the mashed potatoes you made ahead, so call it day. No one here has ever starved."

Ruby laughed. "Well, since you put it that way, I could use some of that mac and cheese about now, and then we could clean up afterward and be done with it."

"I'm on it!" Irene said. "Marlene, our salad is in the fridge, I'll get the mac and cheese out of the warming oven, and we'll all sit down and relax."

"And since you cooked all day, I'll clean up," Marlene insisted. "Don't argue with me, because I can see that you've already washed most of the mixing bowls and utensils."

The two sisters smiled at her. "That's why we love you, Marlene," Ruby said gently.

"*Jah*, you're already jumping in like one of the family, as though you've always lived here," Beulah continued with an approving nod.

Marlene felt warm all over—truly welcome as one of the Promise Lodge family—as they all sat down to their supper. After grace, they filled their plates and talked more about the day at the new bulk store. Irene was delighted that all the pies she and Phoebe had baked had sold by noon, although Marlene suspected she was secretly more interested in talking about Dale than about the other things they discussed.

After enjoying the rich mac and cheese, the salad, and slices of pie, they carried their plates and the food into the kitchen. Headlights approached, and Marlene saw the Mennonite church van proceeding past the lodge and up the hill.

"Looks like Truman and the other fellows are home," she remarked. "They said they were bringing some of our boxes back in the van, so I bet they're going to unload them up by Mose's apartment in the barn."

A few minutes later, when the Kuhns pronounced the

kitchen clean except for the small pile of dishes Marlene was washing, they called it a day and went up the back stairs to their apartments. Irene followed them a few moments later, while Rosetta dried dishes until the van rolled to a stop near the lodge.

"I've got the rest of this covered. Go on home and see to Truman's supper," Marlene insisted. "He's done Mose and me a huge favor, driving us to the farm and helping with the sale these past two Saturdays. Why not take the rest of those cookies on the sideboard for your dessert?"

Rosetta nodded. "Great idea. Truman loves anything with peanut butter and jelly. Have a restful evening and a peaceful Sunday, Marlene. We'll be going to church in Cloverdale tomorrow."

The front door opened and when Truman came in, Marlene allowed the two Wickeys time by themselves in the dining room while she washed the last few dishes. As Rosetta had predicted, her husband was happy to be taking some cookies home with him.

"And how'd the sale go?" Rosetta asked softly.

"It started off slow," Truman replied with his mouth full. "But almost at the end, when the kitchen table and chairs came up, Lester got into a bidding war with an English antiques dealer. He and Mose are bringing the set back in the wagon Monroe bought last week . . ."

As their voices approached the front door, Marlene's hands went still in the warm dishwater. Why on earth did a man in a tiny home want an old table and ten chairs? The table alone—without any leaves in it—would fill most of his main room.

Her heart tightened into a knot of nostalgia, and she had to take a deep breath. Parting with that table had been the most difficult decision she'd made concerning the auction, but practicality had won out: neither she nor Mose had room for the oak table in their new apartments. And when would they ever need it to entertain guests?

She finished the dishes and pulled the sink stopper. After she shut off the lamps and went to her apartment, however, questions about Lester and the table continued to spin in her mind. Part of her was delighted that someone she knew had loved her family's table enough to buy it—yet another part of her questioned Lester's motives.

Does this mean he's planning to build another house sometime soon? Why would he do that, unless—

Marlene sat in her rocking chair by the window, watching until a loaded horse-drawn wagon with two men on the seat passed the lodge on its way to her brother's apartment. She waited until Lester had walked back down the road and alongside Rainbow Lake, which glimmered in the moonlight, before she slipped into her coat. Down the back staircase she went and into the kitchen for the rest of the mac and cheese, which had been cooling on the counter.

Walking quickly with the glass pan, propelled by her curiosity, Marlene made it to Bishop Monroe's place in record time. As she crossed the pasture—which was unoccupied because the Clydesdales were all in their barn stalls for the night—she almost hoped Mose wouldn't confirm her suspicions even if they painted a rosy picture of her potential future. The windows of her brother's upstairs apartment glowed with lamplight that made the outer door's handle easier to see in the darkness.

"Mose? How about some supper?" she called out as she climbed the wooden stairs.

He opened his door, peering out eagerly. "Best idea I've heard all day, even if Lester and I stopped for burgers on the way back."

Marlene gave him a moment to grab a spoon from his drawer and pull out one of the chairs at his small table. As she took the chair across from him, she gathered her thoughts.

"How'd the sale go?" she asked, as though the auction was the only thing on her mind.

Mose shrugged. "It's like folks warned us," he said with his mouth full. "Nobody else thought our stuff was worth nearly as much as we did. But it's done now," he added with a sigh.

When he focused on his food instead of elaborating, Marlene could tell he was keeping some details to himself.

"Lots of folks there?"

Again he shrugged. "Not a bad crowd for a cold, windy day."

She let him eat another bite or two. "Any sign of the Mullets or the bishop?"

"Nope. Didn't figure they'd show. Probably won't ever see them again."

Impatience got the best of her. Mose had always been a man of few words, but apparently he wasn't going to volunteer anything about Lester and the table. She'd have to pry it out of him.

"How much did Lester pay for the table?" Marlene blurted out. It wasn't the way she'd planned to bring up the subject, but it got his attention.

Mose blinked, glancing up at her. "Where'd you hear ab-bout that?"

His stammer revealed even more than his wary tone. Marlene's heart began to thud so hard she thought her brother could probably hear it.

"Truman mentioned it to Rosetta as they were leaving the lodge. I couldn't help overhearing them."

Mose let out a long sigh. "It turned out to be the highest item of the whole day—"

"How much?" she demanded.

As he weighed his words, Marlene held his gaze, silently telling him she wouldn't let him sidestep her question. She awaited her brother's reply, reminding herself that the amount should be immaterial. Yet it wasn't.

"Eleven thousand five hundred," Mose whispered. He leaned across the table, pointing his spoon until it nearly touched the tip of her nose. "That's all I'm going to say, so don't ask me any more questions about the table and chairs, Marlene. A man has his reasons for the things he does and for what he spends doing them. It's not our place to quiz Lester about his . . . intentions. End of story."

Oh, but it's not the end of the story, is it?

For a few more minutes, Marlene made polite conversation about who was at the sale and other inconsequential topics. When Mose had scraped the last of the cheese sauce from the glass pan, she told him good night and headed back to the lodge with it.

"Eleven thousand five hundred dollars?" she whispered as she crossed the bishop's pasture. "*Eleven thousand five hundred dollars?*"

When Lester had given the auctioneer's clerk such an exorbitant amount of money, had he considered it a down payment on her affection? Her adoration? It seemed his gesture had also convinced her brother that Lester Lehman was cut from cloth woven with the same values and principles he and Marlene had been raised with. It sounded as though the two men had become fast friends today.

Marlene knew full well that most women—especially *maidels* her age—would be over the moon if a nice man like Lester Lehman had spared no expense to rescue her family's precious heirloom. But she didn't like the feeling that she'd been bought and paid for—and that several other folks already supposed Lester was going to spring the news on her as the surprise that would win her heart.

The episode kept her awake all night.

Chapter 22

Lester entered the lodge on Sunday feeling like the proverbial cat who'd eaten the canary—a very *large* canary, considering how much he'd paid for the Fishers' kitchen table. Keeping his secret might be difficult, because the ladies at the lodge were astute about people's moods and they'd probably ask him why he seemed so cheerful today.

But he was determined to enjoy dinner and conversation with his friends without letting that proverbial cat out of the bag. The Fishers' table was his secret to share with Marlene, and he would wait until the appropriate moment to reveal that he'd rescued it for her.

Lester inhaled deeply as he walked into the dining room. "Oh, but something smells really *gut*!" he called out.

"Hey there, Lester, and happy Sunday to you," Ruby said as she bustled to the table with a huge platter of sliced pork. "Hope you're hungry! Pork was on sale, so we bought a big roast because—"

"We believe in cooking once and eating at least two or three meals from it!" Beulah finished her sister's sentence. She placed her bowls of mashed potatoes and gravy on the table alongside the meat.

"Nothing wrong with that," Lester put in. He turned as the front door opened behind him. "And here's another fellow who won't argue with today's menu. How are you, Mose? Rested up from our busy sale day?"

The big man nodded as he paused to take in the food the ladies were still carrying out—warm applesauce and glazed carrots, along with the pies and cookies already waiting on the sideboard behind the table. "Still a little tired, but this dinner and a Sunday afternoon nap will help. *Denki* again for all your help yesterday, Lester."

"You're welcome." When the Kuhns sat down, Lester took his usual place at the table. Was it his imagination or was Mose preoccupied, gazing at him as though he had something he needed to say? His dark, expressive eyebrows rose when his sister slipped in from the kitchen and sat down across from Lester without murmuring a word.

Lester suspected that Marlene hadn't gotten much sleep during the night. His heart went out to her, figuring she was caught up in the emotional aftermath of selling her parents' belongings and the home where they'd lived all her life— and for generations before she'd been born. It was yet another form of grief, layered on top of losing her *dat* last fall and her *mamm* a couple of years before that.

She has a lot on her mind, all of it pertaining to loss. Not to mention her unresolved conflict with the Mullets, which has probably left her feeling vulnerable and insecure.

During their brief silent grace, Lester prayed that Marlene would find comfort and peace now that the auction was behind her.

And help me to be a blessing to her, and a gut *listener when she needs one. Slow me down if I come on too fast, Lord, because I don't want to lose her before I've fully won her.*

As the food started around, Lester reached for the platter in front of him. The pork was beautifully sliced and drenched with a rich brown gravy. He could see that it was so tender he wouldn't need his knife to cut it.

"You gals have outdone yourselves again," he remarked. "It's too bad Irene and Dale are in Cloverdale, missing out on this feast. Don't you sisters want to attend your church when we Amish have our visiting Sundays?"

Beulah shrugged, placing a large mound of creamy potatoes on her plate. "We like to go when you folks are having your service, and we're perfectly fine playing hooky on Sundays when you don't."

"We don't have friendships that go way back in the Cloverdale congregation the way Dale and Irene do. They like to have dinner out with friends there in town," Ruby pointed out. "It's a *gut* church service, but we believe we're performing a Christian service by cooking for our friends—"

"And we feel close to God in the kitchen," Beulah added with a little grin. "We're always praying that nothing burns and everything comes out the way it's supposed to. That counts as time with the Lord, *jah*?"

The two men chuckled as they tucked into their dinner. Lester noticed that Marlene seemed so preoccupied, she either hadn't heard Beulah's joke or she didn't find it the least bit funny. It wasn't like her to behave as though she was completely oblivious to the conversation around her. What could possibly be bothering her so much that she seemed lost in her own little world?

"Marlene, I hope you're not catching a cold—or a flu bug," Lester said gently.

Her dark eyes flashed when she focused on him. "Oh, something's *bugging* me all right—and I won't beat around the bush," she muttered. "Too bad you spent so much for that kitchen table yesterday, Lester. I've told you I'll never marry—and I will *not* be bought."

She stood up and grabbed her plate. "Excuse me. Sorry to spoil your nice dinner," she whispered to the Kuhns before she hurried toward the lobby and up the stairs.

Lester sat back, stunned. Marlene might as well have dumped a freezer full of ice cubes on him.

"I should've f-found a way to warn you," Mose said with a sigh. "She came over last night and said she'd overheard Truman telling Rosetta about the t-table."

Lester thought back to the sale, when he and Mose had loaded the table and chairs into the bishop's wagon. "I thought I'd asked everyone to keep quiet about my purchase, so it could be my surprise. But maybe I didn't. Or maybe Truman wasn't around when I—"

"I bet Truman wasn't aware Marlene was still in the kitchen when he came for Rosetta last night," Beulah offered with a sympathetic sigh.

"*Jah*, he wouldn't have knowingly spoiled your secret," Ruby agreed. "But my *gut*ness, Lester, what a lovely gesture. I'd give *anything* to have my family's table."

"Me too," Beulah said, nodding sadly. "Some of the best times of our lives were spent around that table with our folks and for our family gatherings. I suspect Marlene's still raw around the edges about leaving her life in Coldstream behind. She'll come around, Lester."

Lester shook his head forlornly. "You know, I wasn't figuring to buy anything at the sale—because what do I need? I still have the furniture I stored after I sold my house to Phineas and Annabelle," he mused aloud. "It was a spur-of-the-moment impulse to bid on that table, thinking that someday Marlene would be happy to have it."

"Well, *I'm* glad you b-bought it," Mose put in with an encouraging smile. "I wanted to keep it all along, b-but I had no idea where to put it in my apartment. When I've g-got the cash, I'll buy it back."

The growing ache in Lester's heart wasn't something that mere money could heal, however. And why would Mose want to spend eleven thousand dollars for the table and chairs? It was an exorbitant amount to pay for the sake of nostalgia—and for something he'd lived with all his life.

I've told you I'll never marry—and I will not *be bought.*

Marlene's vehement rejection of his gift would sting for a long time, even if her brother repaid him for the table someday. It had never been Lester's intention to buy her affection, or to make her feel obligated to marry him. But that proverbial cat he'd been smiling about when he'd come to dinner had indeed burst out of the bag—and its claws had left a nasty gash on his heart.

He'd offended her deeply. Would she listen to his attempt at an apology? Or would she only become more upset with him? Lester couldn't turn back the clock to before Marlene had overheard Truman, so he'd have to find a way to move forward.

"Your intentions were the best, Lester," Beulah said, gently patting his wrist. "We've all done something we thought would be wonderful, only to have it backfire."

"I bet Marlene will change her tune," Ruby added with a kind smile. "She's not the type to stay upset or hold a grudge—not that she has any reason to question your motives, Lester. I think she was so astounded by your gesture, she took it the wrong way. She spoke before she thought."

Lester appreciated his friends' support, but his Sunday dinner no longer enticed him. He finished his food because it was a sin to waste it, and then he took a couple slices of pie back to the tiny home to have for his supper.

As he entered the little house on the shore of Rainbow Lake, he sighed, suddenly dissatisfied. Allen Troyer's first construction project had been the perfect little home for

Lester over the winter, yet with Marlene's rejection still ringing in his ears he realized that his hideaway was probably sending the wrong signal. Why would a woman want to spend any amount of time with him here—even if they were newlyweds waiting until a traditional-style home could be built for them?

Any man who doesn't have enough space for a kitchen table doesn't come across as husband material. I might as well be back to my days as a penniless young buck just starting out—except I'm forty-five. Why would Marlene take me seriously?

Marlene shoved her dinner plate away before she'd finished even half of the pork and potatoes she'd taken. It didn't escape her that her table was barely big enough for four folks to play cards on—and it had been in one of the rooms here at the lodge when she'd moved in. It meant absolutely nothing to her.

In another fit of anguish, she plopped down on her love seat, hugging her two faded, faceless dolls to her chest. Curiosity had made her pause out of sight on the lobby stairway after she'd stalked away from the dinner table like a three-year-old having a hissy fit, and a few snatches of dining room conversation still haunted her.

I bet Truman wasn't aware Marlene was still in the kitchen . . .

. . .what a lovely gesture. I'd give anything to have my family's table . . .

. . . a spur-of-the-moment impulse to bid on that table, thinking that someday Marlene would be happy to have it.

Your intentions were the best, Lester.

. . . she was so astounded by your gesture, she took it the wrong way. She spoke before she thought.

Marlene began to cry. Why had she been so intent on putting Lester in the wrong? Before she'd even heard what he'd had to say about buying the table, she'd spewed her venom on him and accused him of intentions that nobody else seemed to attribute to him. Even Mose was acting as though he and Lester had become good friends while they'd worked together and shared the long ride back to Promise Lodge.

What's my problem with Lester? He spent two entire Saturdays helping with our sale. He's been patient and understanding when I've become upset about losing my parents and selling the farm—and he was appalled to learn what the Mullets tried to do to me. Would any other man on earth have spent more than eleven thousand dollars to save my parents' table for me?

Marlene shook her head, gazing at poor old Simon and Sally as though they had the answers she needed. She began to cry harder, and then wondered why she couldn't seem to shut off the faucet. Would she ever get past losing her parents and her lifelong home?

If I hadn't shot Lester down, he'd be willing to listen to me, to hold me. He would never make light of my feelings. He wouldn't take advantage of my vulnerable emotional state to take his own pleasure, either.

Sniffling loudly, Marlene sighed as her head fell back against the small couch.

I keep insisting I'll never marry but maybe I deserve to be alone. Why should I subject Lester to my moods? My accusations? He's better off without me.

Chapter 23

On Monday Marlene realized what a blessing her job was. While Dale spent most of the day helping customers and restocking shelves after a busy Saturday, she worked in the back storeroom filling and labeling clear plastic bags—dozens of bags. She started with bulk hot cereals, then moved on to dried noodles and baking mixes, and then filled small oval-shaped plastic containers with jimmies and colored sanding sugars. It was repetitive work that didn't require much thought, and she didn't have to put on a friendly smile to deal with customers.

It's the perfect job for a woman alone. And that's what my life's going to look like from here on out.

As she carefully filled the bags, tied them off with wire twists, and printed their adhesive labels, Marlene wondered if Dale had gone into storekeeping with the idea that being self-employed—and often the only one working in his store—suited *him* for the long haul, as well. He was a meticulous man, and she suspected he had little tolerance for sloppy work habits or other personality traits that didn't measure up to his standards.

Dale was also fastidiously neat, and Marlene was pretty sure he ironed his store-bought shirts and slacks. She'd not been upstairs to his apartment, of course, but she pictured it as clutter-free with swept floors and dusted furniture—much tidier than her own abode. He went to a barber, too, because his steely-gray hair didn't have that home-haircut look that many Amish men wore—chopped around the bottom and across their foreheads.

Lester's hair doesn't look lopped off, either. Who cuts it for him?

Marlene sighed and snapped the lid onto a container of purple sanding sugar. She'd been trying hard not to think about Lester. And she was grateful that the Kuhns hadn't attempted to console her at breakfast—nor had they mentioned Lester's gentle generosity. She wondered if Dale Kraybill had decided as a young man to remain a bachelor, or if he'd simply never met the right woman—or if his high personal standards had scared the ladies away. She could honestly say he did better without a wife than any other unattached man she'd ever met, and he seemed happy. *All* the time.

She could never ask him about such matters, though. Dale would consider her nosy and intrusive, and rightly so.

After she loaded a wheeled cart with the bags and containers she'd filled, Marlene rolled it out into the main room of the store. It was nearly noon, and only a few customers were scattered along the aisles.

"*Gut* morning," she murmured as she nodded to an elderly English woman in the baking section.

The woman glanced at Marlene's loaded cart with a smile. "Oh, look at all these colored sugars! They're like a sparkly rainbow," she said with a chuckle. "My grandkids would love to decorate cookies with such bright colors."

"Help yourself," Marlene suggested, stepping out of the way.

The lady chose containers filled with seven of the brightest colors—hot pink, red, purple, turquoise, and dark yellow among them—and placed them in her shopping cart as though she'd discovered instant fun. "Thank you, dear! The kids and I will have a great time with these, even if I have to sweep a lot of sugar from the floor when they've finished."

The remark made Marlene turn quickly to begin stocking shelves, so the customer wouldn't see the tears that had sprung into her eyes. As a child, she'd adored baking cookies with Mamm. Even when her mother's dementia had altered her personality and ability to focus, the two of them had kept cooking together.

What a shame that you'll never pass along this love of baking to your own daughters.

With a ragged sigh, Marlene continued filling the shelves with her bags of noodles, cereals, and baking supplies. She was her own worst enemy today. Every thought seemed to upset her, but she plugged along until all her bags were arranged on their proper shelves. As she pushed the cart back toward the storeroom, craving the solitude of her bag-filling assignment, the store's front door opened.

"Let me be the first to wish you a *gut* afternoon, Dale!" Irene called out toward the cash register. "I've brought you a fresh supply of pies."

"I'll help you carry them," the storekeeper put in as he hurried from behind the checkout counter. "You and Phoebe must've started baking long before dawn, if you already have pies that are cool enough to cover."

Irene's face glowed as the two of them began toting portable pie shelves in from her van, parked right outside. "We got an early start, *jah*," she confirmed. "It's best to run our ovens before the temperatures rise too high, because our little bakery building gets mighty hot even on these cool spring mornings."

Dale set two pie carriers on the floor near the pie display.

He turned to smile at Irene, gently running a finger along her cheek. "You amaze me, Mrs. Wickey," he admitted in a low voice. "Look at you! Fresh as a daffodil even after hours on your feet—and while working with messy pie fillings, too."

When she beamed at him, she appeared far too young to have a son Truman's age. "Silly man," she teased. "Do you think I'd wear my smeared apron and dress in public— or in front of *you*, Mr. Kraybill?"

When their noses touched briefly, Marlene stood absolutely still so they wouldn't realize she'd been watching them. Their brief moment of affection had given her a whole new outlook on Dale's bachelor state, and the possibility that he might propose to Irene one of these days. As two women entered the store, however, Dale and Irene went about stocking the display as though nothing romantic had happened.

"*Gut* afternoon, ladies!" Dale greeted them. "Can I point you toward anything in particular?"

"We're going to browse," one of them replied.

"It's our first time in your new store—and we're delighted that you've opened it," her companion added.

"As you can see, you're just in time for Irene's pies," Dale continued, gesturing toward the display shelves. "She and her partner just finished their day's baking, so you won't find anything fresher or tastier."

Marlene used the distraction the customers had created to roll her cart along the far aisle as quietly as she could, back into the storeroom. She caught herself smiling for the first time all day. Irene Wickey and Dale Kraybill made a cute couple, even if they were old enough to be her parents. It did her frazzled heart good to see them enjoying each other's company.

Once again, however, the moment of affection she'd

witnessed had only made Marlene recall the times when she and Lester had experimented with kissing. Like Dale, Lester always appeared neatly groomed and he exuded a sense of goodwill and happiness despite the emotional losses he'd suffered in the past year. When he was with her, he looked into her eyes and followed every word she said rather than concentrating on a clever response or comeback. He'd installed two locks on her door without questioning her need for them. He understood why she'd been so excited to find Sally and Simon stashed among her mother's belongings.

And Lester knew how much that kitchen table meant to me without even having to ask. Rather than letting it go to an antiques dealer, he kept bidding until he'd bought it, regardless of how high the price went.

And he did it for me.

Marlene sighed glumly. Even if she held onto her intention never to marry, she owed Lester an apology. She'd treated him badly at Sunday's dinner—and in front of their friends, too.

As she ate the pork sandwich and apple she'd brought for her lunch, she thought about arranging a chat with Lester and what she'd say. The afternoon passed quickly as she filled bags with dried beans, dry soup mixes, and spices. By the time she'd placed these items on their shelves and talked briefly with Dale, it was the end of her shift—and it was raining.

Rather than buying an umbrella from the store, Marlene jogged quickly across the parking lot and past the two Helmuth homes in the pouring rain. She was soaked when she reached the lodge, so she dashed straight up the steps to her apartment. After she blotted her hair and changed into dry clothes, she retraced her path on the stairway and across the lobby floor with a towel. The dreary weather was a perfect reflection of her mood.

The Kuhns and Irene had apparently gone to their apartments after they'd placed a roaster in the oven. Except for the steady *tick-tick-tick* of the battery clock above the sink, the kitchen was enveloped in a rare silence.

Marlene sighed. She was ready for some company after a day spent working alone. As she gazed out her apartment window toward the tiny house perched alongside the gray lake, she hoped Lester would come over to have supper with them.

"This wet weather's supposed to last through the night and all day tomorrow," Truman remarked as the windshield wipers on his truck rhythmically swept away the rain. "Looks like a *gut* day for me to work on Rosetta's honey-do list at home."

"*Jah*, I won't be getting any windows installed tomorrow," Lester put in. "Unless I hear different from you, I'll figure on heading in on Wednesday morning."

"And we'll have *Gut* Friday off, too, remember—and Easter Monday."

"*Jah*, we will." Lester shrugged. "This time of year, we never know how many days the rain might waylay our projects. But it's okay. Mattie's garden plots and all our lawns need the moisture—and the lake's looking a little low."

"It all works out," Truman agreed. "See you Wednesday, most likely."

With a nod, Lester slid down from the truck, closed its door, and bolted across the wet grass. The steady shower was making a million little dimples on the dull surface of the lake. As he stepped into his tiny home, it occurred to him that he didn't have much in the way of a quick-fix supper. And as the rain drummed on his roof, he lost all interest in dashing toward the lodge to eat whatever the ladies had cooked—even though he knew he'd be welcome.

Or would I? Maybe Marlene doesn't want to see my face again anytime soon. Maybe I've permanently worn out my welcome with her.

Lester sighed. After he changed out of his wet clothes, he looked in his miniature fridge. Nothing of interest there. He opened the small pantry cabinet, shaking his head—but he didn't want to dash over to Dale's store for groceries in the rain, either. After all, if he had an umbrella in one hand, he couldn't carry many sacks of food home—and Dale's sacks were paper. The mental image of boxes and canned goods breaking through the bottom of rain-soaked grocery bags gave him reason enough to stay home.

"You're a mess, Lester Lehman," he muttered as he got out his big jar of peanut butter and a box of saltines. "Someday soon you'll have to get your act together and apologize to Marlene. Until you do, it serves you right to eat P B and J on crackers."

Chapter 24

Tuesday morning, Lester lolled in bed longer than usual—because what did he have to get up for? An occasional lazy day could be good for the soul, but as the minutes ticked into an extra hour, he wondered if he might be drifting back into that sneaky state of grief and depression that had plagued him on gray days this past winter.

That thought was enough to get him out of his bed and down from the loft. When he'd dressed, he grabbed an umbrella and headed over to the little white bakery near Christine's dairy barn and the Kuhns' cheese factory. The heavenly aromas of warm fruit pies told him he'd already made the best decision of his day.

"Hey there, ladies, you look like you've already done a day's work," Lester remarked as he stepped inside. He lowered his wet umbrella and placed it on an old rug beside theirs. "Am I in time to put in an order for a couple of pies? You've got quite a selection on your table here, but those are headed for the stores you stock, *jah*?"

Phoebe and Irene smiled at him from their baking area behind the counter. "We don't bake on Wednesdays, so we make extra on Tuesdays," the young blonde replied.

"For *you*, Lester," Irene teased, "we can take fewer pies to the store in Forest Grove this afternoon."

"Take whichever ones you want," Phoebe encouraged him. "We don't have a set number to deliver—and your money's as *gut* as anyone else's, right?"

"*Denki* from the bottom of my heart," Lester said as he pulled out his wallet. "It'll be a real treat to have warm pie for breakfast."

When he'd put his money on the counter, he approached the loaded table where dozens of pies sat cooling. By the time he'd selected an apple and a rhubarb, Phoebe was bringing him two domes and a plastic sack.

"Here you go, Lester," she said as she got his pies ready to carry out. "Not a great day for installing windows or siding, ain't so? Enjoy your time off!"

As he left the bakery, he felt better—and he headed straight to the cheese factory, where Ruby was placing freshly wrapped blocks of cheese in the front refrigerator case.

"You'll need some of this cheddar for that warm apple pie I smell!" she teased.

"You've read my mind," Lester said with a laugh. As he got out his money, he sensed she was watching him, considering what she wanted to say.

Ruby cleared her throat as she placed a small block of cheddar in his pie sack—and then added a block of Monterey Jack, as well. "For what it's worth," she murmured, "Marlene's going around with the same hangdog look on her face that's on yours, Lester. Just sayin'."

Should he respond? The Kuhn sisters always meant well, but sometimes he wished other folks around Promise Lodge would let his business with Marlene be *his* business.

"*Denki*," Lester murmured as he twisted the top of his plastic sack.

He was halfway out the door when Ruby added, "We've

made a big meat loaf for supper. Plenty there for you, Lester, and we'd be happy to have you."

He smiled at her, popped open his umbrella, and then beat a quick path back home. After dropping his wet rain gear in his shower, he sat at his little pull-down kitchen table. With quick strokes of a small knife, he shaved bits of cheddar onto about a fourth of the warm apple pie.

As he attacked the pie with a spoon, not bothering to slice it, Lester realized he was returning to the habits he'd acquired when he'd lived alone. The sweet apples, warm cinnamon, and melted cheddar went a long way toward soothing his soul, however, and by the time he'd devoured a quarter of the pie he felt much better.

Meat loaf.

What other incentive did he need for accepting Ruby's invitation, and for preparing the apology he owed Marlene?

But what did I do wrong? Why should I apologize?

Lester sighed as he cut into the warm, tangy rhubarb pie with his spoon. That little voice had made a point—he'd done nothing to intentionally hurt Marlene. And he'd spent quite a chunk of money on that table, thinking to make her happy.

Okay, I don't owe Marlene anything. But a little kindness would go a long way toward patching things up, no matter who was to blame for the emotional barrier she built at Sunday dinner.

Lester reached over and took a pencil and paper from the countertop beside the kitchen sink. As he indulged in more pie, a basic floor plan for a house appeared almost without any conscious thought—maybe because it was nearly identical to the plan for the house he'd sold to the Beacheys. As the rooms took shape, he recalled the hopes and dreams he'd built into that home he'd planned to share with Delores, and he suddenly missed her desperately.

Lester stood up to look out the window. The rain was still steady, still dreary, but all he could see was his wife's face as she'd looked before that fateful day of the traffic accident.

And Delores, bless her, was smiling at him.

His heart lifted. He doodled on the floor plan some more, wondering if he should ask Marlene's opinion about any of its features. With her, there was the chance for children, after all—and the thought of sharing his bed with a vivacious younger woman propelled him up from his chair with an urgent gasp of yearning.

If he wanted a glimpse of Marlene, all he had to do was walk over to the bulk store, right?

Instead, Lester stepped outside and let the cold rain settle his sexual tension. It wasn't the first time he'd thought about her in an intimate way, but this was no time to come on like a raging bull. The Mullets had frightened Marlene by insinuating they were going to take her by force, and he'd have to tread very lightly and tenderly around that subject—if indeed, he and Marlene cleared up the misunderstanding that loomed between them like an invisible wall.

Lester went inside and changed into dry clothes. It was the perfect day to sketch some new hopes and dreams—and maybe he'd share them with Marlene.

But maybe she'd want no part of his future because she'd mapped out her own chosen path.

Well, that was all right. No matter what decisions either of them made going forward, they would still be living at Promise Lodge, and they could still be good friends.

Lester was hoping for more, but he would accept whatever Marlene was willing to give.

* * *

When the aromas of baking meat and vegetables greeted her after work on Tuesday, Marlene felt incredibly grateful that the Kuhn sisters and Irene were willing—and wonderful—cooks.

"Whatever you've made for supper smells fabulous!" she called out from the mudroom. After she lowered her wet umbrella and stuck it in the laundry sink, she peered into the kitchen, expecting to see two or three smiling faces.

But no one was there.

Figuring the ladies were upstairs, Marlene removed her raincoat and slipped out of her wet shoes. She inhaled deeply as she passed through the big kitchen, and then noticed that it seemed amazingly clean—because all the pans and utensils had already been washed and put away. Her eyebrows rose and she continued toward the dining room—

A vase with two red roses was at the end of the nearest table, between two place settings. The plates were white with blue roses—the china the Kuhns used on special occasions, she was guessing, because she hadn't seen it before. Two votive candles also sat on the table, with a book of matches.

Marlene's heart thudded. She picked up the sheet of paper stuck under the vase.

"'Just for you, dinner for two,'" she read aloud. She looked around, holding her breath. The lodge was completely silent, as though no one else was in the entire building.

Where were the other ladies, and why weren't they eating supper with her? Had Lester put them up to this? Was he trying yet again to win her and woo her?

The front door opened and he called out, "Whatever's for dinner smells awfully *gut*, Beulah!"

It was the same sort of thing he said every time he came over to eat, as though he, too, was expecting the Kuhns, Irene, and probably Mose to join them.

When Lester saw Marlene, however, he stopped in the arched doorway of the lobby. "Marlene, it—it's *gut* to see you—"

"Did *you* arrange it so it's just the two of us eating supper?"

His dropped jaw didn't lie. He was as surprised as she was.

"I had no idea about that," he replied as he walked slowly between the other tables. "When I bought some cheese from Ruby this morning, she said I was welcome to come for meat loaf—that there'd be plenty for *everybody*. I didn't tell her I'd be coming."

Lester stopped, taking in the two china plates and the vase with the two roses. "It seems we've been set up."

Marlene swallowed hard. She'd been hoping to relax and not think about anything after a busy day at the store—and she smelled like the vinegar she'd used to clean the restroom. Hardly conducive to a date night.

"Um, Lester, if you don't want to stay—"

"Oh, I came for the meat loaf," he insisted, fighting a smile. "If you don't want to join me, I guess you can eat upstairs again. But I hope you won't, Marlene. After a day at home alone, with a lot of time to think things over, I really would welcome your company."

Marlene took a deep breath to steady herself. His deep, resonant voice had always appealed to her. He sounded so sincere, so kind. And he'd had no ulterior motives when he'd arrived—it was the Kuhns who'd thrown them together this way.

"Um, give me a minute to tidy up," she murmured. "I just got home from the store."

Before he had a chance to respond, Marlene rushed through the kitchen and up the back stairs.

How awkward is this? The china and candles and roses just shout romance, *but I can't fall into the cozy little trap*

Ruby and Beulah have set! I can't let Lester think he has any chance at a future with me—

But if she didn't go downstairs after she'd freshened up, what sort of message would she be sending him? Marlene still felt bad about heaping her rejection on him Sunday, and there was no excuse for being impolite and childish.

With shaking hands, she yanked off her dress and put on a clean one. She straightened her hair and covered it with a fresh *kapp*. She washed her hands twice, trying to remove the pungent tang of vinegar and bleach. As she went slowly down the back stairs into the kitchen, Marlene focused on maintaining a friendly distance between them as she took their meal from the oven—

But Lester had already arranged slices of meat loaf on a platter, poured gravy into a bowl, and placed the mashed potatoes and the glazed carrots on the table for them. The little candles glowed in their clear containers, simple yet elegant.

"May I?" Lester asked as he pulled out her chair.

Marlene wasn't used to such attention—and reminded herself that he, too, was trying to be polite. "*Denki*, Lester," she murmured as he gently scooted her closer to the table.

After he sat down across from her, he shifted the vase so the roses didn't block his view of her. Then he bowed his head, and Marlene did, too.

Lord, I'm not so sure the Kuhns did us any favors, but at least Lester and I have gotten past my hissy fit. At least we can be friends, as You commanded us long ago.

She knew, of course, that Jesus had actually commanded his disciples to *love* one another as He'd loved them, but she'd purposely kept that word out of her quick prayer. No reason to let God think she intended the feelings between her and Lester to come anywhere near *love*.

Lester handed Marlene the platter of meat loaf. "Well,

we might not be comfortable with the little trick our friends played on us, but at least we get a delicious dinner out of it—and a chance to talk without their listening to our every word," he pointed out. "I love them, but sometimes I wish they'd mind their own business, you know?"

A laugh escaped her, filling the dining room with her sudden mirth. "I do know," she agreed as she place a couple slices of meat loaf on her plate. "But then, I gave them plenty of fuel to fan the flames when I told you off on Sunday, and—and I'm sorry I was so blunt, Lester," she added contritely. "It was very kind of you to realize that I might be attached to that old kitchen table. But I do regret that you spent so much money on it."

Lester cleared his throat as he mounded potatoes on his plate. "The dollar signs rolled around mighty fast when it dropped down to just three—and then two—of us bidders," he admitted. "I know you intend to stay in your apartment for the long haul. And I realize you intend to remain single, too. But the table's yours anyway, Marlene. No strings attached. Honest."

Marlene's eyes widened. A lump rose into her throat as she held Lester's gaze. His gentle, handsome smile looked as open as a book, and she read no ulterior motives or hidden agendas in his clear, dark eyes.

"*Denki*," she whispered in a tremulous voice. "That has to be one of the nicest things anyone's ever done for me. I'll cherish that table forever, even if I can't figure out where to put it."

"You're welcome, dear. Apology accepted—and I'm glad you like your gift."

When she'd filled her plate, Marlene closed her eyes over a mouthful of meat loaf with brown gravy as only Beulah could make it. It surely tasted better because she and Lester had mended fences, and she felt lighter—freer—than she had since she'd spewed out her frustration at him a couple of days ago.

"It was raining today so I couldn't install windows," Lester remarked nonchalantly. "I bought two of Irene's and Phoebe's pies and some fresh cheese at the Kuhns' factory for my breakfast. And I sketched out the floor plan for a house," he added as his eyes met hers again. "Even if you decide not to join me there, I've reached the point where the novelty's worn off my tiny home. It's served its purpose, and I'm ready for rooms full of comfortable furniture again—as well as a real kitchen table."

Marlene smiled. He sounded as gun-shy as she felt, and she appreciated his honesty. "I can understand that," she said as she took a big forkful of potatoes and gravy. "I'm not sure I'd last too long in a tiny home, even if the *idea* of such a small space appeals to me. It's a matter of what you're used to, I guess."

Nodding, Lester took a few more bites of his dinner. His dark eyes shone with affection when he looked at her again. "On a totally different subject, if you were engaged— twice—and broke off those relationships, why did you not consider trying again, Marlene?" he asked wistfully. "And if that question's too personal, you don't have to answer it."

Marlene set her fork down, considering her response. Lester was circling around the subject of marriage even if he didn't mention it specifically—he'd drawn up house plans, after all, and now he was asking about her previous engagements. Yet she didn't feel he was invading her privacy. Now that they'd cleared the air, she trusted him to listen without judgment or ridicule.

"I guess I should start at the beginning," she said in a faraway voice. "I got engaged to Yost Mullet when I was twenty and he was twenty-four. His family's property backed up to ours, so I'd known him all my life—or so I thought," she added with a shake of her head. "I walked over there one afternoon to surprise him with a pan of brownies, just in time to hear him yelling horrible things at his mother as he rushed from the house. Then he kicked his dog, Junior—and the poor thing ran off, terrified, as though it wasn't the first time Yost had mistreated him."

Marlene shook her head as the scene replayed itself in her memory. "I knew right then that I didn't want to live with such a violent man, so I told him straight out that I couldn't marry him. My dreams were shattered—I thought my life was over, of course—but you know, Yost didn't even try to kiss and make up, or lure me back. Mamm told me it was for the best that I'd caught him in such a question-able moment. And she was right."

Lester nodded. He'd put down his fork and was listening attentively. "And do I recall that you dated his cousin, as well?"

"*Jah*—mistake number two," Marlene replied ruefully. "I was twenty-three, and so was Jake. His family lived on the other side of Yost's, so I'm guessing the cousins proba-bly compared notes, although I was too naïve to think of that at the time. Jake was generous with his money and showed me a lot of *gut* times, assuring me that he was much better husband material than Yost.

"I was crazy in love with him," she continued with a sigh. "We'd been engaged for about four months—had our date set, and we were ready to take our vows in about two weeks when we went to a family wedding over in Kirksville. I had used the bathroom and then went looking for Jake, and there he was—kissing another young woman as though he was ready to peel off her clothes right there behind the barn. I knew I could never trust him again, so I called him out while they were still in their clinch and ended the engagement."

Marlene let out a sad laugh. "I was crushed, but I was also disgusted enough with men that I vowed I'd never fall for another one."

Lester was nodding, appearing sympathetic to her rocky past. Before he could say anything, Marlene launched into the final part of her story.

"By the time I was twenty-eight, you can guess how much pressure Bishop Obadiah was putting on me to get married," she said softly. "My *dat* and *mamm* were also determined that I should find a man to make a home with. They were playing their age cards, and we were starting to see a decline in Mamm's mental health. They were so sure that Ervin Yoder was the man God intended for me . . . even if he was widowed and had six kids who needed a mother."

She glanced away, shaking her head again as the memories returned to her. "Ervin was a nice enough fellow—an established cabinet maker, and he made a *gut* living at it. His children seemed well-behaved at church and other social functions, so when he proposed, I said *jah* yet again."

"But the hand of fate—or of God—intervened?" Lester asked gently.

Marlene was grateful for the genuine compassion she saw in his dark eyes, which glowed in the candlelight.

"I was at Ervin's for the day, near the end of summer when he had almost a bushel of ripe tomatoes that needed canning. The kids were carrying the jars up from the basement and acting like perfect angels—which should've been a clue," she added glumly. "The four boys brought the basket of ripe tomatoes from the garden, and out slithered a big black snake. I jumped and yelled bloody murder, of course—which they thought was hysterically funny. Ervin hastened to assure me that boys would be boys, and no mischief had been done—that it was only a harmless black snake—"

Marlene paused to get better control of her voice. Even after years had passed, she could see every detail of that snake—probably two feet long—slithering out from under those ripe tomatoes.

"I had such nightmares about snakes for the next couple of nights that I woke up in a cold sweat more than once," she continued. "I couldn't handle it. So I told Ervin I just wasn't cut out to be a mother—and I *especially* wasn't ready to take on someone else's six kids when I had so little experience handling them. Ervin wasn't happy, but I refused to go along with his promise that such pranks wouldn't happen again.

"So there you have it," Marlene added with a sad shrug. "Three strikes and you're out, *jah*? I'm a three-time loser, Lester. Folks around Coldstream—especially the men—think I have a reputation for being too picky, not to mention for breaking the promises I've made."

She looked down at the remainder of her dinner, awash in the sorrow of her past. To this day, she harbored doubts about her ability to be happily married—or to find a man who truly loved her.

"I guess it's God's way of telling me He intends for Mose and me to live together, a *maidel* and her bachelor brother," she murmured. "After all the opportunities I've been given to marry, I'm probably living the life I deserve."

Lester reached across the table, gently grasping her wrist. For a few moments, they sat in silence as the candles flickered softly. "If you had the chance to relive those years of your life, would you change anything you did with those three fellows, Marlene?"

"Absolutely not! God guided me away from them in the

nick of time." Her heart pounded with the certainty of her reply. When she looked up at Lester again, not a single sign of accusation or blame showed on his handsome candlelit face.

"There's your answer then," he said with a nod. "You did the right thing—three times, Marlene—and those broken engagements are behind you now. You've also escaped the Mullets' vengeful behavior, and you're now safely settled into a new home. You have a lot of years ahead of you, dear, so who knows what God might have in store for you around the next corner?

"You're *not* a loser, Marlene," Lester added emphatically. "You've survived some tough losses and encounters, so now you can focus forward. Forgive yourself and let go of your guilt, sweetheart."

Marlene blinked. She clasped his warm, callused hand. It truly amazed her that Lester didn't consider her previous engagements as a sign that she simply wasn't marriage material.

Forgive yourself and let go of your guilt.

During her entire life in Coldstream, she'd never once heard Bishop Obadiah suggest that anyone should do that. He seemed determined to make folks feel the full weight of their sins forever, without considering that God had sent Jesus into the world as His sign of a forgiveness that far exceeded anything humanly possible.

"You've given me something to think about," Marlene murmured.

Lester shrugged amiably. "No sense in believing your own negative ideas about getting married when God might have something different in mind for you. You've had some tough times with men, but *He's* a fellow you can count on to steer you in the right direction, *jah*?"

Marlene felt the tension leaving her body. "Of course,

He is. And I should contemplate that this week as we remember Christ's death on the cross before we celebrate Easter. Jesus gave us the ultimate gift of forgiveness, after all—and sometimes I forget that."

"We all do." Lester picked up his fork again and cut into his meat loaf.

As she watched him enjoy his mouthful of food, Marlene realized she'd been holding quite an unusual conversation with a man. Although Lester had invested a chunk of money hoping to make her happy with her family's table, he'd taken the time to listen to her and to point out that she didn't have to define herself by relationships that hadn't worked out. She could choose to move forward with a different opinion of herself.

And instead of talking up his own virtues—or making more of a deal about the house he intended to build or the money he'd spent on her—Lester had set aside his own concerns to focus on hers. This was a far cry from the way either of the Mullets or Ervin had behaved—

But after I broke our engagement, Ervin left me alone. And even though the Mullets snuck upstairs to corner me before the sale, they weren't man enough to come back and talk with Mose and me, or offer the forgiveness that Lester and I have been talking about. They chose to leave the situation hanging over our heads.

Marlene blinked. Maybe she'd been a victim of her own faulty, limited thinking. Maybe, with the right man, she had a chance for the sort of happiness Rosetta was always planning for.

"I'm glad you came over tonight, Lester," she murmured as she picked up her fork.

His dark eyes danced as he gazed at her. "Me too. Because think of how strange you would've felt eating this wonderful meal with china, candles, and roses all by your lonesome," he teased.

He'd made her laugh again!

"Oh, but think of the talking-to the Kuhns would've given you if you hadn't gone along with their secret plan," Marlene teased back. "You'd have been in big trouble."

"*Jah*, but I had the rest of those two pies—and their cheese—to fall back on. Not a perfect evening, but I've known worse."

As she scraped the last of the potatoes and gravy from her plate, Marlene envisioned her predicament if she'd found the table set so prettily for two, yet she'd been the only one to show up. For her, it would've meant an evening alone in her apartment, wondering what the Kuhns had intended—and why they'd wanted to rub her nose in the fact that she was alone, without even the company of the lodge women she'd come to enjoy so much.

Maybe she could take a lesson from the independent ring of Lester's words. He was showing himself to be a man who'd learned how to be good company to himself.

"Seriously though," she said as she rose to fetch the cake keeper on the sideboard, "I'm grateful that you've listened to my stories with such patience. You've given me a reason to rethink my attitude, and I really appreciate it, Lester."

When he smiled, the candlelight accentuated the lines that bracketed his mouth and eyes, yet he looked anything but old. Lester was a man who'd lived and loved well, and his face reflected that.

"Happy to hear it, dear," he murmured. "And truth be told, I would not have been very happy eating pie and cheese for my supper—alone—assuming that you and Irene and the Kuhns were over here devouring meat loaf that I'd turned down. I'm glad it worked out the way it did. I don't know where our friends went, but they gave us quite a gift this evening."

Chapter 25

As Lester walked home after supper, he caught himself whistling a tune—something he'd nearly forgotten how to do. He and Marlene had enjoyed slices of angel food cake with rhubarb sauce, and he'd helped her with the dishes. His lips had ached to kiss her goodnight, but he'd refrained. He believed they'd made great progress during their candlelight chat, and he hadn't wanted to push his luck.

Better to leave her wishing for a kiss. She'll want it even more next time.

He laughed at himself as he stepped into the tiny home. *He* was the one who wanted her kiss, *most* of the time now. And wasn't that an improvement over the barren loneliness he'd survived this past winter? After enduring so much unwanted attention from Agnes and Elverta, it was indeed a blessing to sense that Marlene might someday want to share the house he was going to build.

Glancing at the clock on his kitchen wall, Lester decided to walk over for a visit with Preacher Amos and Mattie. As two of the original founders of Promise Lodge, they handled the details when new folks moved to the community and wanted to buy land and build a home on it. The rain had stopped, so he enjoyed the short walk up the main road, past the house on the hill where Phoebe and Allen lived. Lamplight also glowed in the home Mary Kate and Roman Schwartz had built, and then came the smaller Troyer house.

Mattie opened the door with a big smile, playfully swatting Lester with her white towel. "Just in time to help me finish the dishes!" she teased. "But I suppose it's Amos you came to see. He's still at the table, reading this week's edition of *The Budget*."

"*Gut*, I can talk to both of you," Lester remarked as he followed her through the front room to the kitchen. "Hey there, Amos. Looks like you left a bunch of your supper on the front of your shirt, buddy."

The preacher's eyes widened as he looked down in dismay.

Lester laughed. "*Gotcha*, didn't I?" he said as he slipped into the chair at Amos's right.

Amos chuckled, slapping at Lester's shoulder. "You did. But it's a fine thing to see you smiling again now that a certain couple of women have gone back home. What's on your mind, Lehman?"

"Here—finish off this last slice of pie," Mattie said as she slipped it onto the table in front of him. "It is nice to see you looking so happy—nice to see you for whatever reason."

Could a man ever eat too much pie? Lester didn't confess that he'd just finished a big supper—and had devoured about a third of two pies for breakfast—because Mattie's lemon pie, topped with lightly browned meringue, looked too good to pass up.

"I want to buy another piece of land and put a house on it," Lester said as he cut the tip from the slice of pie.

The preacher and his wife exchanged a knowing look. "Do tell!" Mattie piped up from the sink.

"*Jah*, I'm sure there's a story here," Amos said with a

nod. "You seemed snug as a bug in a rug over the winter, living in Allen's tiny house. I can't think all that yammering Elverta and Agnes did finally convinced you to build another full-sized place."

"You're right. It didn't." Lester considered how much he wanted to share as he took another bite of pie. It was only a matter of time before this couple figured out his motives, after all. "I've gotten tired of minimalist living. Seems a shame to have so much comfortable furniture stored away— including a fairly new sofa and my favorite recliner—and not be able to use it."

"Uh-huh," Mattie said, clearly not believing him. "Spring has sprung, and you're feathering your nest along with the other birds, ain't so?"

"And there's nothing wrong with that," Amos put in quickly. "I suspect a certain young woman is making you sit up and take notice these days. Considering the other fellows who've courted her over the years, she's finally made the right choice—for all the right reasons."

Even if they were putting the cart before the horse, it was gratifying to hear the Troyers affirm his relationship with Marlene. They were a prime example of how folks who'd outlived their first spouses had married into even greater happiness the second time around. Lester found that encouraging.

"I've got some floor plans roughed out," he said, dodging their talk of potential romance. "I want a place pretty much like the one I sold to the Beacheys, but with a bigger porch. I don't need much ground with it—"

"But enough for a nice garden and maybe some chickens and a henhouse, *jah*?" Mattie quizzed him. "Better allow for a few more horses and an extra buggy in your stable, too, ain't so—and more bedrooms? Families tend to expand, after all."

Amos smiled indulgently at his wife and then focused on Lester. "All that aside, do you have any idea where you'd like to live? I suspect you've come to love lakeside living, but I doubt Allen would be willing to sell his land."

"And I don't intend to ask him for it," Lester confirmed. "There's still a *gut* bit of property between the Burkholder place and my first house, *jah*?"

The preacher nodded. "There's also a section that curves around behind our row of houses and Truman's land. We'd need to clear some trees and put in another road—but that'll happen sooner or later if Promise Lodge gets more new residents. There's also property alongside the cemetery and the orchard, if you care to take on that sort of enterprise."

"It's a shame nobody's done more with all those nice apple trees," Mattie remarked. Water gurgled as she pulled the plug from her sink.

"That's not my cup of tea," Lester said as he forked up his last bite of pie. "Even if we don't build a lot more houses for new residents, Truman seems to find places for me to install siding and windows. I'm as busy as I care to be."

"Makes a difference that you no longer have Floyd helping with your business, too," Amos remarked. He sat back in his chair, thinking. "You know the lay of this place as well as I do, Lester. I think if I were choosing a spot right now, I'd build adjacent to Monroe's pasture. But that land behind the Wickey place sits high enough that you'd have a nice view of the entire Promise Lodge community. All depends on what appeals to you."

"I'll think about it and get back to you," Lester said. "I'm not familiar with the boundaries of our land behind Wickey's place—"

"So let's you and I walk around up there to refresh my memory," Amos suggested. "I'm pleased you're ready for a new place, Lester. Now that we've finished the two homes for the newlywed Helmuths, I'm free to work on another one."

"Which reminds me," Mattie put in as she joined them at the table. "We've gotten a letter from a gal named Sylvia who wants to rent an apartment in the lodge. She'll be coming next week to look the place over, so you fellows might be doing some painting or remodeling for her."

"That never takes long," Amos remarked. "And we don't know—she might choose one of the unoccupied apartments that's already been redone."

The preacher smiled at Lester. "Tomorrow's Wednesday, so I suppose you'll be heading off to your job site—"

"But I plan to finish there tomorrow. We could do our walk-around on Thursday," Lester put in. He smiled mischievously. "That'll give us both something to ponder during our fast on *Gut* Friday morning—when we're not focused on more faith-based topics, of course."

Amos and Mattie chuckled. "Sometimes God reveals His plans for us on days of meditation," the preacher agreed. "We'll see how things stand after you and I look around, all right?"

"You might want to include Marlene—get her opinion about where she'd want to live," Mattie hinted.

Lester rose to go. "I appreciate your suggestion, but this'll be *my* home no matter who I share—or don't share—it with," he said politely. "God's at work in that relationship, as well, and He's advised me to take it slow, and to not assume anything. Marlene's dealing with issues of her own, and I don't intend to pressure her."

"We'll give God the benefit of the doubt, and leave Marlene out of it for now," Amos agreed with a nod. He rose to shake Lester's hand. "It'll be a blessing to watch your new home rise from the ground up, no matter where you decide to put it, friend. God is *gut*."

"All the time," Lester added.

When Marlene returned from working at the bulk store on Wednesday, she detected a secretive edge to the Kuhn sisters' smiles. Ruby, Beulah, and Irene were in the kitchen baking to prepare for a simple supper on the evening of Good Friday as well as for breakfast and the common meal on Easter Sunday, so the countertops were covered with trays and plastic bins of rolls, quick breads, and desserts.

"Oh, but it smells heavenly in here. Like yeast and sugar," Marlene said as she breezed in to greet them. "Every time I see what you ladies can bake in the matter of a few hours, I'm amazed—and I feel bad that I'm not here to help you."

"Ah, but you're paying rent, which goes into our food budget," Ruby pointed out.

"And now that you're his employee, Dale has told me he's going to give you the same discount that Promise Lodge Pies receives when we buy our aluminum pans and other baking supplies from him," Irene put in. "So we might give you a store list from time to time—if you don't mind bringing our items back with you."

"I'd be delighted to put my discount toward stocking your pantry," Marlene said. "I'll be forever indebted to you for the candlelight dinner you provided for Lester and me last night. It was a lovely surprise."

Beulah smiled at her friend and her sister. "So did it work? Did he, um, want to move forward in a—"

"Did he pop the question?" Ruby interrupted eagerly.

Marlene's jaw dropped. She recalled Lester's words about

these ladies minding their own business, but she decided not to get snippy about it. "You know, it was three weeks ago yesterday that I moved to Promise Lodge," she reminded them. "A *lot* has happened since then—and I'm grateful to Lester for allowing me to handle things in my own way, and in my own *gut* time. Don't count your chickens before they're hatched, ladies."

With that, Marlene snatched a brownie from the countertop and passed through the fragrant kitchen to go up the back stairway. She wasn't irritated about their interest in her love life, but she didn't want to include them in it, either, by playing along with their matchmaking schemes.

No matter how her relationship with Lester evolved, she'd come to respect him a great deal. She was still pondering some of the topics he'd discussed with her over their private dinner, and she trusted Lester not to push for more than she was willing to give him.

Marlene opened her apartment door using the dead bolt lock he'd installed, realizing she'd requested it in a moment of panic that now seemed overblown. The Mullets had ignored the invitation to discuss their encounter with her and Mose. As the days went by, she felt less concerned about them sneaking into her new apartment to repeat their aggressive behavior.

When something fluttered in front of her foot, she glanced down to see a small white envelope that had apparently been tucked under her door. As she picked it up, her heart fluttered wildly. *Marlene* was written on the outside, in a legible but somewhat quirky handwriting with loops and angles that didn't follow the penmanship guidelines taught in school.

Was this the cause of the Kuhns' furtive little smiles? She was betting they'd delivered it—from a man, because a woman could've simply brought it upstairs herself.

Marlene closed her door and sank down onto her love seat before breaking the envelope's seal. As she'd suspected, Lester's name was at the bottom of the page—and her pulse accelerated as she read his note.

> *Dear, dear Marlene,*
>
> *It was delightful to spend time with you over such a special dinner last night. I am honored that you've entrusted me with the stories of your past romances, because now I better understand your insistence that you'll never marry . . . and just maybe we changed your mind about that. I realize you need time to heal after the Mullets' terrifying attack, and that you'll be better prepared to move forward when you've found a way to forgive them.*
>
> *You're like a lovely red rose that feels withered on the vine, but after this faded bloom has dropped off, new rosebuds will emerge, and fresh, vibrant opportunities will bloom for you, dear. Everything in its season.*
>
> *I'll be here, if you want me.*
>
> *Lester*

Marlene's breath escaped in a sigh of longing. Was it possible that the man who'd written her such a beautiful, compassionate letter could truly want to be with her? Her whole being thrummed with his imagery of the withered rose falling off to make way for new rosebuds. She *did* want him, and her attraction felt more innate and intense than it had with her previous beaux.

But Lester had mentioned another important topic, hadn't he? He knew her heart couldn't fully heal until she'd forgiven Yost and Jake. Although it was true that the cousins had avoided meeting with Preachers Amos and Eli and her brother, *she* had also stayed away from the farm that day.

Somehow, she had to find a way to cleanse her heart and soul of the fear and the regrets those men had heaped upon her when they'd cornered her in the storage room. And what better time to do that than Good Friday, so she could truly accept the grace of God in the joy of Jesus's resurrection, come Sunday?

Marlene read Lester's letter again, allowing a few tears to flow unchecked down her cheeks. Lester had come by his patient wisdom the hard way—through his own years of experience and painful loss. If such a stable, compassionate man found her attractive and could believe in her despite her three broken engagements . . . maybe she should give herself another chance to bloom.

Maybe she'd written herself off as a hopeless *maidel* without knowing how lovable she appeared when seen through someone else's eyes—bottomless brown eyes that shone like hot coffee and glimmered in candlelight.

Hope began to shine like a rainbow appearing after a thunderstorm.

She would find a way to believe that true love could be hers, and that she deserved a man like Lester Lehman.

Chapter 26

"As you were saying, Amos, the view from this back boundary is pretty amazing."

Lester gazed out over a panorama that began to his left at the Wickey place and went uninterrupted across the entry to Promise Lodge, Rainbow Lake, the timbered lodge building and its cabins, the Helmuths' nursery and their double home, Dale's new store, and the newlywed Helmuths' homes. A large patch of woods remained along the state highway before giving way to Harley Kurtz's sheep pasture, the home where Harley and Minerva lived, and then came Preacher Marlin's barrel factory. Bishop Monroe's home, barns, and the pasture where his Clydesdales grazed took Lester to the community's boundary at his right. On the road below him sat the widely spaced row of homes where other folks lived, along with the bakery, the cheese factory, the dairy barn and the pasture where Christine's Holsteins grazed.

"And when you consider that only the lodge, the cabins, and the dairy barn were here when we bought the place a couple years ago," Preacher Amos said, "we can't ignore the way the Lord has blessed us with great progress and with the best sort of new neighbors who've come to live with us. Like you, Lester!"

Lester chuckled. "It's been anything but boring since I relocated here with Floyd and his family," he remarked. "And who knew, when I came here, that I'd be looking to build a second house for another fresh start?"

"Any thoughts about where you'd like that house to be? You can take all the time you want to decide, of course."

As he focused on the deep green grass in Bishop Monroe's pasture, with redbud and dogwood trees in bloom along the back border—not to mention the huge red barns and the long stretches of white plank fence enclosing the Clydesdales—his heart knew where he needed to be.

"Let's draw up the deed for the land above Monroe's barns," Lester said, pointing in that direction. "I'm in no huge hurry, but I don't really want to wait for Truman's crew to clear away all the trees up here and then put in a road, either. He's a busy man this spring."

"And you're ready to be out of Allen's tiny home, *jah*?" Amos teased. "To my way of thinking, the best part of your current setup is the view of the lake. The house itself would've driven me insane long ago."

"That about sums it up. And—because Mattie is some-times right," Lester added with a laugh, "let's also figure to build a henhouse and a *gut*-sized stable, and we'll allow for a garden plot that can expand if we need it to."

"You've got it. Shall we head back to my place and mark off your property on the plot map?" Amos asked. "We can calculate your lumber order, too, if you'll bring along your floor plan."

A big smile spread slowly across Lester's face and his pulse settled into a steady, satisfied thrum. This decision felt exactly right. Preacher Amos and the other skilled carpenters here would tackle his new house eagerly and he'd most likely move into it sometime this summer.

"Ah—look who's home!" Lester pointed toward the gray van that was pulling into the drive leading to the two new houses tucked slightly behind Kraybill's store.

"Seems our newlyweds collected so many wedding gifts from the folks in Ohio, they needed a little trailer to bring them all home," the preacher remarked as they started down the rugged path between the old trees. "With the spring weather kicking into full gear, I'm sure Sam and Simon are happy to have Cyrus and Jonathan back to work in the nursery."

"They're *gut* boys," Lester remarked, picking his way carefully so he didn't trip over tree roots or underbrush. "I'm so glad Gloria has found a husband who's every bit as energetic and unpredictable as she is. They'll have a fine life together."

"And the four of them form a bedrock foundation for the younger generation we need to keep Promise Lodge growing," Amos put in. "Before we know it, the Peterscheim kids will be old enough to look for mates, as well as Fannie and Lowell Kurtz."

Lester nodded. Deep inside him, he wondered if he and Marlene might also bring the next generation into play—but that was a topic for more consideration in the future. For now, he felt he was moving forward again, taking the last step away from his life with Delores to start a second family, Lord willing.

After he and Amos started down the paved road and had walked past his former house, Lester glanced up at the second-story windows on the front of the lodge, where Marlene's apartment was. She was working at the store, yet—when Amos wasn't watching—he blew her a kiss.

Maybe she'd feel it when she got home this afternoon.

Maybe she'd know, without the need for words, how much he wanted to share his new home with her.

Good Friday dawned with pastel ribbons of pink and peach in the eastern sky, glowing in the sun's first rays. As Marlene gazed out her windows toward the huge lilac bushes now in bloom at the front of the Promise Lodge property, she felt a stirring inside her. It was a day for fasting until the noon meal, a day of prayer and quiet contemplation of Jesus's death on the cross, yet she sensed a new awakening that made her feel bubbly all over.

She had figured out a way to express her forgiveness to Yost and Jake.

As Marlene took out a pen and a pad of plain paper, she focused inward. What could she say that would cleanse her soul? She would never condone the Mullets' behavior in that upstairs storage room, but if she expressed her forgiveness, she would be living the life Christ expected of His followers. And she could put that painful day behind her.

Dear Yost,

I'm sorry that Mose and I upset you when we sold our property without offering it to you first. We did what we felt was best.

I'm also sorry that you felt compelled to team up with Jake and corner me in the upstairs storage room to take out your frustrations, and that my brother had to pull you both away from me as you tore at my clothes. When Preachers Amos and Eli invited you to the farm to talk things over, and you chose not to show up, it told us all that you had no interest in reconciliation. And I'm sorry about that, as well.

Forgiveness is a pillar of the Amish faith, so please accept my apologies and know that I forgive you for your unthinkable behavior even though you'll probably never confess it in public. Far as I'm concerned, the slate is wiped clean.

Marlene

With only a few cross-outs, the words had flowed from her pen as though they'd been inspired from above. Even so, Marlene realized that Yost and Jake might not think it sounded sincere. She was pretty sure they would both burn their letters immediately after they read them—but if by chance their wives saw her note, maybe it would explain a few things. Who knew what those men had told their women about their black eyes and broken nose?

After she rewrote the letter on fresh paper for Yost, Marlene penned a second copy with Jake's name in it. She realized that she had no control over the Mullets' reactions to her words. She had made the first move. She had apologized—even if most folks believed she'd done nothing wrong—and she had expressed her forgiveness as she'd stated the facts from her own point of view.

It occurred to her that these notes might inspire Jake and Yost to retaliate. She doubted, however, that they'd drive a buggy for three hours in each direction to get back at her—especially because they'd seen the layout of Promise Lodge at Laura's wedding, and they knew that neighbors all around would come to her rescue immediately if they tried to hurt her again.

As she sealed the letters into envelopes and addressed them, Marlene felt as though she was sending away her pent-up fears through the mail, never to return.

She had forgiven Yost and Jake, as Lester had wisely suggested. That didn't guarantee that her nightmares about their attack would immediately stop, but she'd made the effort her faith required.

Marlene went downstairs and out onto the porch to place the letters in the mailbox. All was quiet around Promise Lodge, because most families were observing their Good Friday morning fast and perhaps immersed in prayer and Bible reading. When she looked over at the tiny house on the shore of Rainbow Lake, she spotted Lester stretched out on a chaise lounge on his dock . . . possibly engrossed in a form of meditation that involved studying the insides of his eyelids.

She waved anyway. When he waved back, Marlene blew him a kiss before stepping back into the lodge. She had a feeling he'd be at the table in the dining room to join them all for a quiet supper—and she was looking forward to his company.

Chapter 27

"The message for Easter Sunday rings as true for us today as it did for the disciples who saw the resurrected Christ a few days after He rose." Bishop Monroe filled the lodge's meeting room with his powerful voice and positive energy, his face glowing as he spoke. "In the last few verses of the gospel of Luke, as Deacon Marlin read earlier, Jesus tells His followers to preach repentance and remission of sins—and then He says, 'Ye are witnesses of these things.'"

The bishop paused to make eye contact with a few folks in the congregation, and when he focused on Marlene for a moment, a little shiver tingled up her spine.

"The risen Christ is speaking to *us*, friends. We are witnesses to His life and His preaching *today*." The bishop nodded emphatically. "Some folks bemoan the fact that no new books have been added to the Bible for centuries, and that—apparently—no new leaders like Moses or John the Baptist and no new prophets like Isaiah have appeared to shine light on us, either. But I don't believe that!"

Monroe paused at just the right moment, inspiring the members of his congregation to lean forward in anticipation of what he'd say next. Marlene could understand why folks wanted to live at Promise Lodge, under Monroe

Burkholder's leadership. He was a man afire with the flame of Pentecost every time he preached, and his listeners knew there was no ducking from the responsibilities of a true Christian life. Yet he modeled Jesus as the Good Shepherd rather than as a Messiah pelting them with wrath.

"*We* are to be Christ's witnesses," he reiterated. "We are to repent, and to forgive others of their sins against us. We are to live out that great new commandment about loving the Lord our God with all our hearts and loving our neighbors as ourselves. Jesus never says to wait around for another Moses or another Isaiah—and we're not to wait until we feel stronger or more ready or more inspired. He tells us to get out there and spread His gospel to all by *living* it for everyone to see. Right here and now."

As the church service continued to its close, Marlene was glad she'd written her notes of forgiveness to Yost and Jake. She felt she had done what the Lord expected of her, so she could forgive those men from deep inside herself as well as from the surface of a piece of paper. And because she'd taken that step, she felt free.

When she glanced over toward the men's side, she saw that Lester was watching her from the second row. He, too, seemed to be feeling a joy that radiated on his handsome face—and Marlene wondered what had happened to him since they'd shared that candlelight dinner on Tuesday evening.

After the benediction, Bishop Monroe smiled at everyone. "Today, after the common meal, we'll have an egg hunt for the kids—and right now, our scholars and younger participants are to help Teacher Minerva in the classroom with a special project while a few of our men hide the eggs around the grounds."

"No fair peeking outside!" Preacher Amos teased, shaking his finger at the boys who were most likely to do that.

"And we'll have special prizes for the scholars we see helping the youngest kids find eggs rather than stuffing their own baskets. Let's go and enjoy this fine afternoon together, shall we?"

When folks rose from the pew benches and began chatting happily, Marlene wasn't surprised that Lester found his way over to visit with her.

"How've you been?" he asked amiably. "Anything new and exciting going on here at the lodge?"

"Well, there's been a whole lot of cookin' goin' on," Marlene quipped with a chuckle. "Irene and the Kuhns have outdone themselves preparing food for the Easter Monday gathering tomorrow."

"I'm not surprised," Lester said with a nod. His smile curved endearingly. "You know those walks we shared after Gloria's wedding and again after Laura's, when we first met?"

Marlene nodded, her heart stilling in anticipation.

"Will you join me for another one after we eat? I've, uh, got a little show-and-tell to share with you."

"Sure, I'll go," she said with a raised eyebrow. "But only if you'll sit with me at the meal—and Mose will most likely join us."

"I was hoping you'd ask." Lester glanced around to see what the crowd around them was doing. "Right now I'm helping Harley, Roman, and Allen hide eggs for the kids. Then I'll be back."

He flashed her a smile and strode out to the front door, nodding and greeting other folks as he headed outside. Marlene made her way to the schoolroom, where she'd offered to help with the scholars' special project.

Excitement was running high as the students gathered around the big table to fill colorful woven baskets. Teacher Minerva was setting the small baskets around the edge of the table so the kids could form an assembly line and place the contents inside them. Marlene recognized the baskets—they were small and inexpensive, and she was guessing Dale had sold hundreds of them in the past few weeks.

Lily Peterscheim and Fannie Kurtz, who were fourteen and fifteen, led the way by stuffing fluffy shreds of colored Easter basket grass into the baskets. Their younger brothers, Lowell and Lavern—who worked with the bishop's Clydesdales after school each day—had each opened a bag of wrapped chocolate-covered eggs and began placing two in each of the baskets. Menno and Johnny Peterscheim, who were now twelve and nine, added decorated cookie crosses and jellybeans. Mary Kate Schwartz followed the scholars with her toddler, David, on her hip so he could place a colored marshmallow bunny in each basket.

"Now this is what I call teamwork!" Marlene said as she watched the children make their way around to all the baskets—enough that everyone in Promise Lodge would have a basket to take home. "I'll be sure to tell Dale how you put his baskets to such fine use."

"Oh, we're filling a basket for him, too!" Teacher Minerva said. "And if you could take it over to the store for him, Marlene, we'd appreciate it. We're also making baskets for the two Kuhns and the three Wickeys, and we'll leave those in the kitchen."

"They went to their Easter service at the Mennonite church today," Johnny said matter-of-factly.

"But we like our church—and Bishop Monroe—the best. Right, guys?" Lowell called out.

As the kids chorused their love for their leader, the schoolroom rang with their young voices. When all the baskets had been filled, Fannie and Lily quickly rearranged their contents so they looked more organized—while the boys indulged in a few of the leftover candies. Marlene fetched two wheeled carts from the kitchen so the kids could load the baskets onto them and put one at each place along the set tables in the dining room, where folks would eat the common meal.

When Teacher Minerva and the kids had gone, Marlene and Mary Kate gathered the empty candy bags and leftover Easter grass.

"What an ingenious way to keep the kids from watching the men hide the eggs," Marlene remarked.

Mary Kate gently pried a box half-full of marshmallow bunnies from little David's hand. "*Jah*, and it gave each of our kids a job—and a chance at some extra candy while they worked," she added with a laugh. "For boys of that age range, it's the best incentive. They have bottomless pits for stomachs."

As she rejoined the other women who'd been setting out food for the common meal, Marlene noticed that the four men who'd been hiding the eggs were coming through the front door.

"Great day for an egg hunt—but breezy enough that it's best we're eating indoors," Lester said when he'd come over to help her carry water pitchers to the tables. "Great day for other outside activities, too."

Marlene couldn't miss the mysterious undercurrent of his words. She wasn't sure what Lester had been up to for the past few days, but she suspected she was about to find out.

Lester ate quickly, too excited to linger over the meal even though the cold sliced ham, fresh bread, and various salads and desserts were tasty.

"Looks like your brother has struck up a friendship with Harley," he remarked as he glanced at a table behind him and Marlene. "And that's a *gut* thing. Most of the other men here are either old enough to be his *dat* or younger than he is by several years."

Marlene nodded. "He's developed quite an interest in Harley's sheep, because he can see them from his apartment in the barn loft," she said as she passed Lester a bowl of fluffy pink salad made with cherry pie filling. "And it seems Queenie has taken a shine to Mose, as well."

Lester chuckled, spooning some salad onto his plate. "*Jah*, that border collie might belong to Noah Schwartz, but she considers it her life's mission to herd Harley's sheep."

"I like to think of her as Promise Lodge's version of the Gut Shepherd," Marlene murmured gently. "Whenever I look out over that pasture dotted with sheep and their lambs, and I see Queenie watching them from under a tree, the Twenty-Third Psalm comes to mind. Such a pretty setting there, with the roll of the hills and the blossoming trees and lush, green grass."

The food Lester was swallowing nearly stuck in his throat. Marlene's comment made him dare to believe that she'd be especially fond of the view from the front porch of his new house. She looked serene and pretty as she spoke about the flock—he hoped his news wouldn't backfire when he revealed it in a short while.

Marlene took her time choosing and eating a slice of peach pie and a square of coconut cake. Lester chose chocolate cake and a couple of peanut butter thumbprint cookies he didn't really want—but they kept him from drumming his fingers impatiently on the table. At long last, her smile hinted that she was ready to walk with him—and he suspected Marlene had been dawdling over dessert on purpose, to make him wait.

She had that power over him. And she knew it.

Lester realized he'd spend the rest of his life at Marlene's beck and call if he allowed their relationship to advance to the next stage—but wasn't that one of the deep-down reasons he was building a house? True enough, he'd gotten tired of living in such cramped quarters, but he'd also grown weary of living alone. The sound of Marlene's voice and the way her eyes followed his lips when he talked were only two of the qualities that drove him over the edge, whether he admitted it to himself or not.

"I think springtime's here to stay," she remarked as they stepped outside from the lodge's mudroom. "From here on out, it'll remain too warm for frost—and look at these plots of Mattie's salad vegetables! I think the lettuce and radishes have shot up two or three inches this week. Won't be long until she opens her roadside stand."

Lester tried to think of something besides the weather to talk about, even though it was a safe topic. But what he was planning didn't feel particularly safe, did it? A new home would take both him and Marlene outside their comfort zones—at least until they were officially courting and headed toward the altar. Or not.

"Could be they look so much larger because you've been spending your days inside, working at Dale's store," he pointed out. "I hope that's going well for you?"

"*Jah*, I've learned a lot and I feel pretty confident about all the restocking jobs now," she replied. They were starting up the road, passing Preacher Amos's house, as she continued. "I don't know if Dale ever intends to let me run the cash register, but that's all right. I stay very busy."

"I suspect he'll be wanting to hire another helper or two someday," Lester speculated as he gazed up the hill. "That's a large store—with a huge selection of merchandise—and I bet you were both wishing for more help when the store was so busy at the grand opening.

"And who knows?" he added carefully. "Maybe you won't

want to work there for the long haul. You're of an age that your life could still take a different direction. At the drop of a hat, you might decide to take on another household where you would have a garden again, or—"

"At the drop of a few special words from *you*?" Marlene asked in a low voice.

Lester let out a nervous laugh. Of course, she'd seen through him—he hadn't exactly been subtle lately. "At least you said that with a smile on your face, dear. There've been times when you would've walked away if I hinted at such a thing, *jah*?"

They were passing Lester's former residence when Marlene slipped her hand into his. He grasped it gently— just as he grasped the chance to have this conversation, which would reveal the plans he'd been making.

"I'm a skittish one," she agreed. "I appreciate the way you've listened to my concerns about the men in my past— about courting and getting engaged again, Lester. And I'll tell you that I wrote notes to both Mullets, saying I've forgiven them for their behavior. Whatever they choose to do in response, I've done my part."

"*Gut* for you. I'm proud of you, Marlene. That couldn't have been easy for you."

Was he laying it on too thick? Sounding too much like her *dat*?

Lester inhaled deeply, preparing to tell her his news as they came to the top of the road. From here, they could see Bishop Monroe's white plank fence, with the two red barns and some grazing Clydesdales in the distance.

"So have we almost reached your show-and-tell, Lester? You've been waiting for just the right moment to share it, ain't so?"

He slipped his arm around her shoulders, chuckling. "I can't get anything past you, so I might as well spit it out.

I've just bought this plot of land next to the Burkholder place," he said, pointing in that direction. "And I've drawn up plans for the house I'm going to have built on it—and Amos has ordered the lumber for it."

"Wow! *Wow!*" Marlene crowed as she threw her arms around his neck. "Now that's big news—and a big decision, too. Congratulations, Lester!"

As he held her close for several delightful moments, he thanked God that Marlene had perceived his decision as a positive one—as opposed to backing away from him with a doubtful frown on her face. When she eased away from his embrace, Lester pulled the folded pages of his floor plan from the pocket inside his black vest. His heart was hammering, even though Marlene now knew everything he'd intended to reveal today.

"This is a lot like my previous place," he explained as she grabbed the opposite edges of the page so she could look on with him. "Except I'm going for a larger porch . . . and Amos talked me into a couple more bedrooms, as well as a chicken house."

Marlene's expressive dark eyebrows rose before she flashed a playful smile. "Don't tell me—you're going to take in boarders, so any unattached men who come to Promise Lodge will have a place to live, like the women do now. And you've decided to sell eggs at Dale's store for a little extra running-around money."

Lester laughed out loud. Where had she come up with such ideas—and quicker than the blink of an eye?

"You're a mind reader, Marlene—or one of those psychics who sees all and knows all," he teased back.

Marlene's expression mellowed as she held his gaze. "Maybe I've figured you out because I've spent a lot of time thinking about you lately."

Lester sucked in air and held it. Yet again she'd startled

him with a remark from out of the blue. And her lovely face, so serene and glowing in the afternoon sunshine, told him Marlene was being completely sincere.

I've spent a lot of time thinking about you lately.

"That's encouraging," he whispered. "I—I also looked at property up the hill, where all those trees and the underbrush grow so thick. There's quite a panoramic view of Promise Lodge from up there.

"But when I stood on the other side of the road and looked this direction," Lester continued wistfully, "I saw a picture postcard—Missouri at her finest, with the springtime trees in bloom. And the Kurtz pasture, as well as the Burkholder pasture, will be visible from my new windows, too."

Marlene turned to follow the finger he was pointing, a soft smile overtaking her face. "It'll be like living inside the Twenty-Third Psalm," she repeated. "Especially the part about green pastures restoring your soul, *jah*?"

Was she seeing the surroundings as though they were to be *her* surroundings someday? Or was he caught up in his fondest wishes for their future?

"How soon do you figure to move in, Lester?"

He willed his heartbeat to slow down enough that his words would sound clear and decisive. "You'll soon find out that we have quite a crew of skilled carpenters here," he replied. "Amos didn't name a date, but I won't be surprised if the house is finished sometime in June. We've had a lot of practice at working together. It's a blessing, to have so many skilled friends in one community."

"It is," she agreed. Once again Marlene focused on him, her gaze unwavering. "And when you move your furniture inside, whose table will be in the kitchen—the Lehmans', or the Fishers'?"

How did she keep nailing him with these insightful

remarks? Deciding he should take his turn at that, Lester focused on Marlene's bottomless dark eyes.

"That depends on *you*, ain't so?"

Marlene didn't blink. "Not necessarily. You own both tables, so you can choose whichever one suits you," she pointed out. "So far, I've not been invited to help with any of your decisions, so I have no say about which table you—"

"Marlene."

Had he made a big mistake, not asking her opinions about a new home—or where she'd like that home to be located? Her tone, somewhat teasing yet rock-bottom serious, disguised her true feelings about everything he'd revealed to her.

Was Marlene pushing him to propose? Had she already recovered from her parents' passings, the auction, and what the Mullets had done to her?

"*Jah*? What's on your mind, Lester?" she whispered.

He couldn't take any more of her emotional push and pull, or this exchange of provocative questions. Lester slipped his arms around Marlene and kissed her deeply, cradling her head in his hand so she wouldn't pull away and tease him again. He was vaguely aware that his floor plans had fluttered to the ground.

Her response to his kiss left nothing to his imagination. Marlene wrapped her arms firmly around him as her lips responded to his every move and nuance. Lester's pulse went wild as he opened her mouth with his to further explore it, and she went right along with him. She'd never been married but she'd courted three other men, and they'd taught her a thing or two about kissing.

Her eager response was something that couldn't be tutored, however. When Lester moved slightly, Marlene rested her head against his shoulder and allowed him to take the lead. His imagination went wild. He became so engrossed in the kiss, it took several moments for him to realize that a barking dog was approaching them . . . and he also realized they were on top of a rise, where anyone coming up the road could see them.

With a sigh, Lester eased away from her. Marlene stood looking at him, inhaling rapidly to catch her breath. Neither of them said anything as Queenie loped up beside them. She'd stopped barking but her bushy black-and-white tale was wagging as she pushed her head underneath Lester's hand to get his attention.

He cleared his throat. "I didn't want to stop," he murmured.

"I didn't want you to." Marlene gently stroked his face with her fingertip. "I guess I was afraid of allowing you to get this close, but you're nothing like Jake or Yost or Ervin."

Lester choked on a laugh. "Makes perfect sense that I'm not."

She swatted him playfully. "What I mean is, I'm not afraid to take this to the next level with you anymore, Lester," she confessed softly. "I know now that you don't intend to trap me, or to mold me into the *gut* little woman you want me to be—"

"Woe to the man who tries *that*."

Marlene laughed out loud and embraced him. He knew better than to let this chance go by, even though he'd originally figured on taking a lot longer to speak his piece.

"Will you marry me?" he murmured near her ear. "We can court for as long as you need to—"

"I will," she said softly and quickly.

"—and if you want to change anything about my house plans, you can—"

"I love you, Lester," Marlene interrupted. "How about if you stop fretting over the details and kiss me again?"

Lester blinked. They stood eye to eye, and even with

Queenie whimpering and pawing at his pant leg, he couldn't stop gazing at her in amazement. "You're *gut* with all this? I don't have to keep pleading my case or waiting for you to—"

With a smile that turned him inside out, Marlene moved in for another kiss that defied everything he knew about convincing a woman to want him. Her warm mouth became more insistent, to the point that Lester found it very difficult to control his emotions or his body—because this time, Marlene was in charge. He suddenly knew beyond the shadow of a doubt that she would never shy away from him or need to be coaxed or cajoled into sharing her physical affection.

It was a moment of intense longing, and intense joy. So many men quietly hinted that their wives tolerated love-making because they felt it was their duty, but Marlene wouldn't be one of them.

When they eased apart, she was blinking back tears, yet she appeared radiant with happiness. "I *will* marry you, Lester," she repeated as she traced the outline of his lips with her fingertip. "You're right—there's no hurry. But . . . but I don't want to wait too long, either. At my age I've already missed out on—"

"You haven't missed a thing, sweetheart," Lester whispered. "I suspect we can cover all there is to know about a man and a woman truly becoming one, in short order. *Jah*, that's a magical, mystical concept when the bishop speaks of it at a wedding ceremony, but it'll be another thing altogether when we shut the door on the rest of the world, and it's just you and me, together."

"In our new home."

"In *our* new home," he agreed with a tender smile.

Glancing around, he noticed that his paper plans had drifted off on the breeze—and when Marlene sprinted across the grass to retrieve them, he followed the way her firm body filled out her dress as she reached down to capture them. Would it be wrong to go to Bishop Monroe right this minute and announce that they were ready to tie the knot?

Patience, patience, patience. I should give myself—and Marlene—some time to savor this moment. I'm engaged to her! Praise be to God!

Lester returned the bright smile on Marlene's face, suddenly aware that his world had begun to rotate in a whole new direction.

Everything I've always wanted is now within reach—and if I take the time to do it up right, Marlene will be forever grateful.

"Shall we find a place to sit down, and you can show me these rooms and tell me about this house you've sketched out?" she asked. "I don't know much about floor plans, but I'd like to learn."

"I know just the spot." He folded the plans into his vest pocket again and clasped Marlene's hand. "We can sit on the dock, in the sunshine."

"What if I get our Easter baskets from the dining room, so we can have some candy while we talk?" Marlene suggested. "Everything goes better with chocolate, ain't so?"

Chapter 28

Easter Monday dawned bright and clear. As Marlene gazed out her window toward the lake and Lester's tiny house, the first rays of sunlight illuminated the lawn and made her suck in her breath. Every blade of grass was topped with a tiny, perfect dewdrop. Millions of shiny little water beads shimmered on the lodge's front yard—a sight that made Marlene feel insanely happy.

Lester and I are engaged! It's going to last this time—I just know it!

The excitement of this realization had bubbled inside her all through the night, making it nearly impossible to sleep, yet she felt awake and alert and ready to enjoy this traditional day of recreation. Lester had agreed to keep their news a secret until she chose to reveal it—which would probably happen sometime today. What better event than a family gathering to announce their plans? The folks at Promise Lodge were her and Mose's new family, and she could already anticipate the joy on their faces when she revealed her betrothal. Most folks wouldn't really be *surprised*, but they'd be very happy.

As Marlene showered and put on fresh clothes, she thought about how to tell her brother she was to become Lester's wife. She sensed the two men had become good friends, so she wasn't worried about Mose's reaction—but she did feel bad that her dear twin would probably never tie the knot himself. Although it was true that he'd remained on the farm with her to care for their parents, their family situation had also provided him with a good excuse not to socialize with women . . . because his nervous stuttering got in the way of forming relationships.

When Mose joined her and the other ladies for breakfast in the lodge dining room, Marlene realized that he was speaking easily with the Kuhns and Irene—which meant he felt comfortable with them. She sensed he secretly loved it when these older women fussed over him and watched him devour the food they'd prepared—but that was different from entering into a one-on-one romance with a woman he chose to love and support for the rest of his life.

"Mose, you might as well scrape the last of this sausage-and-egg casserole out of the pan," Ruby said as she offered it to him.

"*Jah*, that way we can wash it up—and fill it with something else," Beulah put in with a laugh. "Although today, we're taking the day off from the kitchen."

"Glad to hear it," Marlene said as her twin went along with the Kuhns' wishes. "You cooked enough food for an army on Saturday—and everyone else will be bringing food to the picnic this noon, as well. You'll have to roll us all away from the table!"

"*Jah*, we might not need the volleyball or the croquet balls. We can just use our friends," Irene teased. She smiled at them from across the table. "This will be the first Easter Monday you Fishers and Dale have spent at Promise Lodge, and we're glad to have you. And truth be told, I'm glad the store's closed so the two of you won't be working there today," she added matter-of-factly. "I suspect this location gets more traffic than the store in Cloverdale did, and Dale should probably be looking to hire more help."

"He's mentioned that a time or two," Marlene remarked. Inside, she was burning with the question of whether he'd need to replace *her* when she and Lester married—but it wasn't the time to bring up that subject. "I'm looking forward to playing badminton and croquet and volleyball—and I understand the fellows are getting up a game of baseball this afternoon, if any of them still have energy left after those other games. And the kids are all excited about their sack races, fifty-yard dashes, and three-legged races. This is a lot more exciting than Easter Monday ever was in Coldstream."

"Every district's different," Beulah remarked. "I'm just grateful that we Mennonites are considered part of the family here even though the bishop's Amish. Monroe's a wonderful-*gut* fellow."

"*Jah*, he is. Easy to work with, too," Mose agreed as he rose from his chair. He smiled at the three ladies. "*Denki* for feeding me again. I'll see you all later. I'm to help set up the nets for the games, so I'd better get out there."

As Marlene finished her food, Ruby and Beulah began strategizing about how to organize the potluck lunch—until they heard Mose close the mudroom door behind him.

"Your brother has come a long way," Ruby said with a nod.

"*Jah*, when you Fishers first came here, he couldn't seem to string three words together without stumbling over two of them," Beulah put in. "I'm glad he feels more relaxed around us now."

"And why wouldn't he, considering the way you gals are always cooking his favorite meals and sending leftovers home with him?" Marlene teased. "But I'm so glad to see him settled into his job with Bishop Monroe, and he's cozy in his new home, too."

"I can recall you saying that you two might eventually build a house," Irene said as she rose to stack their plates. "Do you still see that happening, Marlene?"

Marlene clenched her jaw to keep from blurting out her news about joining Lester in *his* new house. "It's early to commit to that yet—especially since we invested quite a bit to make our two apartments the way we want them, and we've only lived in them a month," she hedged as she also rose from her place. "I've told the Bender sisters I'd meet them to get the prizes together for the kids' races, so I need to skedaddle. See you all later—in time to *eat* again, of course!"

Marlene hummed a cheerful tune as she stepped outside and started toward the Troyer house. She felt so light-hearted—so downright ecstatic—that someone was sure to quiz her about why she was in such a fine mood. And what would she say? How would she inform their friends that she and Lester had said *yes* to each other?

As though he'd sensed she was on the move—or maybe he'd been watching out his window—Lester emerged from his tiny home. His arm shot up in a wide wave and his smile rivaled the sun.

"Wait up!" he called as he jogged toward her.

Marlene paused on the road, watching his trim body move so smoothly. Even in an older pair of broadfall trousers and a slightly faded blue shirt, Lester exuded an air of well-groomed, clean confidence—and she couldn't miss the special sparkle in his dark eyes.

"And how's my girl today?" he murmured.

"Just *peachy*," Marlene replied happily. "And how about you, Lester? Did we make our big move a little sooner than either of us had figured on?"

His dark eyebrows rose as he chuckled. "That's the

question I was going to ask *you*, dear. But I feel *gut* about it all the same. How about you, Marlene? We can take all the time you want to—"

"*Jah*, patience is a virtue," she quipped, playfully tapping his nose, "but maybe it's not one of ours, eh? I think we're both old enough to know what we want. I feel a solid sense of commitment this time around, which I didn't have with those other guys. It's like we're pouring the foundation for the new house, and by the time the walls are up and the roof's on and it's ready for us to move in, we'll be ready, too."

Was it her imagination, or did Lester's eyes mist up for a moment?

"Glad to hear it," he whispered. "And if you want *me* to announce our surprise today, I can do that—"

"Or I can," Marlene put in with a smile. "Let's see how it plays out. One way or another, I suspect today's the day."

Lester nodded. "*Jah*, if I don't say something soon, I might just pop from the effort of keeping our news under my hat," he said with a chuckle. "I feel like a kid again, Marlene, only better. Readier—because I know what we're getting ourselves into. And I know we can handle it."

She wanted to kiss him so badly she could taste it, but she knew that anyone looking out the window would see them. "It'll be a momentous occasion, today."

"It will. And now I need to open the shed by the lake so we can get out the lawn games."

"I'm helping Teacher Minerva and the Bender sisters organize the kids' races." Marlene sighed contentedly. "It's so nice to be included—to feel as though Mose and I already fit in and belong here."

"It'll only get better." Lester held her gaze for a long,

lovely moment. "See you later, sweetie. *I love you*," he added in a whisper.

"And I love you right back," Marlene murmured happily. As they went their separate ways, she felt a great surge of optimism—

And then she noticed Mose. He was standing in the shade of the shed near Rainbow Lake, watching her and Lester.

He can already sense what we've been talking about. I shouldn't make him second-guess our intentions—and I should be the one to tell him.

With a big wave at her brother, Marlene jogged through the damp grass until she caught up with Lester. "We need to tell Mose," she said in a low voice. "Our decision affects him more than anyone else—and we twins have always shared everything."

Lester nodded. "Better that he hears it from you before the others find out," he agreed.

Inhaling deeply, Marlene approached the shed, her heart thumping like a puppy's tail. Mose's gaze flickered briefly from her face to Lester's, but otherwise he stood absolutely still, a tall, broad mountain of muscles—even if a hint of insecurity made him lick his lips.

"Mose, we—Lester and I—well, we got engaged yesterday!" Marlene said in a rush. "We wanted you to be the first to know—"

"Oh, anybody l-looking at you can f-figure that one out," he broke in with a nervous smile. "If you're happy, I'm happy, Marlene. And—and I have to say I f-feel a whole lot b-better about Lester than I did about those, um, other guys."

Marlene laughed, grabbing Mose's hand between hers. "Fourth time's a charm?" she quipped.

"As I told you before, Mose, I'll take *gut* care of your

sister," Lester put in, extending his hand. "You'll probably be pleased to know that I've bought the plot of land alongside the bishop's pasture, and I'm building a new house there. A *real* house," he added with a chuckle.

Mose laughed as he pumped Lester's hand. "A place big enough for an ox like me to visit?" he teased back.

"Any time you care to come over," Lester assured him. "And there's enough land there that if you want to build a place next door, we can do that. Or we can add an apartment onto the house—"

Mose waved him off. "I appreciate the thought, b-but for now I'm happy in my b-bachelor pad above the horses," he insisted quickly. "I—I'm real happy for you."

Marlene launched herself at her brother, and he caught her in the affectionate bear hug they'd shared for most of their adult lives. "So now you know! I figure we'll announce this to everyone else later today—"

"You're flashing like a sign board, Marlene," Mose teased. "I'm betting the Bender sisters will call you out before you have a chance to make your little speech today. And once *they* know, everyone else will."

She shrugged happily, grinning at Lester. "So we'll be bringing even more happiness and excitement to our new friends today. That's not a bad thing, *jah*?"

Lester had spent the morning of Easter Monday smiling and laughing—more than any other day that he could recall. With the men's volleyball games behind them, he went to the big cooler jugs on the picnic table to fill his cup with lemonade again. The weather was perfect for their activities, and everyone was participating in some sport or another, and visiting—the favorite sport of the Amish—in the shade when they needed a break.

Across the lawn, the Kuhns were swatting at the shuttle-cock, trying to keep a game going with the other women despite the way they burst out laughing every time they swung and missed. For these kinds of games, with such a variety of sizes and ages playing, no one really cared which team won. It was all about having fun.

After the opposing side—which included Laura, Phoebe, Gloria, Frances, Fannie, and Marlene—scored three more points in a row, Beulah held up her racket and waved it like a flag.

"It's only going to get worse for us, girls," she predicted to her sister, Irene, and the three Benders. "Let's call a halt and get the food out for our picnic lunch. We can't lose at that!"

The men and boys watching along the sidelines applauded in agreement. Lester filled another cup with cold lemonade and made his way over to Marlene.

"*Gut* game, ladies," he called out as he approached the players. "Watching some of you swing your rackets should be a warning to us fellows when we start up the mixed croquet games after lunch."

"*Jah,* now you know what a fierce, competitive lot we are!" Ruby shot back.

"I'm thinking we all need to fill our cups with something cold so that Lester can propose a *toast*," Rosetta hinted above the murmuring of the others.

Lester chuckled to himself. Of *course,* Amos would've told his wife about the new property sale—and Mattie would've immediately contacted Christine and Rosetta about the house he was building, too.

"All right, I'm all ears!" Bishop Monroe piped up. "Let's

fill our cups so we can raise them high to whatever Lester's going to share with us."

When Lester glanced at Marlene, she shrugged good-naturedly as she accepted her lemonade. "You start, and I'll elaborate," she whispered.

When he saw that folks had filled their plastic cups and were watching him expectantly, Lester held up his glass. "Here's to the new—full-size—house I'm about to build on the hill above Bishop Monroe's pasture!" he called out.

Folks around him laughed and began to drink.

"Glad to hear it, Lester!"

"You go, guy!" one of the Peterscheim boys chimed in.

"So what brought *this* on?" Dale the storekeeper called out. "You seemed very happy in Allen's tiny home—"

Unable to contain her news any longer, Marlene held her cup high above her head. "We also want to announce that I'll be living in that new house with Lester, because we're now engaged!"

The crowd around them went wild, whooping and hollering out their congratulatory remarks. The women gathered around Marlene with bright smiles, hugging her, while the men all stepped over to shake Lester's hand until he thought it might fall off.

What a jubilant feeling that was!

"In that case," Bishop Monroe spoke out above the rest of the crowd, "I propose a toast to the happy couple, Lester and Marlene! God has blessed us with your presence here, and we wish you many happy years together."

Although displays of affection were frowned upon in public, Lester slung his arm around Marlene's shoulders as their friends continued to congratulate them. As her dark eyes sparkled with joy, he was so glad to be the man who'd helped her through her grief, as well as her tense situation with the Mullets.

Folks drained their cups, and the Kuhns began taking lids from casseroles and pans of food so the potluck picnic could begin. Lester spent the rest of the afternoon answering questions about the new house—and playing a very focused game of croquet with Marlene and several of the others.

Marlene was a fine shot. And if she bumped someone else's ball with hers, she didn't hesitate to whack it off in a different direction—which Lester learned from experience. Twice.

When the kids' races began, he saw another side of his intended: as Marlene organized them at the starting line and called out "Three—two—one—*go!*" Lester was bowled over by her genuine enthusiasm for the children. Because there were only six scholars, and they did everything together, Lily and Fannie had agreed to run the fifty-yard dash, the sack races, and the three-legged races alongside their younger brothers.

As Teacher Minerva and Marlene cheered the kids on and assisted them with their burlap bags and with banding their legs together, Lester noted her patience and gentle smiles. Someday, Lord willing, he hoped to be watching her care for *their* children—and he vowed to be a more helpful father with his second family. Now he better understood the energy Delores had invested in child-rearing while managing their household. Marlene wouldn't have to handle so much of that domestic load.

Lester found himself paying more attention to Deborah Peterscheim and her baby, Sarah, as well as to the Helmuth sisters, who balanced little Coreen and Carol against their hips throughout the day's activities. He chuckled as he thought about Marlene growing round with their first child at the same time his young niece, Gloria, might also be in the family way.

Who could've predicted, last winter, that he'd be having such thoughts? Anticipating another home where children's laughter—and crying—punctuated the days of his life? As the afternoon went by, Lester became convinced that the hand of God was indeed guiding him toward a new purpose and a new family with Marlene.

After an evening wiener roast over an open fire—with s'mores for dessert—the kids and several adults spent a couple of hours fishing in Rainbow Lake. When Lester offered to bait Marlene's hook, she thanked him but then deftly centered her worm and shoved it onto the curve of her hook without batting an eye.

"Comes from fishing with Mose and Dat all my life," she explained as she shot a smile at her brother, who stood on the other side of her. "They informed me early on that anyone serious about fishing didn't depend upon somebody else to do the baiting—or the cleaning afterward."

It was a delight to watch Marlene land three nice-sized bass during their time on the shore. When Truman, Bishop Monroe, and Preacher Marlin covered a picnic table in plastic and joined the two of them to clean everyone's catch for a future fish fry, Lester had to admire the way Marlene handled a fillet knife, too.

"I can see I'd better stay on your *gut* side, or you'll have me boned, sliced, and stashed in trash bags before anyone realizes I'm gone," he teased.

Her dark eyebrows rose playfully. "Keep that in mind, Mr. Lehman. The hand that holds the knife rules the world, ain't so?"

As the men around them laughed and teased him good-naturedly, Lester felt sublimely happy. God was good, life was good, and he couldn't wait to enter his new future with this attractive woman at his side.

Chapter 29

Marlene spent Thursday morning restocking the frozen foods near the back of the bulk store. Even though she was wearing her jacket and heavy gloves, it was a cold job—yet she enjoyed the challenge of arranging the boxes and bags just so, to get the most efficient use of the space. When customers wanted some of the products she was stacking, it was a good reason to step away and let her fingers defrost as she exchanged pleasantries or answered their questions.

She was finishing the largest freezer when the phone rang up at the checkout counter. This happened quite often, but Dale's wary expression gave her pause.

"Marlene?" he called out across the store. "Beulah wants to speak with you. It sounds urgent. You can take it on the warehouse extension."

"I'll be right there."

As she quickly picked up the cardboard boxes she'd been emptying, Marlene wondered what could be so important that Beulah would call her. She hurried down the aisle and through the warehouse door, dropping her boxes unceremoniously as she peeled off her gloves to pick up the wall phone's receiver. "*Jah*, Beulah? What's going on?"

Her Mennonite friend cleared her throat and spoke in a

low voice, as though she didn't want to be overheard. "Hate to bother you, dear, but Bishop Obadiah's here with two couples—last name of Mullet," she murmured. "Mose has just arrived, but they want to speak with you, as well."

The bottom dropped out of her stomach. "I—I'll be there as soon as I tell Dale I'm leaving. *Denki* for calling, Beulah."

"Ruby and I are perking a fresh pot of coffee and we've put some coconut glaze cake out for them, but something tells me it won't be enough to sweeten things up. Sorry."

"You have nothing to apologize for," Marlene insisted. "And you don't have to take any static from them, either. *Denki* for playing hostess for us. I'm on my way."

"I'm also going to call Preacher Amos and Bishop Monroe," Beulah whispered. "Seems only fair to fight fire with fire."

Marlene hung up and sucked in a deep, ragged breath. She walked to the checkout counter, grateful that Dale wasn't ringing up a customer. "I've been called over to take care of some unfinished business concerning the, um, farm," she said quickly. "Sorry to leave you, but I have to go—"

"Of course, you do, dear."

"—and I have no idea how long I'll be away." With a nervous shrug, Marlene headed for the warehouse again and strode through the back door. She didn't want to arrive at the lodge short of breath, but she didn't want to keep her un-pleasant guests waiting any longer than necessary, either—because poor Mose would be in a stuttering dither if the bishop, Jake, or Yost started grilling him.

And they would because they loved to upset him.

As she hurried across the lawn, Marlene assumed that her notes forgiving the Mullet cousins had inspired this visit. Her mind raced, composing reasonable explanations for what she'd written to her two former fiancés. She saw a white van parked near the lodge, and spotted a familiar figure seated in one of the wicker chairs on the porch.

"Dick Mercer! How nice to see you again," she said to the English fellow who often drove the folks of Coldstream on their out-of-town errands.

Dick smiled, but it dimmed quickly. "I'm afraid you're in for an inquisition, Marlene," he said softly. "Just between you and me, Yost and Jake have been working on their story—fooling around with the truth, by the sound of it."

Marlene sighed. "I'm not surprised," she muttered. "*Denki* for the heads-up. And feel free to come in for coffee and cake—or just a pleasant chat with my friends in the kitchen."

As she stepped into the lobby of the lodge, she smoothed her apron and straightened her *kapp*. How outrageously were the cousins going to stretch the truth? And if their wives had come along, was it because they wanted a reckoning from Marlene and her brother? Or were they in on the story their husbands had been concocting? And how deeply was Bishop Obadiah invested in this venture?

The voices coming from the dining room were already edged with rancor.

"If Marlene's not here in three minutes, I'll go over to that store and fetch her myself," Bishop Obadiah said in his reedy voice. "What could possibly be taking so long—"

"*Gut* morning," Marlene stated as she entered the dining room—although her brother's flummoxed expression told her that *good* wasn't an accurate description. "What can I do for you folks?"

Five sets of angry eyes focused intently on her as she approached the table where the visitors sat with partially eaten pieces of cake in front of them. Mose's repeated blinking told Marlene they'd already rattled him, which didn't improve her mood. She didn't feel the least bit sorry for Jake, whose nose—after three and half weeks—was still swollen and bruised, with a new bump in it. Yost's eye sported only the pale yellowish shadow of the shiner Mose had given him.

"You call this letter an apology?" Yost demanded, angrily waving a piece of paper.

Jake let out a harsh laugh. "I suppose you feel reconciled to God now because you've *forgiven* us," he said sarcastically. "But far as we're concerned, you've only picked the scab off our wounds and made them bleed again."

With great effort, Marlene held her tongue. If Beulah had called Preacher Amos and the bishop, it might be to her advantage to wait for their arrival—and maybe by then, her two opponents would reveal falsehoods she could throw back at them.

"And imagine our *shock*," Yost's wife, Lovina, said, "when we read about the brazen way you welcomed Yost and Jake into a trap, so Mose could use them as punching bags—"

"For no *gut* reason!" Amy chimed in indignantly. She and Lovina exchanged nods to encourage one another. "Clearly, it's you two who should be on your knees confessing before the Coldstream congregation."

The two women's twisted accusations sounded well-rehearsed. Though they had been her friends, Marlene knew neither woman would dream of contradicting her husband. Marlene frowned, relieved to hear the front door of the lodge opening. Bishop Obadiah's sour expression told her the moment that Amos and Monroe appeared in the doorway.

"This matter doesn't concern you!" the Coldstream bishop declared. "I'm conducting a private fact-finding session for parties involved in the Fishers' confrontation with—"

Preacher Amos held up his hand. "We invited you folks to talk this over with Mose and Marlene twice—before their sale, and at the auction—and none of you cared enough to show up," he reminded them. "What's happened since then that's changed your minds about reconciliation?"

"*Reconciliation*?" Jake shot back. "The so-called *apology* letters Marlene sent us—"

"Where she so graciously *forgave* us for what we supposedly did to her," Yost put in with a sneer.

"—are her most insincere attempt at—well, forgiveness aside, they clearly point the finger of blame right back at her!" Jake continued, triumphantly waving the letter at Monroe and Amos.

The two leaders from Promise Lodge took seats at the table, nodding solemn greetings to Marlene and her brother. Bishop Monroe held out his hand. "May we see this letter, please?"

Preacher Amos's silver-shot eyebrows rose. "Marlene, have either Yost or Jake communicated with you since your sale? Or did they just show up out of the blue this morning?"

"I had no idea they were coming," she murmured as she took the chair next to her brother. "And after you've read the letter, I'd like to see it, too, please."

"Why? You wrote it, so you know exactly what it says!" Yost blurted out defensively.

"*Jah*, it's pretty incriminating. I—I was shocked when I saw it," Amy put in. When she looked to her husband for affirmation, Jake subtly shook his head, as though telling her not to say anything else.

Bishop Monroe rose and plucked the page from Jake's fingertips. "Since you folks from Coldstream have apparently seen Marlene's letter, I'll read it out loud so Amos and I are familiar with—"

"Oh, that's not a *gut* idea," Yost interrupted. "You'll be airing Marlene's dirty laundry, and exposing Mose for—"

"Marlene, may I read this out loud, so we're all up to speed?" the bishop asked her kindly.

Why on earth were the Mullets now acting as though she'd written anything but an apology and words of forgiveness? Her heart thudded, but she nodded at Bishop Monroe. The sooner he revealed the note's contents, the sooner she'd know what was going on.

"The apologies I wrote to these men were identical, except for their names," she said in a thin voice. "I was very upset by the way Jake and Yost cornered me upstairs at the farmhouse, but I was trying to do the right thing by forgiving them in letters, since they didn't come to speak with Mose or me in person when we asked them to."

Bishop Monroe nodded, focusing on the page for a moment before he began to read it to the rest of them. When he cleared his throat, Marlene detected a note of disbelief in the subtle rise of his eyebrows.

"'My dearest Jake,'" he began in a voice that filled half of the dining room, "'I'm sorry that Mose and I upset you when we sold our property to an outsider. We should have offered it to you or Yost first. I'm so glad you two men came to the farm to clear this matter up, and I'm sorry Mose overreacted when the two of you came upstairs to be alone with me—'"

Marlene shot up out of her chair. "I did *not* write that letter!"

Her heartbeat shot up so fast, she could barely breathe as heat rushed into her face. Whose idea had it been to twist everything she'd written into something so suggestive and vile?

Bishop Obadiah was shaking his head, shaming her with his glare. "But the words on the page put it in black and white, ain't so? You were clearly waiting for Jake and Yost that Saturday—or even if you weren't sure they were coming, you didn't turn them away."

Humiliation closed her throat. The four Mullets were

gazing at her smugly, as though she wouldn't dare to defy what the district's bishop had pointed out.

"This isn't the story the Fishers told me when Mose came to confess that he'd struck Jake and Yost," Preacher Amos stated sternly. "And from what I recall about these men's behavior when they were engaged to Marlene, I suspect they have *revised* her letter—"

"Where's your proof?" Jake asked belligerently. "It's the Fishers' word against ours."

"That's your handwriting, Marlene—right?" Yost chimed in. "Is that the paper you use for writing letters?"

When she glanced at the letter, the paper was indeed identical to hers—but then, it had come from the sort of ordinary, inexpensive tablet a lot of Amish women used. The handwriting looked like hers, too, but as her eyes raced crazily over the words that she would *never* have written—

"I'll be right back."

Marlene hurried through the dining room and up the stairs, praying she hadn't emptied the wastebasket in her front room the last time she'd tidied her apartment. She burst through her door with a gasp. When she'd dumped her trash on the table, she searched frantically for the crumpled sheet of paper—

"*Jah*! *Denki*, God!" she blurted as she smoothed out the draft copy of the letter she'd written to the Mullets. "Now, if You can convince Jake and Yost to admit their trickery and send them back to Coldstream, I'll be eternally grateful, Lord."

Clutching the page in her hand, Marlene took a deep breath at the top of the stairs. She wondered why the Mullet cousins had gone so far with this ruse to make her appear at fault, but she could ponder that later. Once downstairs, she reentered the dining room with a sense that right would prevail over wrong. After all, if Bishop Monroe, Preacher Amos, and God were *for* her, who could stand against her?

"Here's the draft copy of the actual letters I wrote to both Yost and Jake," Marlene said as she approached the folks at the table. On instinct, she handed the page to Jake's wife, Amy. "If you'll read this out loud, Amy, we'll all know the truth—"

"That's beside the point!" Jake blurted as he grabbed at the letter.

But Amy had already begun to skim the page, and she refused to let it go. Her expression fell after a few moments, and she began to read.

"'I'm also sorry that you felt compelled to team up with Jake and corner me in the upstairs storage room to take out your frustrations, and that my brother had to pull you both away from me as you tore at my clothes—'"

Amy's breath left her in a rush. She looked from Marlene to Mose, resembling a deer caught in a car's headlights. Then she glared at Jake.

"If this is the way it really happened, why *wouldn't* Mose punch you?" she asked in a trembling voice. "This explains why you didn't answer me when I asked how your nose got broken that morning, ain't so? You told me it was none of my concern."

Lovina was scowling as she got up to look over Amy's shoulder. The more she read of Marlene's drafted letter, the cloudier her expression became.

"*Jah*, I never got much of an answer about why Yost came home with a black eye that Saturday, either," she muttered. "And then yesterday, Yost, when you waved your letter at me, saying we had to come to Promise Lodge and hold Marlene accountable . . . well, it was like all the other times I've had the feeling that you were covering up for something you'd done."

"Not the first time you two cousins did something and then concocted a different story about it, either," Amy put in with a scowl. "And I've seen the way you can forge other people's handwriting, too, Jake. But *this* is inexcusable."

The dining room went absolutely silent.

Marlene realized what a difficult stand both the Mullet wives had just taken, and her opinion of them improved considerably. Only women who'd been misled many times would have the backbone to call out their errant husbands while two bishops, a preacher, and she and Mose were in the room to witness the risk they'd taken.

But maybe they'd fallen victim to their husbands' dubious storytelling skills too many times. And maybe they'd grown tired of it and were airing their grievances while they had credible witnesses.

Bishop Monroe cleared his throat. "So we've established that one of you men rewrote Marlene's letter with the intention of shifting the blame for that Saturday's confrontation to her and her brother. That's pretty low."

Preacher Amos glared at Jake and Yost. "Marlene can also show her torn dress to your wives and Bishop Obadiah, if they'd like further evidence of what went on during your visit," he put in. "In the interest of maintaining our Amish faith—setting the situation right again—I see this as the perfect time for you two men to beg Marlene's forgiveness, and to apologize to her and Mose."

"It would be appropriate to apologize to your wives, as well," Bishop Monroe added tersely. "And if you were in *my* district, you'd be on your knees confessing after your next church service. But that's Obadiah's call, not mine."

Bishop Obadiah, seated at the head of the table, had been glowering at Jake and Yost as though he was disgusted about being dragged into the falsified drama they'd created.

"We'll discuss your confession during the ride back

home," he said tersely. "Apologies to the Fishers and your wives are indeed in order, but that's up to you. You're adults, even if the stunt you just pulled seems more like something a clueless schoolkid would try."

When Yost stood up, Marlene sensed his anger stemmed from the way the two wives had betrayed him and Jake. "Fine. I'm *sorry*," he stated without looking at either Marlene or her brother.

"*Jah*, me too," Jake muttered as he followed his cousin from the dining room.

Amy and Lovina glanced uncertainly at one another before they also rose from the table.

"This was so embarrassing," Lovina murmured. "Marlene, I—I had a hard time picturing a scene where you were so eager to welcome Yost and Jake. Should've known something was fishy about that letter."

"*Jah*, it's given us a thing or two to think about," Amy said with a sad nod. She looked from Marlene to Mose. "I'm really sorry this whole episode happened. I hope you can come to forgive the way Yost and Jake have treated you."

As the ladies headed for the front door, Bishop Obadiah stood up. He shook his head as he picked his hat up from a nearby table.

"Well, this was a trumped-up day all around, and a waste of everyone's time," he muttered. "Like I said before, though, if you Fishers had shown the common courtesy of telling me and your neighbors you were selling your farm—leaving my district—maybe this unfortunate situation wouldn't have developed."

As Marlene watched Coldstream's narrow-minded bishop pass through the dining room, she hoped she was seeing his backside for the last time. Was it a sin to pray that she'd never meet up with him again?

"Some things never change," Preacher Amos said with

a shake of his head. "Obadiah Chupp has no idea that he's the main reason families want to leave his district. But you did the right thing, writing the Mullets' your original letter, Marlene—even if they twisted it around and used it against you. I hope we can all put this matter behind us now."

"I wrote notes to apologize for hitting them, too," Mose said in a low voice. "They didn't mention receiving them— but it's all right. I did my part."

Marlene glanced at the clock on the dining room wall. "I'm going to finish out my shift at Dale's store," she murmured as she rose to go. "Maybe by the time I come back, I'll feel better about this whole episode. *Denki* for your support, Bishop Monroe and Preacher Amos. It means a lot."

When she reached the front door she paused, watching Dick's van turn onto the road before she stepped out onto the porch.

I hope we can all put this matter behind us now.

Preacher Amos's remark summed up her feelings exactly. Marlene just hoped she and Mose would suffer no further repercussions.

Chapter 30

In the kitchen, Lester and the Kuhn sisters sighed as they rose from their seats at the worktable. "I probably should've gone in there to be with Marlene, so those Mullets knew she had another man—a fiancé—in her corner," he said.

"That might've been awkward, as fast as the accusations started to fly," Beulah remarked. "I had no idea about the trouble those men had caused Marlene, trapping her in a room upstairs—"

"And then rewriting her letter to pull the wool over their wives' eyes," Ruby muttered. "It's those two women I feel the sorriest for, because they're stuck living with Jake and Yost for the rest of their days. Marlene got away from them—and we all thank God she's got you now, Lester."

He nodded. "It was *gut* of you to let me know what was going on," he said softly. "See you later for supper."

"We'll be having breakfast again," Beulah said with a chuckle. "We ate plain old oatmeal this morning, so Ruby and I thought sausage patties and scrambled eggs along with hash browns sounded like a suitable reward for being so virtuous earlier today."

"And cheese sauce to pour over everything," Ruby added with a laugh. "*Lots* of cheese sauce!"

Lester was still chuckling as he strolled up the road toward the site of the new home he would soon share with Marlene. His lumber was to be delivered this afternoon—an exciting event that took his dream one step closer to becoming a reality. The rumble of heavy equipment greeted him as he rounded the bend, and a surge of adrenaline made him jog the rest of the way. Truman and a couple of fellows from his crew had arrived while Lester had been in the kitchen, and they were excavating the basement!

Truman waved and shifted the dozer out of gear. He was grinning like a kid when he hopped down from the seat to speak with Lester.

"I was hoping to surprise you—thought we could sneak the equipment past your place and have your foundation dug out before you knew we were here," he explained above the deep hum of the dozer.

"You've made my day, for sure and for certain!" Lester said. "The lumber's to arrive later this afternoon, so it's like Christmas and my birthday rolled into one."

Truman nodded. "The weather forecast looks *gut*, so we'll get your foundation poured within the next couple of days. Congratulations, Lester! You and Marlene are off and running now."

As his friend climbed back into the dozer's seat, Lester knew without a doubt that God's hand was guiding the events that were now falling into place for him.

Elverta and Agnes would be amazed at how fast a house is going up now that neither of them is trying so hard to make it happen.

He smiled, briefly recalling those two ladies and their convoluted plans for romance. His next happy conversation with Marlene would probably involve setting their wedding date for whenever she felt comfortable. It would be only fitting to figure on their courtship lasting a few months, considering that the love of his new life was a first-time bride—and that they'd only met about a month ago. As he imagined the delight in Marlene's sparkling eyes when he showed her the progress on their home this evening, Lester felt as happy as a dog that couldn't wag its tail fast enough.

At supper, as Marlene listened to Lester say he was sorry the Mullets had confronted her this morning— and that he was appalled one of them had rewritten her original letter to deceive their wives—she slowly lowered her forkful of sausage to her plate.

"Why did Yost and Jake even think they could get away with that stunt?" Lester continued with a puzzled shake of his head. "Surely they knew you'd challenge the wording of that faked letter."

"I thought that was strange, too," Mose said, spooning another helping of scrambled eggs onto his plate. "Unless Amy and Lovina insisted they all come here to speak with us."

"They never figured Bishop Monroe would be involved— or that he'd read that letter out loud," Ruby reasoned. "I'm sorry this whole episode occurred, Marlene. And I'm glad both of you Fishers can put it behind you now."

Marlene's mind was racing, trying to put this conversation into logical order. The Kuhns had expressed their sympathy and concern immediately after she'd gotten home from her shift at the bulk store—and she figured they'd been in the kitchen during the Mullets' visit, because they'd been kind enough to serve coffee and cake.

But how had Lester known the folks from Coldstream were here?

"So you're telling me you were in the kitchen, Lester? *Eavesdropping*?" Marlene demanded more tersely than she'd intended. Her temples began to throb with the headache that had been lurking behind her eyes ever since the Mullets and Bishop Obadiah had left.

Lester blinked. "It occurred to me afterward that I should've come out here to be with you—so *jah*, I'm telling you now that I heard what they were trying to pull on you—"

"I'm the one who called Lester," Beulah admitted quickly. "I just thought he should be aware those folks were here, because I knew they were up to no *gut*."

Marlene stood, suddenly upset—even though she sensed she might be jumping to the wrong conclusion. "It just strikes me as sneaky, that you were listening in on this morning's confrontation, Lester, without even letting me know you were here. That's the sort of behavior I'd expect from Jake or—"

A loud *whump* in the lobby made Marlene turn. She saw a small girl with a very large trunk standing in the dining room doorway.

"Sorry to interrupt," the visitor said nervously. "I wrote a few weeks ago to say I'd be visiting Promise Lodge, and I decided to just make the trip once. Sylvia Keim?"

"Oh, *jah*, we've been expecting you, Sylvia!" Beulah called out as she rose from her chair. "You're just in time to join us for supper—"

"And we'll give Rosetta and Gloria—the apartment managers—a ring so they'll know you're here," Ruby said. "Meanwhile, do come and fill a plate. We'll have somebody take your trunk upstairs after we get better acquainted."

"I . . . After the ride here, I need to rest," Sylvia said plaintively.

"I'm on it," Marlene said—and when Lester stood up to

help, she stopped him with a look. "I'm on my way upstairs for the evening anyway."

Inhaling deeply to settle herself, Marlene focused on Sylvia as she passed between the tables. She pasted on a smile, reminding herself that this new resident didn't deserve to be caught in the aftermath of her spat with Lester.

"Sylvia, I'm Marlene Fisher," she said gently. "If you need to lie down, we can find you a quiet room right away and you can choose your apartment whenever you feel up to it."

Sylvia nodded gratefully. She was a mere wisp of a woman, a childlike waif not five feet tall with haunted eyes that looked too large for her slender face. She might've been anywhere between twenty and fifty, so frail and fragile that a stiff wind might blow her over.

When Marlene stopped beside her new neighbor, she felt oversized—too tall and too hefty and impossibly awkward—

And she suddenly realized she had no reason to make her petty complaint against Lester, when Sylvia was obviously dealing with issues that were much more serious. Marlene glanced at the trunk, thinking it looked large enough to be Sylvia's coffin—and then wondering why such a maudlin thought had entered her mind.

"How on earth did you manage to bring this luggage into the lobby?" she asked softly. Something about Sylvia compelled Marlene to lower her voice, to behave more gently.

"My van driver carried it as far as the front door for me," Sylvia replied. "It's not all that heavy—I don't have many clothes—"

Marlene grabbed the trunk's handle and easily lifted it.

"—because, well, I won't be needing them for long anyway," the little woman continued in a voice that nearly disappeared in the high-ceilinged lobby. "I've been diagnosed with a rare, terminal condition. From what I've read about Promise Lodge, it seems like the perfect, peaceful place to spend my, um, final days."

Marlene blinked back sudden tears. "I'm so sorry, Sylvia. We didn't know—"

"I didn't give any details in my letter. Didn't want folks fussing over me."

Not knowing what else to do or say, Marlene nodded toward the double staircase. "Shall we go up and make you comfortable, then? At the top of the steps, open that first door. I'll be right behind you, Sylvia."

Within a few minutes, Marlene had shown Sylvia around the apartment where Gloria had lived before her wedding— the one for which a previous tenant, Maria Zehr, had requested a blue bedroom and a ceiling with puffy white clouds painted on it.

"Oh my," Sylvia murmured, a hint of a smile lighting her tiny face. "You could feel really close to heaven here. And this apartment's not occupied now?"

"No, so it could be yours if you'd like—has a great view over the back lot of the lodge, clear over to Harley Kurtz's sheep pasture, too. But you don't have to decide now," Marlene repeated. "Just let any of us know when you're up to more of a tour, and meanwhile, we'll let you rest."

She paused to give their new renter a chance to catch her breath. "We're glad you've come, Sylvia," Marlene said softly. "I just moved here myself about a month ago, and you're right—Promise Lodge truly is a peaceful place."

"*Denki*, Marlene. You've been a tremendous help."

After Marlene closed the apartment door, she lingered in the hallway. She'd intended to shut herself away in her apartment for the rest of the evening, nursing her wounds, but all the pent-up emotions of her hissy fit had drained away.

The few minutes she'd spent with Sylvia Keim had

reorganized her priorities and put her life into perspective again: time was too precious to be wasted on petty arguments.

Marlene descended the stairs and entered the dining room, where her brother, the Kuhns, and Lester were choosing slices from the coconut cream and the cherry pies Irene had baked in her shop today. Irene, wise woman that she was, had invited her baking partner, Phoebe, to stay in Forest Grove for supper after they'd delivered their day's work to the bulk store and the café there.

Irene's got it right. Life is for living.

"We covered your plate and put it on a gas burner to stay warm, sweetie," Beulah called out as Marlene approached their table. "But if you'd like to join us for pie first—"

"*Jah*, pie first—with ice cream, please," Marlene said as she met Lester's gaze from across the table. "I owe you a big apology, dear man, and I hope we can discuss that after we're done eating."

Lester, ever the gentleman, appeared relieved as he smiled at her. "We can do that. I'm glad you've come back to join us, sweetheart."

As she took her seat beside Mose again, Marlene's thoughts and emotions stopped whirling and came to a crisp, comfortable landing—like a robin settling on its nest. She gazed at the folks gathered around the table, every one of them near and dear to her.

"Sylvia has been diagnosed with—well, she didn't say what," Marlene murmured. "But after reading about Promise Lodge, she thought it would be the perfect, peaceful place to die."

The dining room stilled. The five of them shared a solemn gaze for a few moments.

"After showing her to the apartment Gloria just vacated," Marlene continued, "I realized how healthy I feel, and how happy I am here, and how I have everything to live for. I've been blessed with more than I'll ever need—and with friends and family like all of you.

"And that mess with the Mullets and Bishop Obadiah?" she added. "It's nothing but a hill of beans. Not worth my worry anymore."

"Amen to that," Beulah murmured with a nod.

"I'm on my way to fetch our ice cream," Ruby said. "We should live every day like it's a party, ain't so?"

"Rosetta would say we should plan for happiness," Marlene agreed with a big smile for Lester. "I don't know how much time Sylvia has left, but we should make her feel so welcome and so cared for that—that she won't want to leave us!"

"Hear, hear!" Lester replied, lifting his water glass. "That's the way God would have us all treat one another every day, ain't so?"

...o his eyes. "That's how it was for

...ed that she would understand.

...rmured, "I feel honored that you've

...n her footsteps—"

...your own trail, dear," he said with a

...me down roads I had no idea existed

...ores. And that's as it should be."

...ntented sigh, Lester continued. He was

...thing just right—and yet he sensed that

...ere learning patience with each other's

...o if he had to say something over again,

...ning. She'd still love him.

...to be going a different direction with you

...ife when most guys are plodding along the

...n road—even if it's a loving, comfortable

...ured. "You're giving me such a gift, Marlene."

...one with unshed tears, yet she'd never looked

...are the gift, Lester," she insisted. "After all, I

...omise Lodge figuring to spend the rest of my

...*idel* in my new apartment, yet here we are to-

...nding beside our future home. And it's a home

...door to Mose."

...I *hoped* you'd see that as a point in favor of

...n with me," he teased.

...ne's smile softened. "It's also a home big enough

...Fisher family table and all the gatherings we'll hold

...it," she whispered. "Lord willing, we'll soon be fill-

...ose chairs with little Lehmans, *jah*? What do you

...about that?"

...hen he pulled her close for another long, soul-searing

...Lester lost all ability to think.

...And it didn't matter.

Chapter 31

Lester felt immensely gratified as he sat across from Marlene eating two slices of pie—with ice cream—while she did the same, before eating the supper the Kuhns had set back for her. He hadn't gotten a clear view of Sylvia Keim, but even from a distance it was easy to see that his fiancée was so much stronger and healthier and more robust than their new resident. And for that, he gave thanks. God was giving him a second chance at life and love with a woman who glowed with purpose and enthusiasm.

Marlene was so much more than he'd ever dared to dream about.

"We, um, had some surprises today, and I think you'll want to see them," Lester said as the two of them walked across the lot toward the road leading up the hill. "For me, it was another example of what wonderful friends we have here—folks who just can't do enough nice things for each other."

"We've got plenty of people like that here at Promise Lodge," Marlene agreed. She slipped her hand into his and held his gaze. "And you're one of them, Lester. You've loved and encouraged me in so many ways since I moved here—and I'm terribly sorry that I got so bent out of shape when you said you'd been in the kitchen this morning."

"I can't blame you," Lester countered with a shake of his head. "In your place, I'd have probably seen it the same way. I really do wish I'd come out to stand with you while the Mullets and Chupp were pulling such a twisted stunt—"

"But you know, if I'd said something about you and I being engaged," Marlene interrupted in a pensive tone, "those folks would've seen it as another example of my wayward tendencies—and how I surely must've enticed Jake and Yost into coming to see me that Saturday. I mean, wouldn't *you* assume that a woman who's gone through so many men—and rejected them—was only in it for the thrill of the chase?"

Lester laughed out loud. If Marlene was making fun of her love life, with its unusual twists and turns, it was surely a sign that she'd put the Mullets and their deceit behind her.

"Truth be told, I'd want to meet that woman to see what made her tick," he replied lightly. "It would be the ultimate challenge to win her over, ain't so?"

Marlene smiled, her cheeks turning a comely shade of pink. "Spoken like a true man," she teased softly. "And that's what you are, Lester. A true man in every sense of the word. And I love you so much I can't see straight."

Would there ever be another sweet, sincere moment like this one? Lester threw caution and the Amish *Ordnung* to the winds and pulled Marlene close for a kiss, right there in the road.

"Lucky for you I know where we're going," he whispered after they'd eased apart. "And lucky for both of us that we're already right where God has led us, at the same

From the Promise Lodge Kitchen

Some of the best food we eat is served at family gatherings, right? Cooks always bring their tastiest desserts, and we share our favorite snacks, so this recipe section features great food that Beulah, Ruby, Irene, and the other Promise Lodge ladies have prepared in this story . . . which means that *I* have made these recipes and shared them with friends before I included them! As always, I lean toward ingredients already in my pantry, and—like most Amish cooks—I sometimes start with convenience foods rather than doing everything totally from scratch.

These recipes are also posted on my website, www.CharlotteHubbard.com. If you don't find a recipe you want, please e-mail me via my website to request it—or to let me know how you liked it!

—Charlotte

Coconut Cream Cheese Pound Cake

Coconut lovers, rejoice! This dense, buttery cake is so good it needs no frosting (but if you love frosting, go for it!), and it makes a luscious dessert when served with a simple whipped topping and fruit, or ice cream.

1 cup butter at room temperature
½ cup solid vegetable shortening
3 cups sugar
8 ounces full-fat cream cheese
7 large eggs
3 cups all-purpose flour
1 T. coconut extract
1 tsp. almond extract
1½ cups flaked sweetened coconut, pulsed 4–5
    times in food processor

Preheat oven to 325°. Spray a 10-inch/12-cup tube or Bundt pan with oil spray. Using a stand mixer, cream the butter, shortening, and sugar. Scrape down the sides and mix in the cream cheese until fluffy. Add the eggs alternately with the flour, occasionally scraping down the sides. Blend in the extracts and the pulsed coconut. Pour batter into the prepared cake pan.

Bake for about 85–90 minutes, or until a toothpick inserted into the thickest part of the cake comes out clean. Cool on a wire rack for 20 minutes. Gently loosen the sides and around the center of the pan with a thin knife blade and invert the cake onto a serving plate. Frost, if desired, and store in an airtight container. Freezes well.

Cinnamon Glaze Cake

Here's another cake that looks deceptively plain, but it packs a wallop of cinnamon flavor!

FOR THE CAKE:
- 1 box yellow cake mix
- 3.4-ounce box instant vanilla pudding
- ¼ cup brown sugar, packed
- ¼ cup granulated sugar
- 1 T. ground cinnamon
- 4 large eggs at room temperature
- ¾ cup water
- ¼ cup oil
- ½ cup buttermilk, milk, or white wine

FOR THE GLAZE:
- ⅓ cup butter
- ¾ cup sugar
- 3 T. water
- 2 tsp. vanilla
- 2 tsp. ground cinnamon

Preheat oven to 350° and generously grease or spray a tube or Bundt pan. Pour the cake mix, pudding, sugars, and cinnamon into the large bowl of a stand mixer and combine until brown sugar is fully incorporated. Add eggs, water, oil, and milk/wine and mix well. Pour batter into prepared pan.

Bake 45–50 minutes, or until a pick inserted into the center comes out clean. Set cake on a rack while making the glaze.

Put butter, sugar, and water in a sauce pan, whisking over medium heat until boiling. Boil for 1 minute or until sugar is completely dissolved. Remove pan from heat and stir in vanilla and cinnamon. Pour the sauce over the cake and let set and cool completely. Gently loosen sides and center with a thin knife blade (or you can shake the pan to work the cake loose) and invert onto a plate, then invert onto the serving plate so the glazed size is up. Store in an airtight container. Freezes well.

Baked Chili Cheese Dip

This simple dish is so satisfying that it's often a main dish at our house rather than an appetizer. I love it best spooned over corn chips or corn "scoops," and it's also tasty over baked potatoes! Satisfies your gooey-cheesy-salty cravings—and you can reheat the leftovers in a microwave.

8-ounce block of creamed cheese, softened
1 can chili without beans, any size
2 cups shredded cheddar or Colby-Jack cheese
10–12 black olives, sliced and blotted dry
½ cup diced red and/or green bell pepper
1 bag corn chips, tortilla chips, etc.

Preheat the oven to 375°. Lightly spray a 9" x 9" or 8"x8" glass pan. Spread the cream cheese on the bottom (use a flat spatula or wet your fingertips and press) to cover the bottom of the pan, spread on the chili, then cover entire top with shredded cheese. Sprinkle the olives and bell pepper pieces over the top and bake for 20 minutes, until getting bubbly. Remove from oven and let stand a few minutes. Serve with the chips.

Peanut Butter and Jelly Thumbprints

As soon as I tried this recipe, I had to include it in a book! The peanut butter cookie remains moist and tender, and no matter what flavor of jelly you use, it makes this classic combination a favorite all over again.

10 T. butter, softened
2 cups crunchy peanut butter
1½ cups sugar
1½ cups brown sugar
2 T. vanilla extract
3 eggs, room temperature
3¾ cups flour
3 tsp. baking powder
1 cup of jelly/jam, your choice of flavor

In a large mixing bowl, cream the butter, peanut butter, sugars, and vanilla. Add the eggs until blended in. Mix in the flour and baking powder. Cover the dough and chill at least 30 minutes.

When the dough is chilled, preheat the oven to 350°. Roll the dough into walnut-sized balls and place them on cookie sheets covered with parchment paper. Using the end of a wooden spoon handle, make a hole: insert the spoon handle about halfway into the ball and rotate it gently to make room for the jelly. Stir the jelly to soften it, spoon it into a pastry tube fitted with a large round tip, and fill the cookies.

Bake for about 10–12 minutes, just until the cookies are getting golden around the edges. Cool completely on the pans, and then let set on metal racks until the jelly is set and not sticky anymore. Makes 7–8 dozen. They freeze well stacked with wax paper between layers.

*Please read on for an excerpt
from the next novel in
Charlotte Hubbard's Promise Lodge series!*

Hidden Away at Promise Lodge

*by
Charlotte Hubbard*

Chapter 1

Karen Mercer set her suitcase on the ground and shut the hatchback of her brother's car. "Thanks for the ride, Mike," she called out. "See you next Sunday!"

As he drove away, she smiled at her best friend, Andi Swann, who was tucking a stray lock of blond hair back into her heart-shaped *kapp*. "Well, here we are, following our dream of living Amish for a week—not just reading the books but walking the walk and talking the talk!"

"Look at how this place has changed since we went to church camp here," Andi remarked as they stood at the entry to Promise Lodge. "This must be a new metal entryway sign, because I don't remember it having sunflowers and wheat sheaves, do you? And this plot to the left was a mowed pasture for horseback riding, and now it's planted in green beans and tomatoes—"

"Probably to be sold at this produce stand," Karen said, nodding toward the wooden structure at the roadside. "And look at all the houses! And there's a tiny home with a dock on the far side of Rainbow Lake. How cool is that?"

"The old timbered lodge and the cabins look just the same as I remember them," Andi said wistfully. "Except the Amish here have obviously done a lot of painting—and that looks like a new roof. The summers we spent here as campers and counselors were some of the best times of my life."

"Yeah, they were." Karen pointed toward a large white barn. "And look at those adorable black-and-white cows! Everything looks too neat and perfect to be real—"

"But what about *us*?" Andi interrupted, her smile falling a notch. "Do *we* look authentic? We're wearing these calf-length dresses we made and the *kapps* we ordered from a store in Lancaster County—and we've read hundreds of Amish novels—but what if they call us out as fakes? What if they make us confess in front of everybody at church and then—"

"They can't do that, silly!" Karen reminded her with a chuckle. "We're just taking a little trip down memory lane while we live the Amish life instead of just reading about it. If we stick to our script and imitate the way these folks do things, we'll be fine, right?"

Andi sighed as though she wasn't too sure about that. "But we made our phone reservation request and sent our money as though we were Plain, and the Amish think it's a sin to lie. Maybe we should've—"

"But we didn't," Karen pointed out quickly. Her pulse was pounding with anticipation as she picked up the old-fashioned suitcase she'd bought at a thrift store. "If we follow our plans, we won't have any problems. We're just a couple of Amish *maidels* who've come to Promise Lodge for a week to check it out because we read about it in *The Budget* newspaper—which we did. Let's walk to the lodge before you get cold feet and back out on me."

Side by side the two of them strolled along the main dirt road, gazing at other changes that had been made since their days as teenaged campers. "It must be quite a draw for these folks to have a country store now—and look at how many cars are in the parking lot there," Andi remarked.

Karen, however, was inhaling too deeply to reply. "I smell pie!" she whispered giddily. "And look way up on the hill—at that pasture where the sheep are grazing. What a picture that makes!"

Andi nodded, focused on the rustic, timbered lodge building they were approaching. "That porch hasn't changed a bit," she murmured. "I still remember the night Denny Willoughby kissed me on that swing."

"*Jah*," Karen said with her best Pennsylvania Dutch accent, "but we can't be talking about past stuff like that. According to our story, we've never been to Promise Lodge, remember? Now get your act together, because once we walk inside, we become Annie Stoltzfus and Karen Yoder for the next seven days."

Andi—now Annie—smoothed the front of her deep green cape dress, nodding nervously as Karen reached for the doorknob.

Visit our website at
KensingtonBooks.com
to sign up for our newsletters, read
more from your favorite authors, see
books by series, view reading group
guides, and more!

BETWEEN THE CHAPTERS

Become a Part of Our
Between the Chapters Book Club
Community and Join the Conversation

Betweenthechapters.net